DIABOLICAL

BY JANA DELEON

Chapter One

Belles Fleurs Plantation, 1936

The boy burst out of the back door of the house and ran for the row of azalea bushes that lined the backyard. Storm clouds rolled overhead and blocked the sun, covering the entire plantation in a dreary gray cloak. He slipped between the bushes and ran into the sugarcane fields, traversing the well-traveled path until he reached the tree line that indicated the end of the cane field and the beginning of the swamp.

He stepped into the canvas of thick brush and cypress trees, and everything went several shades darker as the cypress trees choked out what little light managed to push through the stormy skies. Bursts of pain shot through his right eye, and he could feel the skin tightening. It was already swelling and he knew it wouldn't be long before the eye was completely shut. It wasn't his first black eye, but if his plan worked, it would be his last.

The path through the swamp ended at an old slave quarters. His father had plenty of crop workers on the plantation, but they were paid now and all lived in newer quarters closer to the main house. This was the last of the buildings remaining from the old way of things, and the boy and his friends had helped it along by sneaking lumber from the plantation and keeping the structure upright.

He could see light streaming through cracks in the wall and was relieved to know his friends were there. With the storm moving in, he had been afraid they wouldn't be able to come. And tonight was important. Everything depended on it. He pulled open the door and two boys looked up at him, the lantern on the floor illuminating the depressing room that had once served as a home for six people.

Both of the boys stared at his eye but neither questioned it. They didn't have to. They already knew the answer. One of the boys still had yellowish splotches on his own face. Remnants of his own living conditions. The third boy's father was traveling right now, so he'd been bruise-free for two weeks, but his father was due home in three days. The boys' families were all part of the same social circle of the remaining rich plantation owners. They were educated at the same private schools and required to spend so many hours every week learning about the businesses they would inherit.

They'd bonded over the abuse.

At school, the other kids shied away from them. They heard the whispers behind their backs. They knew the other parents didn't want their children visiting plantations that belonged to the fathers of the three. They didn't want their children exposed to the kind of life the three lived every day at the hands of angry, bitter men who took their frustrations with the ups and downs of the sugarcane business out on the weak.

"Did you bring it?" one of the boys on the floor asked.

The boy with the black eye nodded and pulled the crumpled paper from his pocket. It contained a picture of an odd-looking star and a chant. The boy sank onto the floor next to his friends and pulled a piece of chalk from his pocket.

"We need to draw this on the floor," he said. "Then we stand around it and I say the chant."

The two other boys looked at each other, then cast doubtful looks back at him.

"Are you sure that will work?" one of the boys asked. "What if the spirit attacks us instead of your dad?"

"It can't do that," the boy with the black eye said, although he had no idea if what he said was true. But he needed the other two boys to make it work. The spell required at least three people. "The spirit has to listen to us if we bring it here."

Neither of them looked convinced, but this was their last hope.

They were all at the verge—twelve years old—just approaching what their fathers considered manhood. When you were a man, the responsibilities got bigger and the beatings got worse. The boy with the black eye knew it better than any of them. He'd seen his father beat his older brother to death for breaking a plow. The boy wasn't good with his hands, even when he tried to be really careful. He knew he'd make a mistake, and he knew the consequences when he did.

The police wouldn't do anything. They had no power over those with all the money. They accepted any lie the men told and removed themselves from the situation before the men's anger came down on them. No one on earth could help them. But something from hell could.

The boy drew the star on the floor with the chalk and gestured to the two other boys to stand. They rose from the floor, their fear so palpable it was almost visible. The boy lifted the piece of paper and started reading the words. They were in some foreign language, and the boy knew he was probably saying them all wrong, but surely that wouldn't matter.

He was just about to start the second line when the door to the shack flew open and all three boys ran for the back wall, huddling together, certain they had been caught and this was the end. Instead, the son of one of the plantation workers stared at them.

He was older than they were, probably eighteen. His father had worked on the plantation as long as the boy could remember. The son started working the fields six years ago with his father. The son's skin was as dark as the storm clouds swirling overhead, but his blue eyes were a perfect match for the boy's, rather than his Haitian parents' dark brown.

The Haitian looked at the star on the floor and let out a single laugh. "You think you can summon the devil?"

The boy was scared of his father, but he refused to be mocked by a worker's son. "So what if I do?"

The Haitian boy stared at him for several seconds, then nodded. "I know why you want to, but this won't work."

"Why not?" the boy asked.

"Because you don't have the skill. I do. My great-grandmother was a conjurer. I learned from her. This nonsense with chants and stars is the white man's poor attempt at stealing the one thing he hasn't taken from us."

The boy frowned. He didn't understand what the Haitian boy was saying, except for the word "conjurer." He knew that word.

The Haitian boy narrowed his eyes. "I can help you."

"Why would you do that?"

"Because then you'll owe me something."

"What?"

The Haitian boy shook his head. "When the time comes, I'll ask for it. All three of you. Do you want my help?"

The boy looked at his two friends, who'd remained silent the entire time. They were scared, but both nodded. "Okay," the boy said. "What do we need to do?"

"Give me that chalk," the Haitian boy said. "I'll fix this and then I'll call for the demon. Only I will be able to see or direct him. This is your last chance to change your mind. Once I call him and give him an order, he won't stop until he's done."

The boy handed him the chalk.

The Haitian boy smiled. "Then let's begin."

CHAPTER TWO

Friday, July 24, 2015
French Quarter, New Orleans, Louisiana

Shaye Archer fingered the scanned paper, reading the words Detective Elliot had written in. He'd broken part of the code on the document, revealing a list of people who'd sold human beings to John Clancy, the man Shaye had been instrumental in helping the New Orleans police take down a couple weeks before. The name he'd written belonged to the woman who'd given birth to Shaye. Not her mother. Shaye refused to call her that. No mother could sell her child. The woman named on this paper was a monster, just like the man she'd sold her child to. Just like the man who'd bought Shaye from Clancy.

Shaye looked over at Eleonore Blanchet, her therapist and friend, and shook her head. "No matter how many days pass, I still come back to this, almost not believing it's true. Until I look at this piece of paper again."

Eleonore nodded. "Perfectly normal. I've had quite a few moments of incredulity myself, and you know I've heard just about everything there is to hear."

"When will I stop being so angry? Is it even possible?"

"Pop psychology loves to tell you that forgiveness will set you free."

"But you don't agree?"

Eleonore frowned. "You know these sessions are not supposed to be about my beliefs. I posit things so that you dig deeper into your own thoughts and beliefs."

Shaye stared at her. "What I *believe* is that I'd like you to answer the question. Come on, Eleonore. It's not like this is my first day in the chair."

"Okay, then. My answer is no. Personally, I think forgiveness is something that must be earned by the person who wronged you. I don't believe in forgiveness in absentia."

"So you think if someone can't or won't atone, then the victim—God, I hate that word—remains angry forever?"

"Not at all. I believe that eventually, you'll simply let it go. I don't think forgiveness is necessary to put something in the past where it belongs. Letting it go is about your mental health. Not giving someone who didn't earn it a free pass."

Let it go.

"If only it were that simple," Shaye mused.

"I never said it was simple. I'm not ready to let go of the outrage I feel *for* you. I hardly expect you to be in a position to move on without another thought. You're too intelligent and too stubborn for that to happen."

Shaye looked down at the paper again, the penciled

letters seeming to taunt her. "I'm going to launch an investigation," she said quietly.

Eleonore sighed. "I figured you would."

Shaye looked up at her. "I can't let it go until I have answers. At one time, I thought I might be able to, but this seems like it's taunting me."

"I can see how it would feel that way."

"Right now, I have only a small piece of my story." Shaye shook her head. "I always knew my past was bad. It couldn't have been anything else, right? And given the work stories I've heard from Corrine, I always figured that maybe my biological mother was a junkie—someone who traded her child for a fix, or at best, wasn't diligent about the kind of men who came around."

Shaye held up the piece of paper. "But this…I never imagined this."

"None of us did. How could we? Everyone is shocked by what Clancy did, all the way from law enforcement to other criminals. Even the worst among us usually have their lines in the sand. This Clancy stepped right over them without a qualm."

"A sociopath, right?"

"Given what we know, that would be my guess."

Shaye leaned forward in her chair, preparing to broach the subject she'd come here to discuss. "I want your help."

Eleonore frowned. "You already have my help."

"I don't mean for me. Not exactly. I mean to get in the mind of the people who are involved in my past. I don't know anyone who knows more about the deranged criminal mind than you. I can't think like them, but you've been inside enough of their heads to know what's going on."

Eleonore shook her head. "It's not that simple. Every offender I've studied, even the most depraved, all had their own methods. Their own style. For everything that is the same, there's always something else that differs."

"But you would be able to profile things easier than I would. My injuries scream ritualistic abuse. We skirt around the term, but we both know that's the case. The cuts on me are symmetrical, except for the ones on my wrists, and my guess is that I made those. The worst of my dreams have black candles and a red dress, and I'm terrified of both when I'm conscious."

Shaye drew in a breath and slowly blew it out. "And if all that isn't enough, the pentagram branded onto my back clinches it."

Eleonore folded her fingers together and stared at them for some time. Finally, she looked at Shaye. "I know you've read the FBI study on child ritualistic abuse."

"Yes. And I'm well aware that they found it to be a form of hysteria, and that no real cases of abusing children in an attempt to worship demons were ever uncovered. But just because they never discovered an instance, does that mean one never happened? You've profiled cults. Is marrying off little girls to old men with multiple wives—all in the name of Jesus—really any different?"

"In many ways, it's the same. The god that cult members chose to worship isn't relevant, but control is always at the root of it, not spirituality."

"So what if the person who bought me had a small cult—people he'd convinced that he had dark powers and who believed he could do the things he claimed. If he selected members carefully, couldn't he find people who would join him?"

"Evil can always find an accomplice. But even if we assume the person who bought you used you for satanic rituals, why do you make the leap to an entire cult? What if it was just one seriously fucked-up individual?"

Shaye gave her a rueful smile. "Is that your clinical diagnosis?"

"In this case, yes."

Shaye shook her head. "Part of it is my dreams. I see other people there. It's hazy and I can't even latch onto how many or whether they're men or women, but it's more than one person. Also, I…feel like it's more than one person. I can't explain it. It's just there in my mind like it's a fact."

Eleonore frowned. "And maybe you're right, but even if that's true, it doesn't provide you anything that helps. In fact, it gives you an even longer list of perpetrators with not a single clue as to how to locate them."

Shaye took in a deep breath and blew it out. "I want to try something."

"What?"

"Deep regression hypnosis."

"No."

"Why not?"

"Jesus, Shaye, you know why. Anything recalled under hypnosis might be factual but is far more likely to be a conglomeration of things the subconscious mind has put together to answer questions when we don't know the answers or can't handle them. You're already off on this idea that what happened to you was ritual abuse. What makes you think your mind wouldn't put together your thoughts and every late-night horror movie you've ever seen and deposit that answer there for you? Just to make you go away?"

"The truth is neither of us knows what my mind will do. Not unless we try. I hate to do this to you, Eleonore, but I have to tell you that if you won't do it, I'll find someone else who will."

"Damn it!" Eleonore leaned back in her chair and stared at the ceiling.

Shaye knew she had backed her friend and therapist into a wall. Eleonore knew she wasn't bluffing, and while Eleonore didn't believe in hypnosis as a tool, she also knew plenty of the "hacks," as she called them, did. Any of them would be more than happy to take Shaye's money and put her under.

Eleonore leaned forward in her chair and looked at Shaye. "I need some time to research. I'm not interested in making a mistake. And whatever I require for your own safety, you'll go along with or I won't be part of it. Even if it means a heart monitor and an IV."

"Whatever makes you comfortable."

"Not doing it at all is what would make me

comfortable. But I refuse to let some charlatan feed you a bunch of nonsense just to make a quick buck. I'll check with people I know—competent doctors and scientists—and I'll figure out how to handle it the right way. If there even is such a thing."

"Thank you."

Eleonore shook her head. "This is the first time I've ever asked and I hope it will be the last, but can we keep this just between me and you? At least for now?"

"Absolutely." Shaye had no interest in telling her mother. Corrine was an awesome mother who took her role seriously, which made her a great worrier. With Shaye being her daughter and Eleonore her best friend, Corrine would wear the two of them out if she had even an inkling what they were going to attempt.

If she was being honest with herself, Shaye wasn't convinced it was a good idea either.

But if it worked…

Pierce Archer, in his custom-tailored suit and wearing a watch that probably cost more than her car, looked out of place sitting in a lawn chair in Corrine's backyard. But Corrine had insisted on getting some sunlight and air, so if her father wanted to continue harping at her, then he was going to have to do it on the patio.

"I spoke with Police Chief Bernard and the medical examiner yesterday," he said, "and let them both know that if anything about that despicable woman who gave birth to Shaye or that insane man who sold her leaks to the public, then I'll have all their jobs."

Corrine closed her eyes and silently asked forgiveness for her father's complete lack of manners. On a normal basis, Pierce didn't use his considerable wealth or his position as a state senator to manipulate or threaten people, but when it came to Corrine and Shaye, the lines of propriety blurred. She opened her eyes again and stared at him.

"Why would you do that?" she asked. "You know as well as I do that it only takes one person looking to make a quick buck for things like that to get out. We're not the Kennedys, but in New Orleans, we may as well be."

"Damn people are always looking for an easy way to get rich. This is my family. I'm not going to have the Archer name bandied about like a Kardashian."

"It's not the same, and you know it. None of us have done anything to cause the talk, and Shaye can hardly control what was done *to* her. Do you think people will blame her for what happened? I know you don't think highly of mankind in general, but that's a stretch, even for you."

Pierce ran his hand through his hair, clearly agitated. That wasn't unusual. Things outside his control always frustrated Pierce. "How is Shaye? I don't want this to affect her."

"You may as well wish for unicorns then, because I don't see how it's possible for her to remain unaffected. It affects all of us. She's just got the worst end of it."

"And you. If she bleeds, so do you."

"That's true."

"What can I do? Let me send the two of you away for a while. I saw a place the last time I was in Italy. A small castle. I'll buy it and the two of you can go there for a few months and take in the culture, pick out drapes, whatever."

Corrine held in a sigh. Her father held fast to the belief that money could fix anything and refused to think differently, even though all his money hadn't been able to prevent her mother from dying.

"I don't think a vacation will fix this," she said. "Not even one that includes a castle."

"I'm not trying to fix anything. That's Eleonore's department. I'm trying to get the two of you out of Louisiana and away from talk."

"I can't just leave my job for a couple of months to gallivant around Italy. We're already shorthanded, and my being out has already put cases even further behind."

Pierce threw his hands in the air. "You were attacked by a psycho while doing that job. I will never understand why you insisted on being a social worker in the first place, but then you compound the first bad decision by putting yourself in such risky positions on top of it. You're not average people, Corrine. No matter how much you'd like to convince others that you are."

Corrine frowned. She was well aware she wasn't average people. If the mansion she lived in wasn't enough proof, the private security guards parked in front of her gate, courtesy of her father, were a clear indication. Corrine wasn't obtuse. She knew people treated her differently because of who her father was, but that didn't mean she had to act special just because people tried to treat her that way.

"I'm not taking off work," Corrine said, "and that's final. I've missed enough already, and I'm looking forward to going back in another week. But if you want to try to tempt Shaye with your castle idea, then give it a whirl."

He perked up a bit. "You think she'd go for it?"

"Not a chance in hell."

He shook his head. "The two of you are going to be the death of me."

"Probably."

"Then what can I do? I can't sit around doing nothing."

A tiny bit of empathy wormed its way into Corrine's thoughts, and she decided to give her father a break. His intentions were always good even if his execution needed work. And besides, it wasn't as if she didn't have a firsthand understanding of all the worry that a single parent put into their only child. They had that in common.

"I honestly don't know what you can do," Corrine said. "I don't know what *I* can do. I've been struggling with it every minute of every day since all of this mess with Clancy happened. I swear, if I had an answer, I'd share it with you."

The impatient and slightly belligerent expression he'd worn before slipped away and was replaced with remorse.

"I'm so sorry, honey. I know this can't be easy for you, and since Shaye is as stubborn as you are, I know exactly how you feel."

He wanted her to smile, so she forced a tiny one. "I guess I deserve everything I'm getting, right?" she said.

"Maybe a little." He rose from the chair and leaned over to kiss her cheek. "I have to get back to the office, but if you can think of anything, please let me know."

"I will, and thank you."

"Give Shaye my love. I'd like to take you both to dinner this week."

"I'll let her know."

Pierce headed into the house, and Corrine looked across the swimming pool at the beautiful landscaping and lush grass that made up her backyard oasis. She was surrounded by beauty but spent so much time dwelling on the ugly side of life. Why couldn't she have been some simpleton heiress, content with tea parties and charity events? And Shaye one of those girls who loved dresses and talked about weddings and babies?

She frowned. Yuck.

Those women were so far removed from the two of them that she didn't even believe it possible for them to fill those roles for a day without whining. She had to face facts—both she and Shaye had a calling…a bigger purpose than being pretty faces for society paper photos. They wanted to make the world beautiful for everyone.

Unfortunately, they hadn't even put a dent in it.

He watched her as she left the psychiatrist woman's office building and headed down the sidewalk toward her SUV. She was careful, always checking the street before she walked. Always checking the back of her vehicle before she got in. Alarm system. Martial arts training. Nine-millimeter at her waist.

He'd been watching her off and on ever since the night the cop found her. The night she'd escaped. At first, he figured he'd wait until social services put her in one of those group homes, then he'd get her back and go on as usual. But then that Archer bitch had shown up at the hospital and everything had gotten complicated. He decided the girl had to be killed before she could tell his secrets. Before she ruined all his careful work. But the Archer woman made everything impossible. Police guards. Private security. And the hospital played along with her every whim. No one could get to the girl. Not even him, and before now, he'd always been able to find a way.

He followed the story on the news, waiting for the girl to tell everyone what had happened to her. But as the days ticked by and nothing was forthcoming, he started to wonder. Then the news leaked. The girl had no memory of the past. Not even her own name. He wanted to rejoice but was afraid to. What if the memory loss was only temporary? He'd always been careful when he'd taken her food and when he conducted the ceremonies. He'd always worn a mask, as had the other participants. But they hadn't disguised their voices. He'd heard about a case where the victim had identified the man who attacked her by his voice alone. The jury had bought it, and the man was in prison.

Then he'd started to worry that one of the others might get scared and be tempted to say something to the police. That the threat of an investigation backed by Pierce Archer's money might be enough to have them offer up a deal in exchange for their own freedom. So he'd eliminated the others. No one would ever match their voices, because he'd silenced them forever. Then he waited and watched, but weeks, then months, passed and the news reported nothing new and eventually, the entire story faded away.

He wanted to believe he was safe. That she would never remember, but it was impossible to relax with that thought constantly niggling in the back of his mind. He thought again that if he killed her, he'd be done with it forever, but would he? Or would killing the girl be the thing that got him caught? Everyone was watching her now, fawning over the sad little victim. And the Archer bitch had surprised everyone by taking her in. If anything happened to the girl now, he'd have the Archer bitch and all her money pushing to catch him, and he didn't need that kind of heat.

He had one other option. It was a tricky one, but manageable.

But he hadn't needed to use it.

She never remembered.

Nine years had passed and the girl had never done anything to indicate she could recall her past. He'd moved away for years, feeling that a new city was the only safe way to continue his practices, but no matter how many cities he tried, he'd always come back home, even if only for a short while. New Orleans was the only place he'd ever felt the power of the One and True God, and he'd returned for good three months ago, finally allowing himself to slip into the comfort of one who had gotten away with it.

He'd needed to return to the ceremony and ritual that he'd abandoned since the girl escaped. He'd just made arrangements to return to the old ways. To return to the spiritual place he used to dwell. Then that idiot Clancy had gotten caught and he'd started to worry again. The news was filled with stories of notebooks collected from Clancy's work site. What if they were records of Clancy's "other" line of business? He'd given Clancy only his first name, but what if it was somewhere in those notebooks? It wasn't an odd or unique name, but it wasn't overly common, either. If the police started poking around, would they find something to trace the girls back to him?

They were questions with no answers and only one solution.

He'd decided that he needed to clean house, as he should have nine years before. So he started doing reconnaissance immediately. So many people might possess knowledge they didn't even know they had, and if the cops figured out Shaye Archer was one of the girls Clancy sold, they would question everyone all over again. Something that might not have made sense all those years ago might make a whole lot of sense now.

The cops who found the Archer girl. The doctor and nurses who cared for her. They were all on the list. And of course, Shaye.

It was the only way to ensure her continued silence.

CHAPTER THREE

Friday afternoon, Shaye walked into the police station and greeted the desk sergeant, who gave her a big smile.

"You've been busy, Ms. Archer," he said. "That was a fine bit of work you managed with Detective Lamotte."

Shaye felt a blush creep up her face at the veteran cop's praise. "Thank you, but I think I got lucky more than anything else."

"Nonsense. You've got a good gut for this kind of work. I think you've got a big future ahead of you."

"Don't tell my mother that."

The desk sergeant smiled. "Well, mothers worry. That's their job. Still, kids have managed to live their own lives for thousands of years despite it. I'm guessing you will too."

Shaye smiled. "You're very perceptive. You must be a cop."

He laughed. "Stop flattering me and get on back to your meeting. Down the hall where the interrogation rooms are. Second on the left."

"Thanks." Shaye headed down the hall for the interrogation rooms, wondering for the hundredth time why she was being called into the station. She'd answered a million questions already about her last case, which had intersected with a case Detective Lamotte had been working. Her written statement had been lengthy and very detailed. She kept copious notes when working and had been happy to turn them all over to the New Orleans police when her part in the investigation had wrapped up.

It was her second case since she'd opened her own private investigator firm, and she'd been tasked with a single objective—to find a missing street kid named Jinx. She'd been "hired" by another street kid, Hustle, who'd helped her with information on her first case. Her part of the investigation had ended well, with Jinx rescued and reunited with her aunt, who was legally seeking to gain custody. Jinx's future looked bright. Hustle was living with the man who'd saved his life, and who was also a friend of Shaye's, and was helping him with his motel.

But for the New Orleans police, the investigation was just beginning.

John Clancy, the man who'd kidnapped Jinx and other street kids, had been trafficking humans for almost twenty years. Stacks of notebooks containing coded lists of buyers and sellers had been recovered from his office before he'd had the opportunity to burn them. Now the police were tasked with the seemingly impossible job of trying to figure out who the buyers and sellers were and attempt to locate those who were sold. It was one giant cold case that was unlikely to yield any happy endings.

But the police wouldn't call in a private detective for

help with that, and Shaye had no information about John Clancy to contribute other than the small number of facts she'd already given them. So whatever she'd been called here for, that wasn't it. And her…friendship, she'd call it, with Detective Jackson Lamotte was growing stronger, but if Jackson wanted to talk to her, he'd call her himself. And she seriously doubted he'd ask her to come to the police station, especially if it meant his partner and superior officer, the useless Detective Vincent, might use it to cause trouble for Jackson.

She located the second room and rapped lightly on the door. A man's voice inside called for her to enter, so she opened the door and stepped inside. A middle-aged man with graying hair and a dour expression rose from the end of the table and studied her for a couple of uncomfortable seconds.

"I'm Shaye Archer," she said, breaking the silence. "I understand you wanted to meet with me?"

She glanced over and saw Detective Vincent sitting at the far end of the table. He was leaned back in his chair, arms crossed and staring at her like the cat that swallowed the canary. Shaye felt her back tighten. Whatever this was, it wasn't good. She wasn't worried about herself, but if Vincent had found a way to get back at Jackson for making him look like the lazy, incompetent ass he was, Shaye knew he'd use it.

The other man continued to stare and Shaye lost what shred of patience she had. "And you are?"

"My name is Malcolm Frasier," he said. "I'm with

internal affairs."

"Then I'm afraid you've got the wrong person, Mr. Frasier," Shaye said. "I'm not a cop."

He smirked. "No. But I have reason to believe that you have information I'd be interested in concerning Detective Jackson Lamotte."

Shaye stared directly at him. "I can't imagine that I do."

"So you're saying you don't know Detective Lamotte?" Frasier asked.

"I know Detective Lamotte. I know a lot of detectives."

"But you're not getting confidential information from the other detectives you know."

Shaye shot Vincent a dirty look. This was all him. She was certain of it. "I'm afraid you've been misinformed. Detective Lamotte has never shared confidential information with me."

Frasier raised one eyebrow. "Your statement on the Clancy case says that you were in Detective Lamotte's company when you got information concerning your missing persons case and that you asked Lamotte to assist you. That's a convenient way to insert yourself into police business."

"It was certainly convenient for the kids we rescued, and all the potential victims of John Clancy."

Frasier ignored her remark and continued. "If you weren't attempting to make yourself party to a police investigation, then perhaps you'd care to explain why you were in the detective's company in the first place."

Shaye struggled to keep her temper under control, but it took every ounce of strength to do so. The lengths Vincent had gone to in order to discredit Jackson, a man who'd gone above and beyond to find the missing kids, was more than she could stomach.

She looked Frasier directly in the eye and forced her words to remain controlled. "Actually, I don't care to explain anything to you. It was a private matter, so unless my personal life has become the purview of the New Orleans Police Department, then I have nothing else to say."

"You're making a mistake," Frasier said.

"Am I?" The complete and utter condescension was the final straw, and Shaye drew in a breath, preparing to do the one thing she never did. "Did Detective Vincent tell you who I am? Who my grandfather is?"

A tiny flicker of uncertainty passed over Frasier's face and he glanced at Vincent. "I don't see why that's relevant."

"Pierce Archer is my grandfather. State Senator Pierce Archer. I'm sure you know the name."

Frasier did his best to maintain his cool, but Shaye could see the chink in his armor. Vincent had overplayed his hand and Shaye had called his bluff. She turned around and looked at Vincent.

"I'm not a fan of abuse of power," Shaye said, "so I don't say this lightly. Don't screw with me *or* my friends."

Vincent's face reddened but he couldn't work up a response.

"Good day, gentlemen," she said and exited the room, slamming the door behind her.

She marched right back to the desk sergeant, who took one look at her and asked, "What's wrong? What happened?"

"I need Chief Bernard. By any chance is he available?"

The desk sergeant jumped up from his chair. "I'm sure he can be. Just give me a minute."

He hurried off down the hall and Shaye took in a deep breath and blew it slowly out. She'd spent an untold number of years being a victim. Damned if she was going to be bullied by a woman-hating, bloated old windbag. And double damned if he was going to railroad the career of one of the finest detectives in the department because of her.

Vincent had just crossed a line he couldn't step back over.

Detective Jackson Lamotte headed across the parking lot toward the police station. He'd been running down leads on a warehouse burglary all day and had been hoping for a hot shower and a cold beer. Instead, he'd gotten a summons to return to the office. Fifty bucks said it was more bullshit that Vincent had dreamed up. Ever since he'd rescued the kids with Shaye, Vincent had turned up the heat on Jackson, doing everything possible to undermine his work.

For the life of him, Jackson couldn't figure out what

Vincent's problem was. He was certain Vincent thought Jackson was making him look bad—actually working and all—but everyone in the department had known about Vincent's lack of work ethic long before Jackson was saddled with him. Jackson's recent successes had only served to highlight Vincent's laziness, but so what? Vincent wanted to daydream into retirement, so why didn't he? No one would say a word if he sat in his chair and let Jackson do all the work. So why didn't he just shut up and ride his chair into retirement?

Ego.

That was almost always the answer with men and most assuredly with cops, but that left Jackson in the impossible position of either doing a lousy job or constantly having Vincent gunning for him. His own pride and ego refused to allow him to do a lousy job, so he supposed he'd spend the rest of Vincent's time with the department serving as the sacrificial lamb to Vincent's complaints.

He walked into the department and gave the desk sergeant a nod. "Hold up, Jackson," the desk sergeant said.

"What's up?" Jackson asked.

"I'm supposed to send you to Chief Bernard's office."

Jackson stiffened. Maybe Vincent had finally managed to get Jackson in trouble. "Any idea why?"

"Maybe, but it's not my place to say. Don't sweat it. Bernard's fair and he sees more than people think he does."

Crap. Jackson gave the man a nod and headed for the chief's office. It was about Vincent. He should have known. The older detective hadn't bothered to check in with him all day, despite the fact that Jackson had left him several messages, and now he was probably whining about paperwork that wasn't done or something equally trivial. Jackson would just present his side of things, then go home for that shower and beer. Make that beers, plural. He was probably going to need them.

He'd barely knocked on the chief's office door when he heard the summons to enter. The desk sergeant had probably alerted the chief that Jackson was on his way. He stepped inside, and a tiny bit of relief coursed through him when he saw only the chief inside. No witnesses probably meant no reprimand for whatever violation he'd committed according to Vincent.

The chief motioned for him to sit, and he sat across the desk from Bernard.

"You've done some good work lately," Bernard said. "Work that makes this department look good. More importantly, work that's saved people—now and in the future."

Jackson struggled to control his surprise. This wasn't at all where he thought the conversation was going to go. "Thank you."

"There's been some rumbling from Vincent."

Jackson sat back in his chair.

Here we go.

"Talk about you providing confidential information to Ms. Archer," Bernard continued, "and using police resources to aid a private investigator."

"None of that is true," Jackson said. "Shaye's case and

mine intersected. I didn't put her onto it. In fact, she was working it before I was."

"I know that, and don't think I don't see what Vincent is trying to do. I didn't get to this position by being obtuse. But the tension the two of you are creating isn't good for the department. So something has to give."

Bernard leaned forward in his chair and rested his arms on the desk. "Since Vincent seems determined to keep his head tucked in his turtle shell until retirement, I'm putting him on the Clancy files."

Jackson felt a flush move up his face, and he knew if there was any time that he should keep his mouth shut, it was now. But he couldn't manage it. "So Vincent screws off and he gets to run one of the biggest cases in the department's history?" He shook his head in disgust. It was even worse than Jackson getting fired. Not only had Vincent's laziness gotten him on the biggest case the department had ever seen, he'd managed to make Jackson look like the bad guy.

"Vincent won't be running it. Frank will."

Jackson looked back at the chief as some of his anger began to dissipate. Detective Frank Rizzoli was a New York transplant who had made a name for himself with cold cases. He could ferret out criminals with minimal evidence better than anyone Jackson had ever known. He was also Grayson's partner.

"What about Grayson?" Jackson asked. He couldn't picture the high-strung detective spending his days poring over notebooks, no matter how big the case was. Grayson liked to be in the middle of the action. He wouldn't be happy at a desk.

"Grayson needs a new partner. He's requested you."

"Me?" Jackson struggled to contain his excitement. Grayson was a real cop, dedicated to the job and not afraid to go the extra mile to apprehend the criminal. He had probably twenty years or so on Jackson in age and fifteen with the NOLA police department. His case closure rate was solid and the other officers respected him. Jackson couldn't ask for a better situation.

"You two will have your own caseload, of course, but when Frank needs help running down leads on the Clancy files, you'll be assisting there as well."

It just kept getting better. If Jackson had an inroad to the Clancy investigation, then he'd be able to find out if any progress was made concerning Shaye.

And so would Vincent. Shit!

"Uh, sir," Jackson said. "I hope you don't take this as disrespect, but are you sure it's safe to put Vincent on the Clancy files…given that Ms. Archer is one of the victims?"

"I'm aware of the potential for problems, and rest assured that the last person I want picking my job performance apart again is Senator Archer. We spoke at length yesterday. I'm rather hoping to avoid a repeat. Frank will limit Vincent's access. Mostly he'll be scanning and filing. Given his recent propensity for avoiding any real work, I don't anticipate his sneaking documents home and attempting to decode them himself."

A wave of relief passed over Jackson. "No, sir.

Probably not. Thank you."

"For what?"

"For trying to keep Shaye's name out of the news. I know it's going to happen. We can't keep it a secret forever, but if she just had more time to process…"

Bernard tilted his head the side and studied Jackson for several seconds. "At first, I thought you were only infatuated with Ms. Archer. Not that I blamed you, of course. She's a beautiful young lady. Intelligent and intriguing. But I misjudged you."

Bernard rose from his desk and Jackson stood with him.

"Be very careful," Bernard said. "Women like Shaye Archer come with a high price tag. You might find it's one you're not willing to pay."

Jackson knew he wasn't talking about money. Shaye probably had more money than she'd ever use. Bernard was talking about her history, her notoriety. The fact that if he were involved with Shaye, it put him in the spotlight as well, likely for as long as he was willing to stand there. Spotlights didn't just click off on women like Shaye. They tended to follow them quietly around, just waiting for the next event that needed to be highlighted.

"I can afford it," Jackson said.

Bernard nodded. "Maybe you can. Go see Grayson. He'll fill you in on your new assignment. Turn over anything you have on your current cases to Maxwell."

Jackson nodded and left the chief's office. Grayson wasn't at his desk, so Jackson headed for the break room.

Grayson was pouring a cup of coffee and gave Jackson a nod as he entered.

"You talk to Bernard?" Grayson asked.

"Just left there. Thank you for requesting me. You don't know how much…" Jackson trailed off, frustrated with himself for sounding so weak. He'd given Vincent entirely too much control over his emotions.

"You might not be thanking me after you see our caseload. We drew a couple nasty ones and we'll be helping out with the Clancy investigation as needed." Grayson studied him for a moment. "I requested you because I like what I've seen out of you and unlike Vincent, I want you to share your insight with me. Anything seems off to you, let me know. I don't think my radar's as finely tuned as yours, but I've got more years making the pieces fit. I think we can do some good work together."

"I'm looking forward to it."

Grayson nodded. "Frank said he has something he needs to show us." He pulled a set of keys from his pocket and handed them to Jackson. "Would you mind getting a folder from my desk? It's labeled 'Clancy.' I'm keeping it locked up because it's got some information on Shaye. I need to run and talk to the forensic team before we see Frank."

Jackson took the keys and looked at the odd-shaped piece of metal Grayson used as a key fob. "What is this?"

"Huh? Oh, I'm not sure. Something my dad's company used to make."

"Used to?"

"He died when I was in college, and my mother sold the company. He used to have that on his desk at home, so I kept it."

"I'm sorry. I didn't know."

Grayson waved a hand in dismissal. "They're both gone now. They were older when they had me. I think maybe they hadn't been able to have kids before but I never asked. Meet you back here in a couple minutes?"

Jackson nodded and headed to Grayson's desk to retrieve the file. When he got back to the break room, Grayson was already there waiting on him. Grayson took the file and headed down the hall toward the conference rooms. Jackson fell in step beside him, a silent war being conducted in his mind. The question he'd been wanting to ask since he'd left Bernard's office was on the tip of his tongue, but he knew it was a place he probably shouldn't go.

Unable to squelch the desire, he finally blurted out, "Did Vincent do something to prompt these changes? I mean, other than the usual?"

Grayson looked over at him and smirked. "You caught on to that, did you? Radar." He shook his head. "You didn't hear this from me, but word is Vincent went to IA and said you'd given classified information to Shaye Archer. He got IA riled up and one of the suits called a meeting with Ms. Archer today."

Anger coursed through every square inch of Jackson's body. It was one thing for Vincent to mess with Jackson. It was completely another to drag Shaye into his games. "That lying son of a bitch. What happened?"

Grayson let out a single laugh. "Your lady friend told them both off so bad that the suit left here with his tail tucked between his legs. Then she marched straight into Bernard's office, and I don't know what was said, but I would have paid money to hear it. Bernard came out of there apologizing all over himself and yelled at Vincent to get the hell in his office before Ms. Archer had even gotten two steps away."

Jackson grinned. "Good for her."

"Good for all of us. We could hear Bernard yelling clean through the walls, but couldn't make out what he was saying. After five minutes or so, Vincent came stomping out and left, then Bernard called me in to tell me he was moving Frank to run the Clancy files and Vincent would be driving a scanner into retirement. I figured it was as good a time as any to ask if he would transfer you."

Jackson shook his head, still smiling. "I wonder what she said."

"Well, given that the two of you are friends, I was kinda hoping you'd find out and tell me. I wouldn't repeat it, of course. But I have to admit to wanting to know really bad."

"So do I."

Grayson pushed the door to the conference room open and walked inside. Frank was working at one end of the table and looked up as they walked in. He was the only person in the room.

"Lamotte's official," Grayson said. "Bernard just gave

the word."

Frank nodded and motioned for them to come over. "Elliot figured out the code for another notebook. That's four he's been able to decipher so far. It looks like Clancy changed the code every year but some of these are repeats, like he used the original code for repeat buyers."

"Repeat buyers?" Jackson asked.

"Yeah," Frank said. "Elliot found the same names in journals with purchases that are years apart."

Jackson felt his excitement grow. "You have names for the buyers? We can start looking for them?"

"Not exactly," Frank said. "Clancy didn't put 'John Smith' in the books. It's all nicknames."

"Oh," Jackson said, unable to keep the disappointment from his voice.

"Don't despair, Detective," Frank said. "Every little step gets us one spot closer to figuring out a twenty-year horror movie. Anyway, here's what I wanted to show you, and this is for you two only. Bernard's already approved your working this."

Grayson and Jackson nodded.

Frank pointed to a notation in one of the journals. "I matched this buyer amount and date with the transaction in the seller journal for Lydia Johnson."

Jackson drew in a breath. "You found the man who bought Shaye?"

"His nickname," Frank reminded him.

Jackson leaned over and read the word Frank had written above the coded buyer name.

"Diabolique," Jackson said.

"Several of the nicknames have been in French," Frank said.

"But you don't know anything else?" Jackson asked. "Nothing else we could use to go on?"

"Oh, there's something else all right," Frank said, his voice grim. "That's why I sent for you. Take a look at this." He pulled another journal over in front of them and pointed.

"That's the same name," Grayson said. "A fifteen-year-old girl. So this buyer had at least two transactions with Clancy."

"This one was in June." Frank flipped the notebook to the front cover and indicated the date in the upper right-hand corner.

2015.

"Oh my God." Jackson's stomach rolled. "He bought her last month. Another kid is probably going through the same hell that Shaye did. We have to find her."

Grayson nodded, his expression a mixture of disgust and anger. Jackson looked down at the journal again.

Diabolical.

CHAPTER FOUR

Dr. Warren Thompson turned off the television and placed his reading glasses on the end table. He waited a bit before rising from the recliner, allowing his aging eyes to adjust to the dim room. The clock on the far wall began to chime midnight, and he realized he'd been asleep for two hours already. The book that had sounded so interesting in premise hadn't turned out to be nearly as good in execution, and he'd ended up watching television before dozing off. His back and knees protested as he rose, never letting him forget the forty-two years of work and four years of residency he'd put in before finally admitting his body no longer allowed him to practice medicine the way he wanted.

So two weeks ago, he did what he never thought he'd do. He retired.

The first week was all right. It felt more like he was on vacation really, but as Sunday approached and he wasn't preparing his clothes for the upcoming week, the reality of long days with nothing to do stretched in front of him. The second week was a harsh and lonely awakening. His wife, Marie, had passed away five years before. He'd thought he handled her death well, but looking back, he realized he hadn't planned for this reality.

He sighed and headed upstairs, turning off the living room light as he went. Marie had warned him about living only for her and the job. When it was finally clear that the cancer she'd fought so bravely was going to win, she'd made him promise that he'd take up a hobby and make some friends outside of work. Now, with the days and weeks stretching before him, and endless cycle of Netflix, books, and his recliner, he had to admit that Marie had been right.

Even from the grave she'd managed an "I told you so."

Without Marie or his work, to say Warren was at loose ends would be an understatement. His children, one son and one daughter, were successful, busy people with their own lives and responsibilities and didn't have time to coddle a bored, lonely old man. His grandchildren were starting their careers and one granddaughter was pregnant. He was going to be a great grandfather. That made him smile. Marie would have loved it, especially as it was her favorite granddaughter who was pregnant. Warren knew you weren't supposed to have favorites. At least that's what people said, but he also figured they were all liars. Human beings connected with each other on different levels. Why should it be any different just because they were blood?

He climbed into bed and reached over to turn off the lamp. The silence gave him pause, as it always did. Marie had been a noisy sleeper, her snoring interrupted only by her tossing and turning. When he was working crazy hours during his residency, sometimes Warren had slept in the spare room just to get a good night's sleep in. But over the years, he'd grown so used to her nighttime activity that now it felt odd to be so still and surrounded by quiet.

He deliberated turning on the television, but decided against it. Sleep didn't come as easily as it once had. The noise would be worse than the silence. And the news had been filled with stories of that despicable excuse for a human being John Clancy. The only moment of pleasure he'd derived from the stories was when they highlighted the private detective who'd helped expose Clancy.

Shaye Archer was the only patient he'd treated who'd ever given him nightmares. She still remained the worst case of abuse he'd ever seen, and knowing that she'd grown up to be a beautiful, successful, and compassionate young woman made him extremely happy. But that didn't mean that seeing another news story, covering the same tired information, would help him sleep. So he rolled over and closed his eyes, trying not to think of all the things he didn't have to do the next day.

He had just dozed off when he heard a noise downstairs.

He jerked upright, then stilled again to listen, but only the gentle whir of the ceiling fan broke the silence. Had he dreamed it? He didn't think so. He'd barely been asleep, and his racing heart was a clear indication that he hadn't imagined it, either. Perhaps the noise was outside, but even as the thought crossed his mind, he dismissed it. Now that he was alert he recognized the sound. It was the creaking of a loose floorboard in the kitchen. His Labrador had passed a couple years before and could no longer be blamed for noises in the night. The skies were clear and there wasn't a breath of wind. That left only one explanation.

Someone was in his house.

He looked at the security panel in the hall, its green button the only light in the dark, and silently cursed himself for forgetting to set the alarm. He grabbed his cell phone off the nightstand and called 911. Then he swung his legs over the side of the bed, careful not to make a sound, and eased the drawer of the nightstand open. The loaded pistol lay at the back of the drawer where it always had. Warren couldn't even remember the last time he'd removed it, and hoped it was still in good working order.

The 911 operator answered and Warren whispered to her his name and address and told her there was an intruder in his home. The operator immediately dispatched the police and told him to stay on the line until they arrived. Walter moved to the far side of the room, between the bed and the wall, and crouched down, aiming the pistol at the door. If anyone entered the room expecting to find a helpless, sleeping old man, they were in for a rude awakening.

Another creak filled the still air in the house and Warren knew the intruder was coming up the stairs. He sucked in a breath and clenched the pistol with his right hand, his left hand still clutching the cell phone.

"Mr. Thompson? Are you still with me?" The

operator's voice sounded as if it was being broadcast in stereo and Warren hurried to disconnect the call before the intruder could zero in on his location.

Faint footsteps echoed on the bare hardwood floor of the hallway, approaching the bedroom. Warren crouched even lower, until he could barely peer above the top of the bed. His heart pounded so hard that his chest started to burn. He tried to take a deep breath to calm his nerves, but he couldn't do it. His chest ached and his vision blurred as he struggled to take in air, but it was as if he were underwater. He was drowning in an open room full of air.

Sweat ran down his forehead and into his eyes, making his already blurry vision even worse, then his arms went limp and the pistol that had been trained on the door fell over onto the bed, his hands so weak he could no longer hold it.

He was having a heart attack.

What were the fucking odds?

Reagan Dugas lifted her head and groaned. The headache that had been plaguing her for days had grown in intensity until now she felt as if her skull were being pulled apart. She struggled to push herself up from the stone floor but barely made it halfway before she started retching.

He'd drugged her again.

She never knew when the food he brought her would be laced with whatever put her out, but she always knew when he'd done it. The headaches were awful, but they weren't the worst part. She checked her legs and chest and found three new puffy red lines cut into the flesh of her abdomen. Right next to the new marks, old ones were in various stages of scarring, each set of three giving her a clue as to the length of her captivity. She had no idea exactly how long she'd been trapped in the tiny room. With no light and no watch, every minute was the same. Except when he came. The endless minutes in a dark hole were bad, but they weren't as bad as the man.

The last thing she remembered of her life before was sitting at the construction site and watching skaters at the docks. She was pretty sure the skaters were street kids, and she'd wanted to go over and join in, but had been afraid to approach them. In hindsight, she probably should have. Maybe they would have warned her that someone was kidnapping street kids.

The man who'd grabbed her that night on the dark street wasn't the same one who held her captive now. She'd overheard a conversation between the man who grabbed her and someone else she couldn't see. A lot of what they were saying didn't make sense, but enough did. Those men kidnapped kids and sold them, and the man who had her now had bought her from them.

When that realization had hit her, she'd cried until she had no tears left, then she'd gotten mad. Mad at her dad for leaving. Mad at her mom for hooking up with a man who beat her to death. Mad at her aunt for marrying a perv who'd crawled into bed with her and wouldn't get out until she threatened to scream. Ever since she'd hit puberty, men had looked differently at her, including the one who'd killed her mom. Whenever it happened, she felt the need to shower. It was only a matter of time before one of them forced himself on her. She was surprised it hadn't happened before her uncle made his attempt.

So she'd left.

But now she wondered about her choice. That woman from social services, who'd visited after her mom died, had given her a card. It was tucked in a pocket of the backpack she'd taken when she left her aunt's house. She'd even pulled it out once. But she hadn't called. The horror stories she'd heard about foster care had trumped what she thought she'd encounter on the streets.

She'd been so very wrong.

Shaye pulled a brush through her wet hair and tossed the towel on the side of the tub. If she didn't do laundry soon, that towel would be the only semi-clean thing in her apartment. The last time she'd visited, Corrine had suggested that Shaye hire someone to take care of the domestic things that she didn't want to be bothered with. That was Corrine's polite way of saying Shaye was a slob, but then Corrine was anal to the point of arranging her clothes by season, purpose, type, then color.

Shaye supposed she should look for a cleaning service at least. It didn't take a lot of time to clean her apartment, but it was time she'd rather spend doing other things, and her list of things to do had grown astronomically over the last couple weeks. The five-person crew that cleaned Corrine's house was too much for Shaye's tiny apartment, but maybe they could send only one or two of them. She made a mental note to call and ask.

She headed out of the bathroom and into the living room, plopping down on the couch. It had been a long, exhausting, frustrating day, filled with disappointment, anger, and douche bags. Every time she thought about that stunt Vincent had tried to pull, she got angry all over again. Which only pissed her off even more because then Vincent had gotten to her more than once. Given her penchant for perfect recall, Vincent's action had managed to ruin her entire afternoon.

She turned on the television and scrolled through the options, finally settling on a forensics show. The things that could be accomplished with science today amazed her almost as much as the blatant stupidity of many criminals. Of course, stupid criminals weren't something she was going to complain about. It was the smart ones who were the real problem.

She glanced at her laptop and thought about checking email but she didn't feel like it. There wasn't a single thing she could think of that couldn't wait until tomorrow. Besides, if it was an emergency, her cell phone was never far away. She leaned back on the couch and watched as a crime scene unit processed a bedroom where they suspected a murder had occurred.

In minutes, she drifted off to sleep.

The stone floor was so cold she couldn't sit on it without shivering. She hadn't seen the sky in years, but she knew right now it was swirling with angry gray winter clouds. When the man came, the freezing air blew in with him. New Orleans wasn't as cold as the places she'd seen before on television—the ones covered in snow and ice—but sometimes you needed a coat and heat or a stack of heavy blankets to keep warm. She didn't have any of that.

For all she knew she wasn't even in New Orleans.

When she'd first been taken, she'd been drugged for a long time. A girl at school said she wasn't supposed to know about drugs but she'd seen her mother take the different-colored pills, then act weird and sleep for a really long time. One time her mother had been especially aggravated with her and she'd told her to take one of the pills. She didn't remember going to sleep, but she was sick to her stomach when she woke up and her head felt like it would explode.

The man never made her swallow anything, so the drugs must be in her food. At first, it had taken days for the poisons to work their way out of her system. Now she didn't feel groggy and spacey for more than a couple hours after waking up. She thought that meant it wasn't happening as often, but then, maybe she'd gotten used to it.

Even though she had no way of knowing for sure, she thought she was still in New Orleans, or at least in Louisiana. The man had a Creole accent and he brought her shrimp and gumbo to eat sometimes. Besides that, something inside her just felt like she hadn't left the state.

Not that it mattered. No one was coming to look for her.

She went to school for a while, but then people started asking questions that she didn't want to answer—mostly about her mother—so she'd stopped going. It didn't surprise her that no one came to check. Her teacher had called her "disruptive," whatever that meant, and asked to speak to her parents. She didn't have a father. Not that she'd ever known, anyway, and when she'd asked her mother about him, she'd never gotten a good answer.

Her mother never knew where she was and never asked, but this time was different. This time, she'd been gone for a long time. Her mother had made her go with the man, but surely, she realized that he'd never brought her back. But then, if she was still smoking that stuff and taking the pills, she might not care. The smoking stuff cost a lot of money. So much money that her mother traded their food money for it and they went hungry for days. With one less mouth to feed, her mother could buy more stuff. The stuff always made her happier than food.

She pushed a small pile of straw together and sat on it, but the thin strands didn't provide much insulation against the cold stone. The only clothes she had was what she wore now, a pair of jeans that were too big and a T-shirt that was too small. She couldn't even remember what she'd been wearing when the man took her, but she'd been through several sets of clothes since then. They were always used and rarely fit, but she was used to that. She'd never had new clothes that fit properly.

She sat in the silence and listened for the dreaded thunder. If it rained too hard, the floor flooded. She could only stand for so long before her weak body gave out and she had to sit. But the thought of sitting in cold water when she was already freezing brought tears to her eyes, and not many things did that anymore. Cold water and the red dress were the only two things that still made her cry, and sometimes she worried that even those things would no longer matter. That she'd give up entirely and figure out a way to end it all.

She knew how. She'd seen it on television. Two long cuts across her wrist would do the trick.

So far, she'd always found a reason not to do it, but she was afraid that might change. Lately, the man had looked at her with his dark eyes and instead of just raw fear, she'd felt her skin crawl and then the overwhelming feeling of wanting to cover up her entire body so that he couldn't see any of it. Something else was coming. She didn't understand what, but she knew it was different from before.

A thunderclap boomed overhead and she pulled her knees up to her chest, lowered her head to them, and began to cry.

Shaye jerked awake, her heart racing. She tried to force all the details from her dream into her awakened mind, but they were already slipping away. Damn it! Her frustration grew as the harder she tried to remember, the quicker she forgot.

She'd been back in the stone room again and it had been cold, but there was more this time. Things about her mother that she'd never dreamed before. But now she couldn't remember them. She rose from the couch and headed to the kitchen to fix herself a snack. Then she'd head to her office and work.

There was no use to try sleeping again.

Not after one of the dreams.

CHAPTER FIVE

Belles Fleurs Plantation, 1936

The Haitian boy hid in the shrubs and watched the plantation owner through the window of the big house. The owner was in the fancy room with a huge desk and bookcases. The Haitian boy knew it was supposed to be a place to work, but the owner had never worked a day in his life. Everything that hadn't been given to him, he'd taken. He was evil and cruel, but he wasn't the only one who could use those traits to make himself rich and powerful.

He watched as the man left the room. It was dinnertime, and he'd sit in an even fancier room while servants fed him, his pathetic wife, and the weak boy. The man would return to the working room when dinner was over and unlock the cabinet that held his expensive whiskey. He'd pour glass after glass and if he was in a foul mood, which was usually the case, he'd head upstairs and beat his wife or son, or he'd leave the house and beat one of the workers.

The Haitian pulled a burlap bag out of his pocket and jiggled it in his hand. The whiskey bottle would work. The locked cabinet presented no difficulty, nor did the window. No one would ever know he'd been inside.

He smiled. The owner's son believed they had conjured a demon, but that was a lie. His great-grandmother didn't know how to make demons appear, but she knew everything about the old magic. A person could do anything with roots, if they knew how.

Even kill someone.

CHAPTER SIX

Saturday, July 25, 2015
Ninth Ward, New Orleans, Louisiana

Shaye hesitated before entering the apartment building. She'd been here once before, to the apartment that Lydia Johnson, her biological mother, had occupied. Nothing had been familiar, leading Shaye to believe at the time that she'd never lived there. The date in Clancy's journal and Lydia's occupancy date of the apartment confirmed what Shaye had felt. She'd never been inside the apartment until the night she entered it with Jackson.

But Lydia had lived here for twelve years. In that time she must have talked to someone, maybe even mentioned Shaye during a drug-induced haze. If Shaye could figure out where Lydia lived before she moved here, maybe it would spark Shaye's memory of her past. If she could remember her time with Lydia, then she might remember her time with her captor. All the answers she needed were right there, locked away in her fragile mind. If she could just figure out a way to access them, all of this could be over.

Healing could begin.

She took in a deep breath and blew it out, then walked into the building and headed toward the apartment her mother had occupied. She stopped at the apartment across the hallway from her mother's old unit and knocked on the door. She heard movement inside and after a short wait, the door opened and a woman peered out at her through the crack in the door, the chain latch still in place.

"Who are you?" the woman asked, looking her up and down.

"My name is Shaye. I'm trying to get information on the woman who lived across the hall from you—Lydia Johnson?"

"Already talked to the cops. Didn't know nothing about no Lydia then. Don't know anything now."

The door slammed, and Shaye heard the dead bolt slide back into place. She stared at the door for several seconds, assessing the situation. The apartment manager had told her the woman had occupied the apartment across from Lydia's for four years. How was it possible that she didn't know who Lydia was?

The bottom line was it wasn't possible.

The woman simply didn't want anything to do with the police or anyone else. Unfortunately, it was common behavior. People didn't want to get involved, especially when they could lose their benefits if someone clued in to any illegal activity. Like Lydia being a junkie.

Shaye sighed. Given what she was up to, Lydia probably hadn't spent a lot of time chatting with other residents. But still, four years? Surely there was a conversation in the laundry room or in the back courtyard smoking at some point. She moved on to the next door and knocked again. It was a long shot to get information, but damn it, it was one of the only things she had to go on.

An hour later, she slumped into the drivers' seat of her SUV, completely frustrated. She'd been through the entire building. Of the people who'd bothered to answer their doors, none had claimed knowledge of Lydia Johnson. They were lying, of course. Shaye could see the distrust and fear in their expressions. But what could she do about it?

Nothing. That's what.

She started her car and pulled out of the parking lot. While she was on this side of town, she'd stop and see Hustle. She hadn't checked on him in person in a while, although she'd spoken with Saul regularly and he'd reported the teen was doing fine. Seeing Hustle doing well would definitely improve her day.

It was just shy of 1:00 p.m. when Shaye parked her SUV in front of the Bayou Hotel. She yawned and blinked several times, trying to get her tired eyes to focus correctly. After the dream and her impromptu hour of work, she'd never managed to get back to sleep properly, instead tossing and turning the rest of the night, barely dozing and jumping awake at every little sound. Consequently, she was exhausted but knew if she tried to sleep, her overly active mind wouldn't allow it. By tonight, she'd be so tired her mind wouldn't have a choice. She was already counting the hours until her collapse.

She hopped out of the car and headed inside. Saul

occupied his usual perch at the front desk and smiled at her as she walked inside.

"I was wondering when you would pay us a visit," he said.

"I'm sorry I haven't sooner," she said. "I've had some stuff…"

"You don't have to explain things to me," Saul said. "Besides, I've got this under control."

She smiled. "I knew you would or I wouldn't have asked."

At the center of the human trafficking case that Shaye had assisted the New Orleans police with was a street kid named Hustle. He'd helped Shaye on her first case and when his friend Jinx had gone missing, he'd sought out Shaye to see if she could help. Jinx had lived through a terrifying ordeal but was now reunited with her aunt, a good woman who would give Jinx the life she deserved.

Hustle had been happy for Jinx, but worried about his own future. With no parents and still a minor, he should be a ward of the state, but he'd fled foster care to escape an abusive foster parent and had zero intention of returning to the system. During the investigation, Saul had not only given Hustle a place to stay while Shaye looked for Jinx, he'd saved Hustle's life by shooting one of the kidnappers as he was about to kill Hustle. Then Saul had gone a huge step further and agreed to foster Hustle when all the dust had settled and Jinx was safe.

"How's he doing?" Shaye asked. "How are you doing?"

"We're both doing fine. The kid's a hard worker, and you weren't kidding about the artistic ability. Come look at this."

Saul walked around the desk and headed down the hall to the small dining area used to serve continental breakfast. He clicked on the lights and Shaye gasped. The walls had been painted with scenes of New Orleans streets, but from past times. Men and women in fancy dress, Mardi Gras parades, and other New Orleans traditions all came to life against a background of French Quarter buildings.

"This is incredible," she said. "I knew he was talented, but I had no idea…"

"I took some pictures of this and he agreed to let me send them to some art schools. I can't imagine they wouldn't take him, and I'm guessing he'd get a scholarship besides."

Shaye nodded. "I think you're right. What about high school?"

"He's doing the homeschool classes online. I thought it would be a bit of a fight, but he hasn't said a word of complaint. We set a schedule for him with work and school and he's stuck to it by the minute. He's a sharp boy. It won't take him long to get his GED."

"I figured as much. What about other things?"

"You mean all the touchy-feely stuff? Well, that's a little harder to navigate being that I'm a crotchety old Marine and he's a skittish teenager, but we're doing all right. He's shared some stories about his mom with me, so that's a good sign."

Shaye felt as if a huge weight had been lifted from her shoulders. "You don't know how much I appreciate what you're doing, Saul."

"Yes, I do, but it's not necessary. I would have taken the boy in whether you asked me or not. He's a good kid, and he's going to make a fine man. Doing what he did to find his friend…that's serious heart, and you can't teach a person heart." Saul looked down at the floor for a minute and shook his head. "He reminds me of a member of my platoon. He would have been a fine man, if he'd made it back."

"Well, whether it's necessary or not, I still appreciate it. You know I would have been happy to take him myself, and Corrine wouldn't have batted an eyelash if I'd asked her, but I think he needs a good man in his life. He's never had that."

Saul nodded. "Too many people discount the importance of fathers, including a lot of fathers. It's a shame." Saul cocked his head to the side and stared at her for a couple seconds. It was clear he wanted to ask something but wasn't sure if he should. Curiosity must have won out because he finally asked, "Have the police figured anything out on those journals?"

Yeah, they've figured out I was one of Clancy's products.

The words ran through her mind, unbidden, but she couldn't bring herself to say them. Not yet. Not that way. "I'm not exactly in the loop on everything the police are doing, but I know they're working on deciphering them," she said. "But it's a lot to cover. The journals date back almost twenty years."

Saul's eyes widened. "Jesus. I had no idea…"

"No one did. How could we? It's the most incredulous and awful thing we've ever seen here. The police are as shocked and disgusted as the rest of us."

He shook his head. "I can't imagine trying to work all that out. All those victims…it must be heartbreaking. Is your man working it?"

Shaye felt a light blush creep up her neck. She'd gotten to the point where she'd readily admit to others that Jackson was a friend, and sometimes she'd admit to herself that she thought about him being even more, but she wasn't anywhere near ready to call him her man.

"He's not mine," she said, "and as far as I know, he wasn't assigned to work on the Clancy journals, but I haven't talked to him in a week or so."

Not since the last time she'd run into him at the station, after one of her many meetings to go over her statement concerning the Clancy case. He'd called a few times and left messages, but she hadn't returned the calls yet. Something about Jackson made her so comfortable she actually wanted to talk to him about the things she never talked about. But she wasn't ready for a conversation about the journals. He'd probably already been informed through police channels, and he was respectful enough not to bring the subject up unless she did, but she wasn't ready to do that. Not quite yet, but the time was coming.

Saul raised his eyebrows a bit but he was smart enough to let it drop. Pushing Shaye for information was a waste of time. It only made her more silent. "Hustle's painting." he said. "Room 12."

"Thanks." She headed off, following the sound of rock music that trickled down the hall. It wasn't loud. Saul wouldn't allow that as other people were staying at the hotel, but with the room door open, the lead guitar and pounding drums echoed a bit.

She stepped into the room and took a moment to appreciate the cool blue Hustle was putting on the walls. The sad tan would soon be a thing of the past. She smiled, knowing good and well that Saul hadn't picked the color. He was too traditional, but at least he'd been wise enough to take Hustle's advice. The blue gave the room a relaxed feel.

"You do good work," Shaye said.

Hustle gave a bit of a start and whirled around, grinning when he caught site of her.

"Saul just showed me the dining room," she said. "It's incredible."

The teen blushed and looked down at the floor, still not used to receiving compliments, especially from adults. "Thanks," he said. "I was surprised he let me do it. I figured he'd think it was too much. It wasn't cheap, either, all those colors."

"I'm guessing the blue was your idea too?"

"Yeah. I thought it looked like the ocean. I went there one time with my moms when I was really little. I don't remember much about it but I'll never forget that shade of blue."

"It's going to look great. Come sit with me for a minute," she said and pointed to the little breakfast table in the corner.

Hustle put the paint roller down and slid into the chair, looking slightly uneasy.

"How are things going?" she asked. "Are you doing all right here? Because if it's not working okay for you, we can find something else."

His eyes widened. "No! I mean, it's great here. Every morning, I wake up and I still can't believe my luck. I thought the school part would be really sucky, but it's not as hard as I thought it would be. I do the classes in Saul's office. They're more boring than anything, but Saul says it won't take long to get my GED. At least that way I don't have to go to actual school."

Shaye smiled. "I'm so happy for you. You deserve something good in your life."

Hustle dropped his gaze and shrugged. "People don't always get what they deserve—the good or the bad."

Shaye's smiled slipped away. Having experienced too much too young was something she and Hustle shared. They knew better than most that the bad things that came at you weren't often warranted. But they'd both survived. Shaye was accomplished and successful, and she had no doubt Hustle would be as well.

"Are you all right?" he asked.

She tried to force the smile back but she knew it wasn't very convincing. "I'm fine."

He shook his head. "Don't do that. Don't lie to me. If

you don't want to say what's wrong, then that's okay, but don't say things are fine when they're not."

Instantly, Shaye felt contrite. One of the things that had finally convinced Hustle to trust her was that she'd been honest with him about everything from the moment they'd met. "I'm sorry. There's some things I'm dealing with…hard things…and most of the time, I don't feel like I'm doing a very good job."

"The police aren't hassling you over Clancy or me, are they?"

"No. Nothing like that. The police have bigger fish to fry than worrying about me or you."

"I'm glad. I wouldn't want you getting into trouble for doing something good. So is what's wrong a secret or is it too personal?"

Shaye considered how to answer. The real answer, she supposed, was yes to both questions, but the secret part was bound to come undone sooner than later. So far, news of her biological mother hadn't leaked to the press, but Shaye knew it was only a matter of time. The question was, did she want Hustle to hear about it on the evening news or from her?

"It's personal and secret," she said, "but I know it won't stay that way." She drew in a breath and slowly blew it out. "They found my biological mother."

Hustle jerked up straight in the chair, his eyes wide. "No shit? Wow! No wonder you're freaked out. Have you talked to her? What did she say? Did she know what happened to you? Sorry. I'm throwing all this at you."

"You're fine. Trust me, I have plenty of questions myself. Unfortunately, she wasn't alive to answer any of them."

Hustle's face fell. "Oh. I'm sorry."

"I'm not. She was a junkie. She died of a drug overdose."

Hustle was silent for a bit. "I don't get it, you know? How the drugs take hold of somebody. I mean, I seen it happen a lot, but I can't wrap my mind around it. Seems like you ain't gotta suffer from it if you never do it to begin with."

"If only that bit of wisdom crossed everyone's mind."

"She didn't leave anything that might help you figure out what happened?"

Shaye bit her lower lip, still wavering. Did she tell him everything now or hope the information in the journal remained confidential for a while?

"The police know what happened," Shaye said quietly. "I'm going to tell you this because I want you to hear it from me and not some slimy news reporter, but I'd appreciate it if you keep it to yourself."

Hustle looked confused. "Okay."

"My mother's name was in Clancy's journals. I was one of his products. She sold me."

"What?" Hustle jumped up from his chair and paced the tiny kitchen. "No fucking way." He looked at Shaye. "You're not shitting me?"

"I wouldn't do that. Especially about this."

"Of course you wouldn't. What the hell am I

thinking?" He ran his hand through his long blond hair. "I'm thinking it's a horror movie is what I'm thinking. And I don't blame you for not caring that she's dead. I swear, if I could, I'd bring her back to life and kill her myself."

Shaye felt tears fill her eyes. "You're a good friend, Hustle."

He stopped pacing and looked down at her. "We are friends, right? I mean, for real friends?"

She nodded. "I don't have a lot of them, but you're definitely my friend."

He sat back down and leaned forward, over the table. "Then let me help you."

"I don't know what you can do. If there was anything…"

"There is. You went to her house, right? That woman who had you."

"She lived in government housing—an apartment. And yes, I went there, but I never lived there. The dates in the journals confirm it. Nothing inside was familiar, and she wasn't nice enough to leave a letter explaining why she sold her child. Not that I need it spelled out for me. I think we both know what happened."

"Did you try talking to people there who might have known her?"

"I talked to the apartment manager the night I went to see the place but he has his head in the sand. If he's not aware of it then he doesn't have to report it to the police, you know? I went back this morning and tried to talk to the neighbors, but no one had anything to say."

"Let me guess. You got a bunch of doors slammed in your face."

"Yeah. They wouldn't even admit to knowing who she was."

Hustle shook his head. "They're not going to talk to you. Even though you're not one, some of your habits scream cop. And your clothes and haircut tell them right away you're not one of them. But they might talk to me."

"No. I can't let you do that."

"Why not? She's dead. Clancy's dead. The danger is gone, right?"

"I…well, I don't know."

"Do you have any reason to think it's not?"

"There's still the person who bought me."

"And he hasn't come after you all these years. Maybe he's not around, either."

"Maybe not." That thought had only crossed her mind about a hundred times a day.

"Then let me take a run at them. I'm still a kid. I look street and I know how to talk it."

"What will you tell them?"

He frowned. "I don't know. I'll lie, I'm sure, but I'll have to see them to figure out what will get them talking."

Shaye's emotions warred. Hustle was right that the neighbors might talk to him when they wouldn't talk to her, but it wasn't his responsibility to help her. She was the adult. He was the child.

"If they give her name on the news," he said, "I'm going to do it without your permission, and by then, it will probably be too late to get anything out of them because reporters will be camped out on the sidewalk."

She smiled. "Playing hardball?"

He shrugged. "Sometimes you have to get a little pushy when you know what somebody ought to do."

She knew exactly what he was getting at. She'd all but strong-armed Hustle into listening to her idea about Saul fostering him. And she knew he was stubborn enough to do exactly what he was threatening to do—investigate on his own as soon as he had the address. Unfortunately, he was also right about waiting. Nothing would seal people's lips faster than knowing cops or reporters were looking at them.

"Okay," she said, "but you cannot go there alone. I'll take you."

"It won't work if you're with me."

"It will work if I stay in the car, and you wear a wire so I can help if there's trouble."

He grinned. "You're all James Bond and shit."

"I'm working on it." She rose from the chair. "I have time tomorrow afternoon. Does that work for you?"

"Tomorrow morning is better."

"Really? Why?"

"Because tomorrow morning is algebra class?"

Shaye smiled. "I'm afraid you're going to have to suffer through it. You know I have to tell Saul what we're doing."

"Saul's cool. He'll want me to help if I can." Hustle shuffled a bit. "Does he know…about your mother and stuff?"

"Not yet, but he's about to." There was no use putting it off any longer. "Thanks, Hustle."

"For what?"

"For being my friend."

Jackson leaned back in the conference room chair and blew out a breath. He'd arrived at work that morning, ready to launch full speed into finding the girl Clancy had sold, but before he even finished pouring coffee, he and Grayson had to take a homicide call. It had turned out to be a simple one as far as police and legal work went. A man tweaking on something had broken into a woman's house and attacked her. She managed to get a shot off in the struggle and it went straight through the perp's heart.

Open and shut on their end. Unfortunately, the perp was the woman's brother, so it wasn't over for her, maybe never would be. Still, she had a restraining order against him due to a previous attack and he was wanted for stabbing a man two nights before, so the ADA had taken one look at the facts and said he wouldn't pursue charges.

But even the simple ones took time. Time to process the crime scene. Time to interview witnesses. Time to put the facts together and present them to the ADA. So it was midafternoon before they grabbed some takeout Chinese food and headed back to the police station.

For the last hour, Jackson had been reviewing files for missing children in New Orleans and calling to get updates if any were available. He tossed his pen on the conference table in disgust. Over twenty missing children, and that was the ones who got reported. How many others had slipped through the cracks in the system and taken off from a bad situation at home? Six fit the age range of the teen Clancy had sold, but two had returned home, another was found living with the noncustodial parent, and the fourth had been picked up working at a strip club.

"Anything?" Grayson's voice sounded behind him as he walked into the conference room.

"Two still missing that fit the criteria, but neither feels right."

Grayson looked over Jackson's shoulder at his laptop. "Why not? Looks like either one could work."

Jackson hesitated a moment before replying. The theory that had bounced around his mind the entire time he'd searched the database seemed sound when he was keeping it to himself, but now, when faced with saying it out loud, it sounded like a huge guess with nothing to back it up.

"Out with it, Lamotte," Grayson said. "I told you if something got on your radar, let me know. Leave it up to me to reel you in if I think you're too far out in left field."

"Okay, well, I was thinking that the child he bought this time was the same age as Shaye when she escaped."

Grayson's eyebrows went up. "I hadn't thought about it that way, but you're right. You think that's significant?"

"I don't know, but what if he wanted to pick up where he left off?"

"Nine years later?"

"I know it sounds crazy, but if that was what he had in mind, then I was thinking he might want a girl not only the same age but who also looked like Shaye. One of these girls has blond hair and the other red. Both were overweight and fairly short."

Grayson frowned but didn't dismiss Jackson's theory. "So nothing at all like Shaye, physically." He put his hands in the air. "Okay, so let's say you're right and it's neither of these two. Where do we go now? Broaden the search to Baton Rouge?"

"We can, but we know Clancy was working New Orleans at the time this girl was sold. She could have come to New Orleans from another city, but it's more likely she's from New Orleans or somewhere nearby."

"If that's the case, then we've got a big hole in our data. If this girl was off-grid as far as social services is concerned and the parents are a no-show, she might never be reported."

"I know." Jackson struggled to control his frustration. He tapped his desk, staring at the monitor as if a solution were going to materialize on the screen. "What about this? If the girl is local and not reported, then she's got a crap home situation, right?"

"That's probably a given."

"Then chances are social services would have been called in, at least once."

Grayson shook his head. "There's no way we can check up on every fifteen-year-old that social services took a peek at. Hell, for all we know, they could have seen the kid years ago, if they investigated her household at all. It would take days to go through that amount of data, even if we only went back a year and only in the New Orleans area. And that's assuming I could get this witch hunt approved in the first place. We don't exactly have the manpower to spare."

Jackson's expression must have shifted at the words "witch hunt" because Grayson put his hand up to stop him from replying.

"I'm not saying *I* think it's a witch hunt," Grayson said. "I'm inclined to think you're onto something, but we'd never get departmental resources approved for a search. Not right now. And besides, I can't see how knowing who the victim is would help us find her now."

Jackson slumped back in his chair and blew out a breath. Grayson was right. Even if they could convince Captain Bernard that this course of investigation was viable, they didn't have the staff to pursue it, not with so many resources already pulled for the Clancy investigation.

"I guess I was hoping if we could identify her," Jackson said, "then maybe someone has seen her—you know, could give us a place to start looking." Then an idea swept through his mind and he straightened up. "What if we had someone else do the research? Someone who already has clearance?"

"There's no one with clearance that isn't already assigned to a double workload."

"Corrine Archer is still on medical leave. She'd have

access to the files at social services. Surely she could be cleared to have information on the missing girl."

Grayson's eyes widened. "Whoa, I don't know. Sure, Corrine has access and she's one sharp cookie, but her daughter was also this guy's prisoner."

"Which gives her more reason to want him caught than anyone else in this city except Shaye."

Grayson stared over Jackson's head at the wall, and Jackson could tell he was weighing the risks and possible rewards against the potential for the entire thing to blow up in their faces. Finally, he nodded. "We'll have to run it by Bernard."

"Of course."

"No time like the present," Grayson said. "If he goes for it, we can give Ms. Archer a call and see if we can go talk to her."

Jackson nodded and hopped up from his chair. He was glad they were going to talk to Corrine in person, assuming Bernard approved this line of investigation. Jackson couldn't fathom telling Corrine over the phone that another child had been sold to the same man who'd purchased Shaye. Apparently, Grayson felt the same way. It ticked the senior detective up another notch in Jackson's estimation. He'd already known Grayson was a good cop. It appeared he was a good man as well. Jackson's overall attitude about his job and his future with the department had improved by a mile in the past twenty-four hours.

Bernard was in his office and Grayson took the lead, explaining their theory and the desire to ask Corrine for help going through records at social services.

"That's a bit of a stretch, isn't it?" Bernard asked.

"Yes, sir," Grayson said, not even trying to hedge. "Unfortunately, a stretch might be all we have to go on with this case."

Bernard nodded, his expression grim. Jackson knew the mayor had already paid Bernard a visit, and word around the water cooler was he'd received a call from the governor as well. The amount of pressure on him to get those journals deciphered and put more of these despicable people behind bars must be practically crippling. Jackson did not envy the man his position. Not one little bit.

"Okay," Bernard said finally. "If Ms. Archer is willing to do the research, I don't see how it could possibly hurt." He gave them a strained smile. "I always did like betting on a long shot."

He stepped out of the alley and into the parking lot, clutching the long, ornate knife in his right hand. Her car, a Lexus, was parked on the back row, making his job easier. No one paid any attention to a man walking across a parking lot, and on the back row, he was out of sight of the sidewalk as soon as he stooped down. The gap between the front bumper of the car and the concrete wall that formed the rear of the parking lot made the perfect hiding place.

He crouched and peered around the car, pleased to see that the front row of vehicles, mostly made up of contractor vans and SUVs, effectively blocked him from street view. All of the businesses in this area had security cameras, but only one was nearby and it was at a jewelry store across the street. That camera would be focused on the sidewalk and road in front of the store, not a parking lot across the street and certainly not the back row of the parking lot.

Despite the relative seclusion provided by the row of vehicles, he wouldn't have chosen this place for the work at hand if there had been another option. Public places were never best, especially during daylight hours. But the woman lived in a secured high-rise with valet parking and in the days during the past two weeks that he'd tracked her, he'd never seen her leave the building at night. Her daily schedule, though, had been simple to ascertain. Work, gym, dinner, home. Monday through Friday. Breakfast, then teaching senior aerobics at a community center on Saturday.

The building that housed her physical therapy practice was in a busy area and had full-time security guards for the building and parking lot. The community center, however, was located some distance from the nearest parking area and it was one of those unmanned lots where you shoved some bills in a slot and went on about your business. Saturday was his best option.

He checked his watch and frowned when he saw it was a good ten minutes past the time she should have arrived at her car. The street was lined with retail shops between the community center and the parking lot. If she'd gotten distracted by the displays and decided to waste time shopping, it would put him behind. He had other targets to locate and eliminate, and some of them were proving harder to find than he'd originally thought. Nine years had given people time to change jobs, homes, spouses, and even states. As soon as this one was taken care of, he was headed to Florida for the next on his list, which is why the current delay was making him antsy.

He peered around the car again and caught a glimpse of her on the sidewalk in front of the parking garage, looking down at her cell phone. She walked slowly into the lot, both hands on the cell phone as she went. Probably texting. The entire world was obsessed with technology. He found it exhausting.

Finally, she shifted the phone to one hand and pulled her car keys out of her purse with the other. The car beeped, signaling that the doors were unlocked. Clutching his ceremonial knife, he crept around the front bumper and to the passenger side of the vehicle. As she moved toward the driver's door, he slipped around the side of the car and then to the rear as she stepped up to the door.

She was reaching for the door handle when he struck. Quick and stealthy as a cat, he moved behind her, put his left hand over her mouth, and slit her throat with the knife. She didn't even have time to struggle. He heard a gurgle as air and blood pushed through the incision, and then she collapsed.

He grabbed her purse and hurried away from the car along the back of the parking lot, then entered the alley, making sure he never looked toward the street as he walked. When he got into the alley, he removed the surgical gloves he'd been wearing and grabbed the backpack he'd stashed behind a Dumpster. He cleaned the knife with a towel and placed it in the leather sheath, then he put the towel, the purse, and the gloves into a plastic bag, wrapped it tightly, and stuffed all of it into the pack.

The alley led onto a residential street. He'd parked two blocks away. He grabbed the pack and hurried out of the alley and set off down the sidewalk. No police sirens wailed in the distance. No one pointed. No one even looked at him.

Two down.

CHAPTER SEVEN

Harold Beaumont hung up the phone and grabbed a beer from the refrigerator before heading out onto his back porch. It looked out over Santa Rosa Sound with its blue water, tons of birds, and excellent fishing. The sun was setting now, and bursts of yellow and orange glittered on top of the water like a disco ball. It was a nice view—one that usually brought out a smile from a tired, cynical old cop. But today it didn't so much as elicit a twitch of his lips.

Even though he'd left New Orleans shortly after retiring, he'd kept up with the local news. You could talk the cop into retirement, but that just meant he wasn't getting paid anymore. It didn't stop the mind from processing crime, especially when it was in your home territory. Especially when it was headline news, like the Clancy case.

He took a swig of beer and sat in a lawn chair, mulling over the information he'd just received. All the news reports had been filled with drama and outrage but few facts. Harold knew that was usually for one of two reasons—there weren't any facts to be shared or the police were holding back facts to help eliminate suspects. In this case, Harold would have bet his million-dollar view on the second option, and he was right. The phone call he'd just received confirmed it.

The news was all regular folks had, but Harold wasn't regular folk. He had an inside source that kept him in the loop with what was happening at the NOLA police department. Sergeant Robert Royer had worked beat with Beaumont for two decades before he had to give it up because of a bad knee. If you could just shoot them if they ran, he probably could have put in another ten years, but department policy required you to chase them instead. At least, that's the way Bob liked to tell it. It always got a smile from other cops. Civilians were usually less amused. They didn't understand the things cops dealt with day in and day out, so they couldn't wrap their minds around firearm humor as a coping mechanism.

So Bob had moved off the streets and behind the front desk, running the show from the inside, as Harold liked to say. And things had gone well. Harold had thought moving Bob out of the action would set him straight to private work, but Bob surprised Harold by not only taking the desk sergeant position but claiming he enjoyed it.

Bob always had been the biggest hound dog for information that Harold had ever met, so he supposed he could see the appeal on that level. The desk sergeant was the hub of the police station. Nothing happened that didn't pass in front of them, and since Bob had been around for a long time, most of the guys stopped to share their stories or to run theories by him. The end result being that Bob knew more about crime and politics in New Orleans than anyone else in the department.

Usually Bob called Harold with a juicy bit of gossip about who'd just gotten their asses handed to them by Bernard or a crime that was outside the norm, but this time, the call was one Bob hadn't enjoyed making.

Shaye Archer.

Harold couldn't even think her name without the hair on the back of his neck standing up. Even after all these years, he could see her standing in the street, illuminated by his patrol car headlights, covered in blood and God only knew what else, white as a sheet, and staring straight through him as if he weren't even there. In thirty-two years on the job, Harold had never seen anything so horrible and he hoped he never did again.

That idiot he'd been partnered with after Bob moved to the desk had immediately dismissed her as a runaway junkie, but Harold knew better. Whatever had happened to the girl had been so horrible she'd stepped outside of her own mind. She might have been drugged, but that wasn't the only thing going on. Her expression was that of someone whose life was so bad, she'd mentally escaped it. As soon as she'd been admitted to the hospital, Harold had called Corrine Archer. If anyone could help the girl, he thought, it would be Corrine.

And he'd been right.

Corrine had not only personally taken the girl in but had gotten her the best of everything—doctors, psychiatrist, physical therapist, tutors—everything she needed to recover from a horror she couldn't remember. And despite all odds saying that Shaye Archer didn't have a chance at a normal life, she'd managed one, at least on paper.

On paper, she was a first-class student, a hard worker, and generous with charity, and she appeared to have all the makings of an excellent private investigator. Harold had allowed himself to slip into a good place when it came to Shaye. They'd won. Good had triumphed over evil and Shaye was proof.

Then Clancy happened.

Calling it a can of worms was the understatement of the century. This was Pandora's box. In all his years on the force and all the years he'd listened to his own father talk about cases, Harold had never heard anything like the Clancy case. Sure, you saw things on television—those true-crime documentaries and such—but this was different. This was his town and his people.

He'd known the day would come when Shaye would want to talk to him. For years, he'd stiffened slightly when the doorbell rang, thinking it was time, but the years had passed in silence, and he'd finally assumed Shaye was determined to put her forgotten past behind her. He couldn't blame her. He would have done the same thing.

But this was different. Everything had come home to roost and Harold had no doubt that Shaye was right in the thick of things, trying to ferret out her past. He couldn't blame her for that, either. If someone flung the door open right in your face, it was hard not to step through it. Which also meant something for him.

It was time.

Time to head back to New Orleans and schedule a visit with Ms. Archer. Time to live that night one last time, for her sake and for his. Because it wouldn't truly be over until the man who'd tortured Shaye was identified and punished. But right now, he had a more pressing problem than a four-hour drive and figuring out how to start the conversation he'd never really wanted to have.

Someone was watching him.

He was careful about it. Never coming close enough to the house to set off the motion lights or get caught on a camera, but Harold knew he was out there. He could feel him watching. Maybe from the wooded area surrounding his home. Maybe from a boat anchored in the sound. But definitely somewhere nearby and more than once.

The first time Harold had felt him was the week before when he'd been in the garage working on his bass boat. He'd grabbed a spotlight, pulled out his gun that he still kept on him at all times, and headed across the road to the undeveloped acreage that spread out miles in front of him. He'd found a set of footprints in the bushes close to the edge of the property and had tracked them a couple acres through the woods to a road, but there were no houses nearby, so no one to question about a car parked there or the man driving it.

Since he'd arrived in Florida, Harold had kept mostly to himself. The only person who knew him by name was the guy who owned the bait shop, but Harold couldn't picture Old Joe making his way through the woods with his cane to spy on Harold in his garage. And for what purpose would someone watch him anyway? Harold had arrested plenty of people in his day, but he couldn't think of a single one who would waste time tracking him down today.

No. This was about Shaye. He had no proof, but he knew it as surely as he knew the sun would rise tomorrow. Which meant whoever was watching him was getting scared. All these years and no one had ever taken a peek at him. Clancy gets exposed along with his journals and now Harold is suddenly interesting. It wasn't a coincidence. And if Harold was important enough to watch, then Shaye was probably in danger.

He polished off the beer and headed back inside. It was time to put his plan into action, because the last thing he intended to do was set out for New Orleans with some psychopath on his tail. He reached for his cell phone on the kitchen counter and dialed.

"Joe? Remember that favor I asked you about last week? Well, I need it tonight."

Corrine opened the door to the two detectives and motioned them inside. They both greeted her politely and followed her to the kitchen, where Eleonore was seated at the kitchen counter, drinking tea. Jackson wasn't surprised to see the psychiatrist in attendance. As Corrine's best friend and Shaye's therapist, she'd be in on everything going on with the Archer women.

"I hope you don't mind Eleonore being here," Corrine said. "When you said it was about the Clancy journals, I asked her to come. I want her in the loop on everything that has to do with Shaye, even if it's not directly related to her."

"Of course," Grayson said, and extended his hand to Eleonore. "I don't think we've ever met formally, but I'm a big fan of your work. I'm Detective Grayson."

Eleonore shook his hand. "It happens, I'm a big fan of your work, too." She smiled at the detective and Jackson saw Grayson's shoulders relax a bit. Corrine Archer and Eleonore Blanchet might be the two most intimidating women in New Orleans. It made him feel a little better that Grayson was as careful around them as Jackson was.

"Have a seat, gentlemen," Eleonore said. "I'm getting a crick in my neck."

They slid onto stools next to Eleonore, and Corrine stepped behind the counter across from them. "Would you like something to drink?" she asked. "I know you're on the job but I have sweet tea, soda, and water. I can make coffee if you prefer that."

"Sweet tea would be great," Jackson said, and Grayson nodded.

Corrine removed two glasses from the cabinet and fixed the tea while Eleonore uncovered two plates of cookies and pushed them over.

"When Corrine is stressed, she bakes," Eleonore said. "When I'm stressed, I eat. Since I need to lose some pounds, it isn't a good situation for either of us. Please put a dent in those cookies and save me from myself."

Jackson picked up a cookie and took a bite. "This is great, Ms. Archer. You can't beat homemade."

Corrine gave him a small smile, but Jackson could tell she was a bundle of nerves, waiting to see why they'd requested this meeting.

Grayson took a drink of tea and looked at Corrine. "The reason I requested this meeting is to ask for your help."

"My help?" Corrine looked confused. "I'm not sure I understand."

"We have a situation," Grayson explained. "Some of the names in the journals have been decoded."

Corrine sucked in a breath. "You know who bought Shaye?"

"Only his nickname," Grayson said. "All the buyers that have been deciphered so far have been nicknames. But this particular buyer appeared again in a journal dated June of this year." Grayson glanced over at Eleonore. "There's no easy way to say this. The man who bought Shaye purchased from Clancy again last month—a fifteen-year-old girl."

Corrine's hand flew over her mouth. "Oh my God."

"We've checked the missing children database and have a couple that fit the age range," Grayson said, "but Lamotte has a theory about why they might not be a good match. I'm going to let him explain it to you."

Corrine and Eleonore both fixed their gazes on

Jackson, and he felt like he'd been called to the front of the schoolroom. Now that he was sitting in front of a social worker and a psychiatrist, his idea didn't seem to have nearly as much merit as it did down at the police station.

Or maybe you're afraid to disappoint Corrine Archer.

Fine. So there was that, too.

He drew in a breath and started talking. At this point, he had nothing to lose but his self-respect. Surprisingly, no one rolled their eyes or stopped him in the middle of his somewhat long-winded explanation of how he'd arrived at his theory, and when he finished he looked at Corrine, then Eleonore, but neither spoke. Corrine wore a pensive look and Eleonore was straight-out frowning.

"This is the part where you can tell me I'm crazy," Jackson said, "and that I should never waste your time again with my nonsense."

"I don't think you're crazy," Corrine said. She studied him for a while, then gave him a rueful smile. "I think you're a good man who wants to find a very bad man. And I think this case is more important to you than any other because of Shaye. I'll be honest with you—I was prepared to not like you, but you're making it really hard."

Jackson stared. Of all the things he'd thought Corrine might say, that wasn't on the list. "Thank you."

"As for your theory," Corrine said, and turned to look at Eleonore. "What do you think?"

"You mean is it psychologically viable?" Eleonore asked. "Absolutely. But just because something is a viable option doesn't mean it's happening in this case."

"I know it's a long shot," Jackson started.

Eleonore held up her hand. "You didn't let me finish. Shaye tells me you have good instincts, and I believe her because she would know. She's pretty intuitive herself. So if this idea latched onto you, then it's for a reason and I think that reason is worth pursuing." She looked over at Grayson. "Obviously, you do as well or you wouldn't be here."

Grayson nodded. "I think Lamotte has a good feel for things. I call it radar, and it's the reason I asked the chief to assign him to work with me."

Jackson felt the tension in his back and neck loosen, and he shifted from stressed to slightly embarrassed. "Thank you. I know it's a lot to ask, going on a feeling, especially when all identifying the girl is going to do is support my theory that this guy is trying to pick up where he left off."

"It tells us about his psychological state and lends itself to intent," Eleonore said. "That could be useful in identifying him when you get closer."

"What exactly do you want me to do?" Corrine asked.

"Assuming the girl was on the street," Grayson said, "we figured she probably had a less-than-stellar home life."

Corinne nodded. "And you thought social services might have a record of a call to the house." She leaned back in her stool and blew out a breath. "How far back are you wanting to search—six months, a year? Our office probably handled five hundred reports in the last six months alone."

Grayson's eyes widened. "Five hundred? Holy

smokes."

"They're not all abusers," Corrine explained. "Some reports are made by people trying to cause trouble, and many are unhealthy situations due to poverty or ignorance, but yeah, that still leaves a lot of kids with less than what they deserve."

"I didn't realize it would be so many," Jackson said. "I completely understand if you can't help. That's too much to ask."

Corrine whipped around and pinned her gaze on him. "Not help? Now you're talking crazy. When it comes to finding the man who hurt Shaye, I'm the second-most-vested person on the planet. Of course I'll help. I'll do anything I can to save another girl from going through that hell. But it's going to take some time. Fortunately, I'm still on medical leave for another week, but I can't see it taking less than that to sort through all the records for the last year and try to verify that the teens who fit the description are accounted for."

"I'll help," Eleonore said. "All I have scheduled next week is a conference, but I can cancel. There's nothing worse than sitting around listening to people talk all day."

Eleonore winked at Jackson and he smiled.

"Thank you, both," Grayson said. "I can't tell you how much we appreciate it. With so many people working on the journals, we don't have the manpower to run down these kinds of inquiries. If you need anything, please let me know, and I'll do everything I can to accommodate you."

"There is something you can do for me," Corrine said.

"Catch this evil son of a bitch."

"That's exactly what we intend to do," Grayson said.

Corrine nodded. "And then give me five minutes alone with him."

Shaye hurried into her apartment, secured the locks and dead bolts, and turned on her security system. She grabbed the packages she'd dumped by the front door and headed into the kitchen with them. Her face felt flushed so she grabbed a cold bottle of water from the refrigerator. It was hot and humid, and the combination of that and all the running around had probably caused the faint feeling.

That's what she tried to tell herself, anyway, but she knew better.

The flush was from what was contained in the bags on her kitchen counter and what she intended to do with the contents. If anyone knew what she was planning, they would have told her not to do it, especially her mother and Eleonore. But Shaye wanted answers. The hypnosis she'd strong-armed Eleonore into would take time to set up, mostly because Eleonore would be hyper careful to make sure nothing could go wrong.

But every second that passed, Shaye felt as though she was falling further behind—that the answers she wanted were slipping deeper into her unconscious, making them harder and harder to draw out. She had to grasp on to them while they were still there. Before her untapped memories faded away into nothing.

She polished off the water and looked at the packages. She could wait until it was completely dark outside, but that would just be stalling and she wasn't going to be any more prepared thirty minutes from now than she was already. Besides, the sun was almost gone and with the blinds closed and drapes drawn, the inside of her apartment would look no different than it would in the middle of the night. She reached into the first bag and pulled out a box of black candles. Just four round pieces of wax, and yet they were so much more. She placed the box on the counter and hurried to close the blinds before she changed her mind.

With the apartment completely dark, she used her cell phone to guide her back to the counter. She pulled off her shoes and all her clothes except her underwear and placed them on the counter next to the packages, then she reached into the second bag and pulled out a red dress. It wasn't the same, of course. This was actually a nightgown, but it was the closest she could find to the color and style in her dreams. Her hands shook as she pulled the nightgown toward her head and she paused when she reached her forehead.

You can still change your mind. You can stop now.

And accomplish what? Doing this might not yield any results, but not doing it certainly wouldn't. She shoved the nightgown over her head and the silky fabric fell down her bare skin. It was supposed to be luxurious, but it was one of the most uncomfortable things Shaye had ever put on her body. Everywhere the fabric touched her skin, it felt as if it were burning. She knew it was all in her mind, but that didn't make it any more comfortable.

She took the candles out of the box and placed them on the kitchen floor. The bricks were cool and would be a good representation of the stone altar from her dreams. The granite countertop was probably an even better choice, but she didn't want to risk falling off if a flood of memory took over. The floor was safer.

She lit the candles and placed them on the floor forming a square. It wasn't the same as the dream, which featured more candles than she could count, but it would have to do. Hopefully, the effect would be enough. She crouched down, then sat on the floor. Her breathing grew more rapid and she felt her pulse increase. She took a deep breath in and slowly blew it out as she leaned back until she was lying flat on the floor.

The coolness of the bricks immediately penetrated the thin fabric, and she felt a chill run through her. She closed her eyes and forced herself to recall the dreams—the man with no discernable face, the huddled movement of others behind him, the glow from the candles.

And she slipped away.

The cold was almost unbearable, especially to her foot, which still wasn't right. It always hurt worse with the cold. The candles flickered all around her, creating shadows that jumped on the walls, their ominous shapes seeming to grow in size and proximity. Then she heard the quiet footsteps of the man coming up behind her. He touched her face with his finger, running it down her cheek, and she jerked her head away. She hated his touch but she knew this was only the beginning.

He moved to the side and she saw the flash of the knife as he positioned it above her. The laces on the front of the red dress were already loosened, exposing a good portion of her bare chest. He lowered the knife to her chest and made a single cut.

She wanted to scream but knew if she did, he'd only cut her deeper the next time, so instead, she bit her lip until she could taste blood. The cuts always came in threes, so she had two more to endure. He took his time inflicting the next two cuts on her chest, and she squeezed her eyes tightly shut, biting down harder on her lip. When the knife lifted from her skin after the last cut, she opened her eyes.

He leaned over and she looked at his face, hoping it would come into focus, but it was a blur of black and red, as it had always been before. He reached down and grabbed the end of the dress and pushed it over her hips, exposing her naked lower body. Her legs twisted inward, involuntarily trying to cover her nakedness. The man leaned over again and dipped his fingers in the blood on her chest, then brought his fingers up toward his face.

And that's when she saw it—the mask.

Shaye screamed and bolted upright from the floor, knocking one of the candles over as she backed away. Her lungs burned and her head ached from her pulse pounding in her temples. She struggled to take in a breath, almost unable to manage it. The candle she'd kicked over rolled into her foot, and she choked back another scream before grabbing it up and throwing it in the sink.

It was a demon.

The mask was a horned goat.

Chapter Eight

He watched from the woods as the old man backed his truck up to the garage and climbed out, using his cane to steady himself. Beaumont came out the front door and waved, then went back inside. A couple seconds later, the garage door opened. He lifted his binoculars and spotted the two of them loading boxes into the back of the man's pickup truck. It took them several minutes to get the boxes in and a strap around the back to secure them with the tailgate open, then Beaumont pulled two beers out of the refrigerator and they stood outside by the truck, talking.

Wasting my time is what they're doing.

He checked his watch. Eight p.m. As soon as the old man left, he'd strike. He'd been ready to make his move earlier when he'd heard the old man's truck approaching. It would have been simple to kill the old man, but he had performed the ritual only for Beaumont. The One loved sacrifice in his name, but he required obedience, and ceremony was important. Killing the old man would require acts of penance, and he didn't have the time or inclination for that right now.

The One also required death by his hand. It was

supposed to be visceral and personal. Things that separated him from the sacrifice—like guns—were profane and therefore forbidden unless for self-protection. Killing them both by hand was possible, but it presented more difficulties, especially as he anticipated the cop might be a challenge. It was best to wait for the old man to leave. After all, how long could he possibly be? It was probably past his bedtime already.

Mosquitoes buzzed around his head, sounding as if they were in stereo, but they never landed on his skin. Even insects knew his power and were afraid. Soon Shaye Archer would understand his commitment to the One. Soon, she'd know what real sacrifice meant.

Finally, the old man handed Beaumont the empty beer bottle and began the climb back into his truck. Beaumont headed up the porch and waved to the old man before walking inside, closing the door behind him. It took the old man a while to get into the cab and situated, but finally, the truck started up and the garage door began to close. The headlights came on and a couple seconds later, the old man pulled out of the driveway and headed down the road toward town.

The front room of the house was dark, but he could see light in the back of the house. He'd found an old real estate listing for the property and knew the kitchen was in the back corner where the light was coming from. He'd originally thought he'd wait for Beaumont to go to bed before breaking in, but his patience was running short and it was a long four-mile walk back to the grocery store parking lot where he'd left his car. Besides, the thought of seeing Beaumont's face when he realized who he was and what was going to happen was giving him a hard-on.

Power was an incredible thing. Power over life was the ultimate.

He pulled on his gloves and mask and stepped out of the woods. The porch light trailed across the front lawn, making his passage to the house an easy jaunt. When he reached the house, he skirted the edge of the porch and located a window for one of the spare bedrooms. It took him only seconds to cut out a piece of the window pane and open the window. He paused for a moment, waiting for an alarm, but as he'd suspected, Beaumont hadn't set it yet.

Silently, he slipped through the window and into the room, the thick carpet masking the sound of his passage. Country music wafted down the hallway and he grimaced. He couldn't stand that redneck crap. Only the lowest of the species thought such trash had merit, but then Beaumont was a cop and a Roman Catholic to boot. It went without saying.

He did a quick scan of the other two bedrooms and the two bathrooms before heading for the front of the house. He crept down the hall, pausing for a second when the floorboards squeaked, but continued when he heard no movement from the other end of the house. When he reached the opening for the kitchen, he flattened himself against the wall and pulled out his knife.

He said a quick prayer to the One and took a step

around the corner, arm lifted and ready.

The room was empty.

He frowned and scanned the room. Two other doors. One led to the patio and the other to the garage. He crossed the kitchen and checked the patio door, but it was locked. That left only the garage. Maybe Beaumont was out there working.

He inched over to the door and leaned against it, but couldn't hear anything over the obnoxious, blaring sound of steel guitars. Deciding he was well over all of this, he turned the doorknob and stepped into the garage, prepared to strike.

The garage was empty.

What the hell was going on? He'd seen Beaumont go back into the house and the old man leave. The bedrooms and bathrooms were clear, and he'd walked through the living room. The kitchen was empty and the back door was locked. Unless Beaumont was hiding in a closet, the only other place he could be was the garage, but he wasn't here, either.

Maybe he *was* hiding.

Maybe he'd heard the man enter the house and had closed himself in the pantry. Beaumont was a cop, so anything was possible. He walked back into the kitchen and that's when he saw it—the message on the chalkboard hanging on the kitchen wall.

You missed me, asshole. Smile for the cameras.

Cursing, he slammed his hand on the board and rubbed off the mocking words. Beaumont must have sneaked out the back door, maybe escaped in a boat. But how did Beaumont know he was coming? He'd been careful. He'd never been seen or caught on the security cameras. How could Beaumont have known?

It was pointless to ponder that fact now. The bottom line was that Beaumont was gone and now he had to start the search for him all over again. And now that Beaumont knew someone was tracking him, he'd become even more elusive. He could be anywhere.

He needed to move faster and more efficiently before this got away from him.

And he had to find Harold Beaumont.

Harold climbed out from between the boxes in the bed of Old Joe's truck, a little worse for the wear due to the bumpy road, but a lot better off than he might have fared if he'd remained in his home. Sure, he could still shoot like Clint Eastwood, but every cop knew that if a man was stalking you, he'd eventually get you.

He headed up to the cab. "Thanks for the help."

Old Joe nodded. "I figure if a man who carried a badge as long as you needs to sneak out of his own home, then that's serious business."

Harold nodded. "The most serious kind of business. You're going straight to Mississippi, right?"

"Yep. My son is expecting me. The bait shop is closed and goes on the market next week along with the house. I packed up everything personal this morning and sent it off in a U-Haul. I ain't got no reason to be seen around these parts again, so don't you go worrying about anybody tracking me down. "'Sides, my son's got plenty of ammo and a bit of a temper." Old Joe grinned.

Harold shook his hand. "Good luck to you, Joe."

"You too. Don't let me see you on one of them damned true-crime television shows, all zipped up in a plastic bag. That would piss me off."

"Me too."

Harold patted Old Joe's truck as he drove out of the parking lot. Then he grabbed his duffel bag and headed for the small prop plane sitting on the private airstrip in the middle of a field. The pilot greeted him as he walked up.

"Uncle Hal," the pilot said. "You ready?"

Harold nodded. "I'm as ready as I'm getting."

"You gonna tell me what all this is about?"

"Not just yet. You're going to have to trust me on this one."

"Of course. But if there's something I can do…I mean, to help with whatever…"

"There is something."

"Name it."

"Don't tell your mother."

His nephew grinned. "Neither one of us wants that kind of grief."

Jackson parked in front of Shaye's apartment and deliberated whether or not to knock. It wasn't too late to visit a friend, but time had moved beyond the casual drop-in range. Still, he needed to talk to Shaye about everything that was going on and he preferred to tell her himself. Hearing it from Corrine would make him look and feel like a coward, and he wanted no part of that. Resolved to the task and the time of night, he climbed out of his car and heard a scream from Shaye's apartment.

He pulled out his gun and bolted for her front door, then began pounding on it and yelling her name. No way could he break it down. The door was solid steel construction with a wood overlay. The windows had bars on them. Short of calling the fire department or running his car through the building, there was no way he was getting inside.

He yanked out his phone and was just dialing 911 when the door opened and Shaye peered out at him through a crack. Her face was devoid of color and her eyes were wide with fright.

"What's wrong?" he asked. "Are you all right? Let me help."

What if someone was inside with her? What if they were holding a gun on her? Could he shove the door open and apprehend the perpetrator before he got off a shot?

All those thoughts ran through Jackson's mind, and every millisecond of hesitation from Shaye allowed time for another question to spool into the reel. It seemed like forever, but was probably only a couple seconds before she removed the chain on the door and stepped back to allow him to enter.

Jackson walked inside and glanced around, wondering what the hell was going on. The apartment was completely dark. The blinds and drapes completely covered the windows, blocking any light from the streetlamps that might attempt to creep in, and not a single overhead light or lamp was turned on. For someone who slept with lights on, it seemed an incredibly odd situation.

Shaye didn't speak at all, but trailed through the front room, which served as her office, into the kitchen. Jackson followed her and drew up short when he saw the candles on the floor, their flickering flames the only source of light in the otherwise dark room. Shaye turned on the kitchen lights and he got a better look at her. Something was definitely wrong. First off, she was wearing what appeared to be old-timey-looking lingerie. Granted, he had no idea what her normal sleepwear was, but somehow, this didn't fit the mental image he'd constructed. She reached for one of the candles on the floor, and he saw her hesitate before lifting it. Her hand shook as she put it in the sink with another candle, and he grabbed the remaining two and placed them with the others before blowing out the flames.

"Maybe you should sit down," he suggested. "I'll fix you something to drink."

She nodded and moved around the kitchen counter to sit on the couch. He opened her pantry and pulled out a bottle of whiskey. He fixed her a stiff shot of the whiskey and carried that and an iced tea into the living area. He placed the iced tea on the end table beside her and handed her the whiskey. She took a big drink and closed her eyes. He could see her chest rise as she took in a deep breath and slowly blew it out. She opened her eyes and took another drink before looking at him.

"Thank you," she said.

"Did something happen?" he asked, and sat on the coffee table in front of her. "I'm always here to help…I just need to know with what."

Her expression shifted from exhausted to grim. "I was stupid," she said.

"I find that hard to believe," he said.

She gave him a rueful smile. "You're great for my ego, but it doesn't change the facts. I did something reckless and I wasn't ready for the consequences."

He thought about the dress and the candles and none of his conclusions were logical or good. "Can you tell me what happened?"

"I was trying to remember. I have these dreams that seem so real, but since I have no conscious memory of my past, I could never be sure that the dreams were really glimpses of my past."

"But you think they are?"

She nodded. "There's things in them—like my ankle that aches when it rains and some of my scars—that correspond with injuries I have. I know my mind could be creating fiction and bringing my reality into it, but that's not how it feels. I don't know how to explain it, but I'm certain my dreams are trying to show me what happened."

"If you feel strongly about it then you're probably right. I don't pretend to know stuff about the brain like Eleonore does, but what you're describing sounds reasonable to me."

He frowned. But where did the dress and candles come in? And what did they have to do with her dreams? He wanted to ask, but he knew how much weight Shaye was already toting with her biological mother being found and her name in the Clancy journals. She was the strongest woman he'd ever met, but everyone had a breaking point. The last thing he wanted to do was be the final straw—the one statement or question that pushed her back into the shadows.

But he couldn't help her if he didn't understand what was going on.

"The candles and dress," he said. "Are they part of the dreams?"

"Yeah. In the worst of the dreams, I'm wearing a red dress and surrounded by a bunch of black candles. I'm tied down on a stone altar and a man approaches and other people are huddled in the background. In the dreams, all their faces are blurred. The man steps up to the altar and pulls out a knife. He cuts my chest with the knife and licks the blood off of it."

She pulled her knees up to her chest and wrapped her arms around them. "Sometimes I wake up then. Sometimes I don't wake up until he pulls the dress up." She looked directly at Jackson. "I never wear red and just the sight of candles is enough to send my pulse racing. I have flashlights and kerosene lamps in my house in case of a power outage. So does Corrine. I won't eat dinner at certain restaurants because I know they light the dining area completely with candles at night. I've been known to leave charity events that do the same, pretending I'm ill."

Jackson's chest constricted as she talked, empathy and anger warring inside him. No one should have to live with such things. No child should have to endure them.

"I wouldn't call that pretending," he said.

She relaxed a little. "No. I guess it's not."

Now that Jackson knew about the dreams, he could make an educated guess as to what Shaye had been doing and why she said it was stupid.

"So you put on a red dress," he said, "lit the candles, and lay down on the floor, hoping you'd remember."

She nodded. "Stupid, right?"

"I was going to say brave."

A flush crept up her neck and she looked down. "I'm not brave. I'm broken."

Jackson reached over and put his hand on her arm. "We're all broken. Some of us are just in more pieces. It's how we handle it that makes us brave, and from where I'm sitting, you're the bravest person I've ever met."

She looked at him again and he could see the disbelief in her eyes, but finally she managed a small smile. "You believe that," she said. "You have a lot of positive attributes, Jackson Lamotte, but the thing I love about you the most is your sincerity. It's rare that someone can always tell exactly where they stand with another person, but you don't have an ounce of guile in you, do you?"

"When it comes to police work, yes. But when it comes to relationships, no."

Especially when it comes to you.

He didn't say it, but it was right there at the forefront of his thoughts.

"Did you remember?" he asked.

"Yes," she answered, her voice barely a whisper. "It was just like my dreams, except this time, I saw his face."

His pulse quickened. "You can identify him?"

She shook her head. "He wore a mask. A horned goat."

No way in hell would he ever admit it, but the image in his mind creeped Jackson out. No wonder she'd screamed.

"I'm sorry," he said. "I can't imagine how horrifying that was."

"I suspected something along those lines. Eleonore isn't willing to jump completely on board with my theory yet, but I think I'm right."

"Right about what?"

"It was ritualistic abuse." She held up a hand before he could reply. "I've read the FBI study and I know all the facts of other cases, but that doesn't change the facts here. Black candles, a red dress, a stone altar, and all the cuts on my body. The brand—"

"Wait," Jackson interrupted. "What brand?"

He'd been through all the medical records in her file and none of them had made mention of a brand.

She frowned. "I thought you read my file."

"I did. There's nothing about a brand in there."

"That's strange. I know it was documented in my medical records. I have a copy of the records myself."

"Maybe it wasn't scanned in when the department converted everything to digital."

"Maybe not." She rose from the couch and turned around with her back facing him. She pulled the gown up over her hips and up her back.

Jackson took one look at the pentagram on her midback and felt his stomach roll.

"It's been treated with lasers more times than I can count," Shaye said as she dropped the gown and sat back down. "But they can't remove it. It used to be worse. I had the protruding skin surgically removed. It's better now. At least I can't feel it when I lean back."

"I am so sorry." He struggled for words but couldn't think of any that would properly express everything he felt. "I…I can't even imagine, but I see why you feel it's ritualistic."

"You think I could be onto something?"

"Do I think there's a satanic cult operating in New Orleans—I suppose anything is possible, but it's more likely it's one insane person."

"Except there are other people in my dreams. I didn't see them today but if we assume my dreams have been recall, then there were other people involved."

Jackson shook his head. It was bad enough to assume one demented, evil individual was still loose on society, but if he had coconspirators, that opened things up to a whole different level of horror.

"If I hadn't screamed," Shaye said, "I might have remembered more. I should have been better prepared. I knew what might come out of this, and I rushed into it without preparation. I think I was afraid if I took time to think it through, I'd change my mind."

"I can see that, but even if you'd waited, what possible preparations could you have made for something like this?"

She frowned. "I don't know. Video, for one. At least if I said something during the recall, it would be recorded."

"Do you think you said something that you don't remember?"

"No. I didn't have any lapses in recall. I'm sure I didn't say anything."

"Then it wouldn't have made a difference," he pointed out. "Look, I'm sure you could have done yoga or had a stiff drink or any of a dozen things to try to calm down, but I don't think they would have done a bit of good once you were on the floor. I can't imagine what would have, so stop chiding yourself. You did it to get answers and you got some. Not everything you were looking for, but it's an important start."

"Yeah. I guess so." But she didn't sound convinced.

"You remembered something from your past. Have you even thought about how huge that is?"

She stared at him for several seconds, then he saw a tiny flicker of excitement. "I guess I hadn't thought it out. What if this opened the door for my mind to release all those things it's been holding back? If I could remember how I escaped that night, I might remember where I escaped from. We could find him. We could find the man who bought me."

It was hard to contain his emotions at what this breakthrough might mean to Shaye and to the investigation, but Jackson knew that the return of Shaye's memory probably came at a huge cost. Her medical records told part of the story that her mind couldn't, and it was dark and evil. If seven years of torture and abuse flooded back into her memory, could she handle it? Corrine's love and Eleonore's expertise still had their limits, although Jackson had zero doubt as to their commitment to Shaye.

"I think you need to take things slowly," Jackson said. "You only got a quick glimpse of the past and it was bad. If it all comes racing back in…"

"I can handle it," she said. "I know it doesn't look like it, but this was a wake-up call. I'll be prepared for it next time."

Next time? He should have known her experiment wouldn't end here. Shaye had spent years deciding whether or not she wanted to pursue remembering, but now that she'd made up her mind, there was no putting on the brakes. The discovery of her biological mother and Clancy's records had only upped the ante.

And she didn't even know about her captor's recent purchase.

Jackson knew he had to tell her. If she heard it from Corrine, she'd be mad at him for withholding the information, and the last thing he wanted was for Shaye to get angry with him and cut him out of her life. She needed people around her she trusted. People who would have her back no matter where the chips fell, and he was one of those people. But he wouldn't be for long if she felt she could no longer trust him.

Still, now wasn't the right time. She needed to calm down. To clear her head of the thing she'd just done. To get back into private investigator mode, thinking logically and impartially about information. As impartially as a victim could be, anyway.

"Promise me," he said, "that you won't do this again unless I'm here."

"You don't have to do that," she said, but he could tell she wasn't exactly opposed to the idea.

"I just want to see you in your nightgown," he said, "although skimpier and blue is more to my taste."

She smiled. "The only blue I sleep in is a blue T-shirt. It is shorter, though." She rose from the couch. "And now that you've mentioned clothes, I think I'll go put on something normal. This makes me feel…I can't even describe it."

"I recommend a hot shower and a change of clothes."

She nodded and started to say something, then hesitated. Finally, she said, "Will you stay for a while? I mean, unless you're working or already had plans. I don't want to hold you up, but we haven't talked in some time, so I thought we could catch up."

"Unless I get a phone call, I'm officially off the clock, and my only plans were dinner. Are you hungry? Because

I'm starving."

"Always. There's a great Chinese place that delivers. The menu is in the drawer next to the sink. Get me crab Rangoon and chicken fried rice. You like Chinese food, right?"

"You had me at crab Rangoon."

She headed for the hall, then stopped and turned around. "Thanks, Jackson."

He nodded and she slipped through the doorway and disappeared down the hall. A couple seconds later, he heard a shower turn on and he rose from the couch and headed into the kitchen to find the menu. He placed the food order and opened the refrigerator, figuring Shaye wouldn't mind if he helped himself to something to drink. He pulled out a cold beer and then noticed a Tupperware container on the cabinet that held round items that looked suspiciously like cookies. He pulled the lid back and sighed when he saw the same cookies he'd had earlier at Corrine's. Unable to help himself, he grabbed a couple out of the container and headed back to the couch with the beer and cookies. He located the remote and turned on the television, determined to find something to watch that didn't have any news coverage. The day had been grim enough already. He didn't need to be depressed even further with all the evil in the world.

As he flipped through the channels, he thought about what Shaye had done. It was definitely outside the box, but he had a keen appreciation for creative solutions. Most importantly, it had worked. Not only had she determined that her dreams were most likely glimpses of her past, she'd forced her memory to give up one of its closely guarded secrets—the mask.

It might just be the tip of the iceberg.

He only hoped she was ready for the meltdown.

Chapter Nine

Reagan stiffened when she heard the door creak open. It was at the top of a set of narrow stone steps and was solid wood. She'd tried pounding on it but it barely moved, and no matter how much she shouted, no one ever heard her. Wherever this hole was, it wasn't near people, or it was so well insulated that sound didn't carry far enough for others to hear. The bottom line was, the door offered no way out, and it was the only way into the room.

The man's footsteps sounded on the steps and she backed into the corner. It was a reflexive action that did no good. The man locked the door after entering. Even if she could run past him, she didn't have the key to get out. And despite the fact that she was in good shape and fairly strong for a girl, there was no way her ninety pounds was any match for his six-two, two-hundred-pound frame. She'd tried kicking him once, a really good shot right in his crotch, but he'd laughed at her and said she was turning him on. She never tried it again.

Light from the lamp he always carried trickled down the stairs and into the room. A couple seconds later, she saw his blue jean–clad legs as he descended. She flattened against the wall even more, hoping this was one of those times he left food and went away. It was worse when he spoke to her. He paused at the bottom of the steps and she sucked in a breath. No matter how many times she saw the mask, it chilled her to the bone. She'd never seen anything so horrific in her life. She'd never been so frightened of an inanimate object.

The mask turned slowly and his eyes locked on hers. Immediately, she dropped her gaze, unable to take his dead-eyed stare through the demon mask. He laughed and despite the heat and humidity, a chill ran through her and she shivered. His laugh was almost as bad as the mask. Mocking her fear. Excited by it.

He reached out with his left hand and dropped a paper bag on the floor. The scent of cooked ground meat wafted over to her and her mouth watered. He only brought food once a day, sometimes less, and it was never enough. Sometimes one hamburger, sometimes two. Once a small pizza, but never enough food to keep her strength up. Every day she grew a little weaker, and she assumed that was exactly what he wanted.

He stared at her several more seconds, then turned and headed back up the steps. She waited until she heard him lock the door before moving to the center of the room to feel for the food. She located the bag and sank onto the ground beside it, digging inside to see what he'd left.

Two hamburgers today.

That meant he either was being generous or wasn't planning on coming at all the next day. He'd done that before. She pulled out one of the burgers and took a huge bite, washing it down with the soda he'd put in with the burgers. She barely chewed before swallowing and started to take another bite but hesitated. If she was ever going to get out of here, there was only one way, and that was catching him by surprise.

Locked in this dungeon, the one thing she did have was plenty of time to think, but no matter how many ideas she'd rolled around in her mind, only one was viable. She had to get the jump on him to steal the key and get out the door. She'd found a piece of stone that had broken off at the end of the wall where the steps entered the room. It was a little longer than her hand, and she'd been sharpening it against the stone wall for a day now. The edge was getting sharp. She just needed to get the end more pointed and it would be ready. Kicking him in the crotch might not have inflicted enough pain but surely stabbing him there would.

The hard part was faking being unconscious. That meant figuring out when the food was drugged and not eating it, which meant taking a single bite and waiting to see if she felt any aftereffects. Taking a single bite and waiting, even though she was starving.

As the aroma of the burger filled her nostrils, her stomach growled and clenched, begging her to take another bite and ease its discomfort. But she couldn't do it. Not if she was going to escape. If she could escape, she'd find another way to live. Maybe call that social services lady.

And she'd never, ever go hungry again.

Shaye stood under the stream of hot water, letting it run over her shoulders and down her back and chest. She'd already scrubbed every inch of her body with exfoliating gel and no longer felt the slick red fabric on her skin. The overwhelming urge to burn the gown as soon as she got out of the shower dominated her thoughts for a while, but ultimately, she convinced herself that the garment might be needed in the future. The last thing she wanted to do was have another shopping trip over that particular item, so she'd find someplace to lock it up, along with the candles, until she was ready to use them again or until this was over for good.

Her relief at seeing Jackson at her door was huge. She'd dreaded looking through the crack because her first thought was that it was her mother outside. If Corrine knew what Shaye had done and had seen the direct effect it had on her, Shaye would never have another moment's peace again. Corrine would have badgered her to move back in with her, and when Shaye refused, she would have insisted on the bodyguards Pierce kept threatening her with.

Shaye knew she was extraordinarily lucky to have Corrine, Pierce, and Eleonore taking care of her, but sometimes it made her feel claustrophobic. She worked hard to control her aggravation when it felt as if they were pushing her too hard toward what they wanted rather than listening to what she wanted. Meeting Hustle had made her even more aware of what it was like to care about someone and feel hopeless to help them, so it wasn't as though she couldn't empathize. But lately, everyone had gotten more intense. The Clancy journals and her biological mother's turning up had put an enormous strain on everyone, and she was feeling the pressure.

Jackson was a safe island in a stormy sea. She knew he didn't necessarily like or agree with the risks she took, but he never once suggested that she stop. Instead, he requested only that she be well prepared for the undertaking and ask him to help when the risk was too great. She'd scared him today. That had been apparent. His asking her to never attempt a repeat performance unless he was present was indicative of his fear, even if his expression hadn't been a dead giveaway.

In the past, and with anyone else, she would have been annoyed by the request, but Jackson never made her feel as though he was intruding. His presence always felt like assistance and sometimes guidance, but never control.

Admit it. You like him.

Fine. So she liked him. What wasn't to like?

You like him as more than a friend.

She turned off the shower and reached for a towel. Her feelings for Jackson had moved beyond just friendship a while back. Or maybe they'd been that way from the beginning. Certainly, she'd never felt so comfortable with a man, especially so soon. But right from the start, she'd known that Jackson was different. The question was what she intended to do about it.

Her life, which was always complicated at best, was in a huge state of turmoil right now. It probably wasn't possible to find a worse time to pursue a romantic relationship, and yet every day that passed that she had avoided seeing Jackson in person, the more she'd missed him. The more she'd thought about him.

She dried off and pulled on yoga pants and a tee, then headed back into the living room. Jackson was sitting on the couch, watching car racing and eating a cookie. He looked up when she walked in.

"I hope you don't mind," he said. "I helped myself to a beer and cookies. You mom is a dangerous woman in a kitchen. Does she bake like this all the time? These are the best cookies I've ever eaten."

"When she's stressed, she takes it up a notch. Right now, she's taken her notch up a notch. I'll be on a treadmill for the rest of the year working those things off. But how were you so sure I didn't make them?"

She meant it as a joke, but the flash of guilt on Jackson's face told an entirely different story. He stared at her for several seconds, like he was assessing her.

"Are you feeling better?" he asked.

"You came here to tell me something, didn't you? My mother baked those particular cookies this morning, but you wouldn't know that unless you'd been to see her. Why?"

"A lot has happened today," Jackson said. "We have some time before the food gets here. Maybe you should sit down."

She chided herself for not seeing this coming. Jackson wouldn't stop by just because. Their relationship wasn't so close that drop-bys were the norm, but she'd been so relieved to see him when she'd opened the door that she hadn't taken that thought a step further and wondered why he was there. She sank onto the couch and waited.

When nothing was forthcoming, she said, "Look, I know it can't be good or you wouldn't be here. So lay it on me. I promise my head is clear and I'm ready for whatever you have to say."

"This is confidential information, but as it concerns you, I have permission to let you know," he said finally. "The team reviewing Clancy's logbooks have made some headway in breaking the code on parts of them. One of the names they decoded was the man who bought you."

She jumped up from the couch, staring at Jackson as if he'd lost his mind. "You know who he is and you're sitting there? Why aren't you mounting a cavalry? Why aren't you busting down doors?"

"Because it's not a formal name. It looks like Clancy listed all the buyers by nicknames."

"Which was?"

"Diabolique."

Shaye blew out a breath. "Diabolical. Jesus. How appropriate."

Jackson nodded. "His actions were enough to warrant it, but now that you remembered the mask, it's downright creepy."

She sank back down onto the couch. "So you still

don't know anything about him. Not really."

His expression turned grim. "We know one thing. He purchased another girl last month."

The blood rushed out of her face and her stomach rolled. "Oh my God. You're sure?"

"It's the same nickname. I can't imagine that Clancy would reuse one."

"What about Reaper—Clancy's son? He wasn't working with Clancy when he sold me, but he was last month. He has to know something. I know he's refused to help decode the journals unless he gets to walk, but I'm beyond caring about his rights. Go to the jail and force it out of him or let me."

"It was the first thing the lead detective thought to do. Unfortunately, it wasn't an option. Reaper hung himself with his bedsheet last night. The story hasn't been released to the press yet, but it will probably hit tomorrow."

The momentary hope she'd felt dissipated completely. "Coward."

"Definitely."

"Have you started the search for the girl?" Shaye asked. "Do you know who she is?"

"We've started a search to identify her. That's where your mother came in. The database for missing and exploited children didn't turn up anything."

"So you thought my mother might be able to find a match in one of the case files." Jackson's visit to her mother's house made sense now.

He nodded. "It's a long shot, but we have to start

somewhere."

"What do you know about her?"

"Only the date of purchase and her age—fifteen years old."

"The same age I was when I got away."

"Yeah. I have this theory about that," he said, and explained what he'd shared with Grayson and her mother and Eleonore.

She leaned toward him, focusing on every single word, her mind processing the facts and the theory. When he finished she sat back. "You think he's picking up where he left off? Nine years later?"

"Maybe. God knows, it wouldn't be the craziest thing we've seen lately, especially given what you remembered tonight."

"That's true enough, but..." She blew out a breath. "What can I do?"

"I don't think there's anything you can do except what you're already doing—trying to remember." He ran one hand through his hair. "Look, I told you all of this because I knew you'd hear it from Corrine anyway, and I didn't want you to think I was giving her information concerning you behind your back, but I didn't know you were going to do something like you did today."

"What difference does that make?"

"It was risky. It took a hell of a lot out of you. I don't want you to feel additional pressure to remember. If anything, putting more pressure on yourself will make it even harder to unlock your memory. And I don't want you taking even bigger risks. You have your own health to consider."

Irritation coursed through her. "Do you think I'm that fragile? That I'll break?"

"I think you're the strongest person I've ever met. And I think everyone can break."

It wasn't the answer she wanted to hear, but it was an honest one. So far, she'd managed to maintain control of her emotions, with only a few lapses, like today. But she knew better than most that everyone had a breaking point. Sooner or later, the brain turned off to protect itself. Like with her memory loss. She had no doubt her missing memory was self-preservation, and believed that it was only returning now because she was emotionally healthy enough to handle it.

Maybe she'd been wrong.

Maybe she was forcing an issue rather than allowing it to develop in its own time. But with another child missing, she couldn't back off now. She'd set off on this path, and she was more determined than ever to see it to the end.

The doorbell rang, and Jackson jumped up from the couch. "I've got it," he said.

Shaye watched as he paid the deliveryman and returned with a large paper bag. He placed it on the coffee table and pulled out the containers.

"Don't get up," he said. "Just tell me what you want to drink."

"Diet soda," she said, her emotions shifting from horrified to angry.

Jackson sat a soda on the coffee table and took his seat again.

"We're going to get this son of a bitch," she said.

"Yes. We are."

She reached for a crab Rangoon and something Jackson said struck her. "Why was Grayson with you at my mom's?"

"Because I officially have a new partner."

Shaye perked up a bit. That was really good news in a sea of crap. "Congratulations! That's great."

He nodded. "I'm sure I don't have to explain to you how happy and relieved I am. I also owe you, big time."

"Me?"

"Yeah, I hear Vincent tried to railroad me with IA and you took him down."

"All I did was report my displeasure at being accused of impropriety to Captain Bernard."

"Well, I would have loved to have been a fly on the wall. Grayson said Bernard yelled so loud the walls shook."

"What did he do with Vincent?"

"Moved him to work on the Clancy journals. But—" He held up a hand before she said anything. "He will only be scanning and filing. He won't have access to any information concerning the decoding, and the detective in charge is under strict orders that Vincent is not to ever have knowledge of anything concerning you."

"And you think that will hold?"

"Only a few people know about your name being in those books. Vincent is too lazy to attempt to solve a case, and he has no reason to suspect that digging into the Clancy files would produce something that he could use against you."

She shook her head. "I know everyone is doing what they can, but you and I both know that this information won't remain secret forever. Quite frankly, I'm surprised nothing has leaked before now. Every day I turn on the news and wait for the bomb to drop—at least about my biological mother. More people know about that, and even more people have access to those records."

"And when it happens, we'll deal with it, but with any luck, the secrets will hold for a while longer, at least until we find this guy."

"I hope so. If this gets out, the media storm will be worse than a hurricane. If he knows we're onto him, even a little, he'll kill the girl and flee."

"That's not going to happen."

"You think if you keep telling yourself that, then it will come true?"

"You have a better idea?"

She sighed. "No. I guess not."

CHAPTER TEN

Sunday, July 26, 2015
French Quarter, New Orleans, Louisiana

Harold Beaumont leaned back in the chair and looked out his hotel window. Despite the fine furnishings and comfortable bed, he'd barely slept at all and his body was sore from all that bouncing around in the back of Old Joe's truck. The effects of aging often annoyed him but at the moment, he'd moved straight past annoyed and directly to aggravated. His mind was as good as it had always been, and for that, he was thankful, but when it came to the physical side of things, he wasn't near the man he used to be. And that bothered him more than he'd ever admit out loud, especially right now, when he had a feeling a little more strength and endurance might come in handy.

He'd just finished off an excellent breakfast, courtesy of room service, while he waited for Bob to wake up and get moving. Sunday had always been his day to sleep late, and Harold couldn't think of any good reason to force his old partner out of bed when there was nothing he could do with the information Harold was going to give him until tonight. Besides, if he woke Harold up on Sunday, his wife would know something was up. Susan was a great woman but she had a nose like a bloodhound. If she thought Bob was poking his nose into an open investigation, especially anything that involved Shaye Archer and John Clancy, Bob would never hear the end of it.

He checked his watch and decided that eleven o'clock was a good enough time as any to call his friend. "I'm here," he said when Bob answered. "Can you talk?"

"Yeah. Susan just ran out to pick up some lunch. You made it all right then?"

"Went off without a hitch. You got that information for me?"

"Of course." He gave Harold Shaye's home address and cell phone number. "You aren't thinking of going to her apartment, are you?"

"No. Not after I saw the footage from my security cameras. I'd hoped I was wrong—that an old cop was just being paranoid—but no such luck. I can't afford for him to know I'm here, and I have to assume he's watching her when he's not out doing whatever the hell else evil he's up to. Both of us in her apartment would be like shooting fish in a barrel."

"So what are you going to do?"

"I'll figure something out. Thanks for the information and watch your back. I know you were already driving the desk, but we were partners for a lot of years. We have no way of knowing how far he plans on reaching."

"You know me...three big dogs and too many guns to name. If none of those work, I'll send Susan after him."

"That will do it."

"Call me if you need anything else."

"I will."

"And Beaumont...be careful."

Harold tossed his phone on the bed, rose from the chair, and grabbed his duffel bag. It contained what he considered the necessities—a single change of clothes, three pistols, and more ammo than he took to the gun range. He'd hidden his rifles in the attic before he left, not wanting the killer to get his hands on anything that he could use to kill people. If someone were killed with one of Harold's guns, he wouldn't be able to forgive himself. The three pistols were the only other guns he owned and they were all right there with him, along with holsters for his hip, shoulder, and ankle. The only other item in the bag was his bulletproof vest.

He pulled it out and ran his hand over it, his fingers dipping into the holes the three bullets had made. He'd been lucky the guy wasn't a better shot. If he'd aimed just six inches up, Harold's head would have been gone and the vest would have been cataloged and handed to another detective. They'd allowed him to keep this one. Since it was damaged, it wasn't as effective as it was before, but Harold was superstitious about some things. The vest had saved his life once before. If he got into a situation again, he wanted to be wearing it.

He placed the vest on the bed and picked up his phone

again. The app for the security cameras was right there next to his in-box and he pressed it to watch the clip he'd saved from the earlier footage. He watched the killer's back as he crept down the hall toward the kitchen, and the same anger he'd felt when he saw it the first time coursed through him all over again. That man had come there with only one purpose in mind—silencing Harold forever.

But why the knife?

That was the one thing Harold hadn't been able to figure out. He'd expected the killer to whirl around the corner with a pistol, ready to empty a magazine into him. The knife didn't make any sense, but then, maybe there was no making sense of evil. It usually had its own reasons for things that normal people would never understand.

When he walked into the kitchen, the hood on the sweatshirt blocked his face from view but as before, Harold could tell the shape of the hood was odd. When the killer came out of the garage and faced the camera, Harold could see why the hood was misshapen.

In all his years of police work, he'd been cautious but never scared.

Until now.

The afternoon was half gone when Shaye pulled into a parking space in the corner of the lot of the apartment building where her biological mother used to live. They were getting a later start than Hustle had expected, but

Shaye hadn't offered an explanation as to why. He could tell by her strained expression that something had happened. Or maybe it was just everything was weighing so heavy on her that she was getting exhausted. Either way, she wasn't in the same mood as the day before, and that bothered him, but he didn't want to ask and put her on the spot. Whatever it was, she was still thinking on it hard and he didn't want to get in the way of that.

She looked over at him, and he waited for the inevitable question that he knew was coming.

"Are you sure you want to do this?" she asked.

"That's the third time you've asked me and that's just in the car. My answer isn't going to change."

"I know. I just don't feel right having you do my job for me."

"It's your job to get answers, right? You already tried and these people won't talk to you. It's Saul's job to keep the hotel maintenance up, but that don't mean he's doing it all himself. I don't mean no disrespect but you're not qualified for every job you need done."

She smiled. "So what you're saying is that picking the right person for the job *is* my job? I guess I can live with that. Is your microphone still in place?"

He pulled out the collar of his T-shirt and glanced down. "The microphone is in place. I'm sure I want to do this. I have a couple things worked up to tell them depending on my assessment when they open the door. If anything looks or feels weird, I'll leave and come straight back to the car. Can we get this show going? This tape on my chest itches."

She nodded. "Get out before I annoy you even more."

He grinned and climbed out of the SUV. Shaye was great but she was a professional worrier. Not that she didn't have plenty of reason. But she didn't get these people. She didn't understand how their minds worked, but he did. His mom had worked hard, often holding down two jobs, but a high school education didn't get you much in the way of pay. They'd never lived in government housing, but the tiny house she rented was on the same block as a big complex and a lot of HUD homes. He knew these people better than Shaye ever could.

And no way would they talk to someone like Shaye. Even in jeans and a T-shirt, she would never look like she belonged down here. Everyone would assume she was a cop or social worker, and doors and mouths would shut so fast she wouldn't even have time to introduce herself. But a skinny kid with long scraggly hair and cheap secondhand clothes wasn't a threat. Saul had taken him shopping for new clothes, but Hustle had insisted on keeping the jeans and shirt he wore now. They were the last things his mom had bought for him, and he planned on keeping them forever. When they didn't fit, they would get one last washing, then he'd stick them in a drawer. It was a good thing he'd been so sentimental. No way would his new clothes have passed with these people, and he would have felt guilty tearing them up, even though he had a good reason.

He pulled open the door to the apartment building and

headed down the hallway toward the unit where Shaye's biological mother had lived. The building was run-down and dingy and he'd been in Dumpsters that smelled better, but none of that bothered him. He'd lived in worse conditions than this, but it was a good reminder of where he could be if he didn't take advantage of everything Shaye and Saul were offering him.

He located the apartment across the hall from Shaye's mother's old unit and knocked on the door. There was some rustling inside and finally the door opened and a woman peered out at him. She was probably thirty or so, but she looked at least fifteen years older. Drugs aged you fast, and based on the acne she had on her chin and cheeks, Hustle was betting her drug of choice was meth.

He heard a baby squeal inside and struggled against the urge to shake the crap out of her until she realized what kind of life she was dooming her child to, but he knew it wouldn't do any good. He'd seen it too many times before.

"What do you want?" she asked.

"I was looking for Lydia Johnson."

"She's dead."

"Yeah, I know. The manager told me."

"Then what are you knocking on my door for?"

"Lydia was my aunt. She had a daughter, my cousin Cindy. Anyway, I was trying to find her."

"Ain't never heard of no Cindy. Ain't never seen Lydia with a kid."

"Maybe Cindy wasn't with her when she came here. You have any idea where Aunt Lydia was before?"

The woman narrowed her eyes at Hustle. "If you don't know where your cousin is, you ain't seen her in a while. Why you need to find this girl now?"

"My dad worked road construction and we moved away for a while. Aunt Lydia didn't have a phone so I lost track of them. We moved back to New Orleans a couple months ago, but my dad died. He had one of those things at his job—you know, where they give you some money?"

"Insurance."

"Yeah, that's what the man called it. Anyway, the man said I had some money coming and I thought maybe Aunt Lydia, Cindy, and me could use it to get a better situation, you know? But since Aunt Lydia's gone, it's just me and Cindy."

"What about your mother?"

"She died having me. Couldn't afford no hospital."

"Sorry about that, and your dad. You're young to lose them both."

He shrugged. "Shit happens, you know? You just keep going until you can't go no more."

The woman stared at him for a bit, then nodded. "I don't know the exact address, but Lydia said she used to live in a house on Tupelo close to the river."

"You know the cross street?"

"Around Douglas maybe? I can't remember for sure, but that sounds right."

"Thanks, I appreciate it."

"Good luck finding your cousin. Maybe you can get her out before she goes the way her mom did. If she hasn't already."

The woman closed the door and he headed out of the apartment and back to the SUV. He could have tried the other units, but he didn't think anyone would know more than what the woman had already told him. He had no way of knowing if the house on Tupelo was where Shaye had lived, but at least it was a start. Assuming, of course, that the house hadn't been wiped out by Katrina.

He hopped into the SUV and was instantly greeted by an ecstatic Shaye. "You are incredible," she said. "I couldn't even get that woman to admit she knew Lydia."

"I don't look like no threat."

"Apparently not. Do you think that story will work again at the other address?"

He shrugged. "Hard to say. She wasn't too old and had a baby inside so I figured I'd go with the 'trying to break out' angle. They get too old and they aren't even desperate anymore. They all accepted that's their life. But if they haven't gotten to that place, thinking someone has a chance to get away from it gives them that little spark of hope that maybe someday that knock on the door will be their ticket out."

Shaye frowned. "I wish you didn't know all of this."

"I'm not mad about it. My moms didn't always do things smart, you know, but she was a good person and I know she loved me. A lot of people ain't even got that."

"That's true."

"Besides, knowing all this—how hard it is to live this way—makes me work even harder to never be back here.

You and Saul were my ticket out. I'm going to make sure you never regret it."

"I could never regret knowing you. You're going to do great things."

Hustle looked at the dashboard. Every time Shaye said things like that he felt weird. Not bad weird. More like uncommon weird. He was so used to people blowing hot air about everything that Shaye's sincerity was something he didn't have a lot of experience with, especially when she was complimenting him. He liked it but he didn't wear it all that well. It made him kinda itchy, like the microphone.

Finally, he nodded. "Just like you. So get to driving. We have a bad guy to catch and your memory ain't gonna just walk up and write his name down for you."

Shaye smiled and pulled out of the parking lot, making her way to Tupelo. She turned onto the street a couple blocks away from the river and drove slowly until they reached Douglas, where she parked at the curb, close to where the streets crossed.

"Lots of houses are gone," she said, and he could hear the anxiety in her voice.

Hustle nodded. It was exactly what he feared—that the place where Shaye had lived with her mother might not be standing anymore. If that was the case, then they were back to zero and just the thought of that had him feeling frustrated and helpless. Shaye had done so much for him and if there was anything he could do to help her, he would be first in line to volunteer. She deserved to know what happened to her, and the man who did it deserved to be tied up and tossed into a river of alligators.

"Does anything look familiar?" he asked.

She scanned the street up and down, her brow wrinkled in concentration, then shook her head. "Nothing stands out. I was really hoping something would."

"If the house is still here, it probably looks different now. And all the trees and stuff is grown up a lot from back then too."

"That's true," she said, sounding a little more optimistic. "Where do you want to start talking to people? I mean, do you get a feel for any house over the other?"

Hustle studied the structures that Shaye had charitably referred to as houses. Run-down was a polite way of describing them. Beaten down by time, weather, and lack of maintenance was more accurate. Most were probably rentals and the tenants were paying with vouchers. The question is, which ones might have been there long enough to have known Lydia and returned after Katrina.

A house with peeling white paint and ugly green trim caught his eye. There were pot plants on the sloping front porch. People didn't like to cart pot plants around because they were heavy and messy. Usually, the people who had them had been in one place for a while.

"I'll start with that one," he said.

Shaye nodded. "I'll circle around and park far enough back where my car isn't as noticeable. Be careful, and if anything feels wrong, get out of there."

"I will," Hustle said as he climbed out of the SUV. She didn't have to tell him twice. He'd been stalked and almost killed. If anyone knew when to run, he did.

He walked up the broken concrete that made up the sad path to the house and stepped onto the porch. The boards creaked under his weight and he prayed that the rotted wood held while he was standing there. He knocked on the door and listened for any sign of movement inside. After a minute or so of nothing, he knocked again. This time, he heard rustling inside and the door opened a crack.

The woman who peered out at him was probably in her fifties. The deep wrinkles on the sides of her lips were a dead giveaway for a long-term smoker, and if they hadn't been there, the smell of stale smoke coming off of her would have been enough to know. Her hair looked as if it hadn't seen a brush in a while, and her ratty T-shirt had worn spots and stains down the front.

"What do you want?" she asked, one hand on the door, ready to slam it at any indication of trouble, the other arm reaching toward the wall where she probably had her hand wrapped around a bat or some other form of protection. It was a position Hustle knew well as he'd seen his mom do it any time someone came knocking that she didn't know.

"I'm looking for Lydia Johnson," he said.

Her eyes narrowed. "Why you looking for her?"

"I'm her nephew. My dad moved us away years ago and I lost track of her and my cousin. We moved back a couple weeks ago and I'm trying to find her. She used to live around here, but I can't remember where exactly."

The woman studied him for a while, sizing him up as

far as threats went. His lie and his appearance must have registered favorably, because she answered. "Looks a lot different now than it did when Lydia lived here."

"Yeah, I guess so. I was just a little kid then anyway, so my memory ain't that good. Besides, looks like Katrina did a number down here. You said 'when' my aunt lived here. She don't anymore?"

The woman shook her head. "Moved a couple years before Katrina. Said she got an apartment. Smaller and on higher ground. Don't have to rain for an hour around here for shit to flood. Streets back up quick."

"You don't happen to know where the apartment is, do you?"

"If she said, I don't remember. Been too long. 'Sides, it might not be standing anyway. Not like these slumlords keep anything up. Probably caved right in when Katrina hit."

"That's true enough." He looked up and down the street. "Which house was it? I mean, if it's still standing."

The woman pointed across the street and down the block. "That blue one with the weeds tall as the porch. It's been abandoned since Katrina. Not fit to live in, but then a lot of these places aren't."

He looked at the house and frowned. "Doesn't look familiar, but I guess I shouldn't expect it to. Was my cousin still with Aunt Lydia when she moved?"

Based on the date the woman had given him, Hustle already knew Lydia had sold Shaye before she moved, but he wanted to know what she'd told people.

The woman shook her head. "Lydia said social workers took Trina. I remember her saying she was trying to get her back, but I never saw Trina again. I guess she couldn't make it happen."

He struggled to control his anger. That junkie had sold her daughter to Clancy and then blamed her disappearance on the government. He'd bet money she never told the government she no longer had a child, otherwise her benefits would have been reduced. If asked to produce her, Lydia would have just borrowed someone else's kid. He'd seen it done before.

"I remember my dad said some people went and talked to her about Trina," he said, and sighed. "I guess my chances of finding either one of them ain't that good."

"Not unless you know someone down at the government. Ha."

"No, and I ain't trying to. Not in this lifetime. Thanks for your help."

She nodded. "Good luck," she said before closing the door.

He headed back down the steps and started walking toward the house the woman had indicated. Storm clouds were forming overhead and his shirt was sticky from perspiration as the humidity level spiked.

"Circle around the block and park on the street behind the house," he said, hoping that the feed was still working and Shaye had heard him.

He wasn't afraid the woman would be a problem, but he didn't want her spotting Shaye's vehicle, either. They might need more information, and if the woman caught sight of Shaye or her car, she would know something was up besides the story Hustle had given her. That was a sure way to make her forget everything she ever knew about Lydia.

Hustle crossed the street and walked up what was left of the sidewalk to the house. The weeds had taken over the lawn and were growing through cracks on the walkway. He pushed them out of the way, but the stalks rubbed against his arms and made them itch. The porch was missing planks on one side and he pressed his foot on the boards, testing them, before taking a step off the concrete steps and onto the failing structure. He moved slowly to the front door, avoiding the boards that showed the most signs of rot until he reached the entrance.

The door wasn't even closed all the way, much less locked, so he pushed it open and stuck his head inside. A squatter could be inside, and they didn't like people walking into their territory. He scanned the room but saw no signs of life. The dust and grime on the floor was free of footprints or any other indication that someone had passed through recently. Two of the four windows were still boarded up, but the others were open to the elements, the glass broken out long ago, by either storm or human. The broken windows allowed some light to enter the room, but with the clouds thickening overhead, it was only enough to cast a dim glow across the depressing room.

He stepped inside and heard a creak from the back of the house.

"Shaye?" he called out.

"It's me," she said. "I figured it was better if I came in the back."

He smiled. She caught on quickly. Or maybe it was her subconscious, bringing out the things she would have understood from her time living with Lydia. Shaye was eight years old when she'd been sold by Clancy. You didn't make eight years in the Ninth Ward without developing some street smarts.

A door in the back of the room swung open and Shaye stepped inside. Her expression was serious and it was clear she was concentrating on the house, trying to force herself to remember. He stood silently and without moving, not wanting to break into her thoughts.

He'd done his part. The rest was up to Shaye.

CHAPTER ELEVEN

Shaye stepped into what must have been the living room and moved to the center before stopping. She scanned the walls with their peeling light green paint, trying to imagine herself here. There would have been a couch or chairs, maybe even an old television. Would the couch have been against the side wall or the front? She looked at both, trying to imagine furniture in the space, but nothing was forthcoming.

Trina, sitting on a couch or maybe the floor, watching cartoons.

She shook her head. Even the name didn't jog her memory any. She'd thought if she could find her birth name that it might unlock everything, but the name sounded as foreign to her as this room felt. Clamping down on her rising frustration, she moved off to a door on the opposite side of the room and pushed it open to find the kitchen. She stepped inside and sucked in a breath. What was left of the yellow wallpaper with red cherries was hanging in long strips off the wall, surrounded by big stretches of crumbling drywall.

But those strips were all she needed.

She heard quiet footsteps behind her and turned to

look at Hustle, who stood in the doorway. "I remember the wallpaper," she said, struggling to contain her excitement. It was just one small thing. It didn't mean anything yet.

Hustle nodded and she knew he was being quiet so he didn't interfere with her process. She moved forward until she stood next to a row of cabinets where a stove used to be. None of the appliances were there any longer. They'd probably been removed or stolen long ago. But when she looked at the empty space, she saw the yellow stove that used to be there. It was dark yellow, almost gold, and had big dials on it.

She turned and took two steps to the eating area and lifted a long strip of the wallpaper. "I picked this paper," she said. "There was a big, sweaty man. He brought a book of colored paper to the house and my mother told me to pick."

She whirled around and stared at Hustle. "Oh my God. I remember her."

Hustle motioned with his hand for her to keep going.

"She was sitting at the breakfast table right here. Her hair was twisted on top of her head in a messy knot and she was wearing a dirty pink bathrobe. The man must have been the landlord. I remember standing at the table on my tiptoes, looking at the pages as he flipped them over."

"You were young," Hustle said, finally breaking his silence.

Shaye frowned, not getting the correlation, then realized he had clued in to her barely being able to see onto the table. "You're right. I must have been a lot younger than eight. Four, five maybe? Guess it depends on how fast I grew."

Hustle nodded.

She blew out a breath. "I need to remember much later."

"You just got here. Give it time."

We don't have time.

It was the most prevalent thought in her mind ever since Jackson had told her about the other girl. But Hustle didn't know about the girl and she wasn't about to tell him. He'd promised not to ever investigate on his own again, but if he found out the man who'd held Shaye hostage had another victim, Shaye knew he'd be combing the streets looking for her. He had too big a heart to sit at the hotel and hope for the best.

"I'm impatient," she said. "I know. Let's find my bedroom."

She headed out of the kitchen and back into the living room. There was an opening to a hallway on the far wall. She went down the hall and poked her head into the first room. It was small and had brown walls. Nothing tickled her memory, so she kept walking. The bathroom was next but the tile and tub had been redone sometime in the last ten years. The design was too recent to have been there when she'd occupied the house.

She continued to the last door and stepped inside. This was it. Her bedroom. A big window on the far wall looked into the backyard. A shrub below the window had grown so large, it blocked almost any light from entering, but she knew she'd spent hours standing at this window, watching thunderstorms. She crossed the room and pulled open a door to the tiny closet. It couldn't have been more than two feet square, but her belongings still hadn't filled it. She could picture the precious few garments hanging inside, the colors faded, the material threadbare. The two pairs of shoes—one a pair of worn brown loafers and the other a pair of cheap pink running shoes—and a purple backpack.

She took a step closer and a flash of the past coursed through her so intense, it took her breath away. This is where she used to hide when the men were here. She didn't like the men. They brought the stuff that made her mother sleep for days and they always looked at her in a weird way. So when the men came, she hid in this closet.

The child, Trina, didn't know why the men's staring bothered her, but the very adult Shaye knew exactly why. Had the abuse started before Clancy bought her? Had her mother traded her for drugs? She didn't think so, but she couldn't be certain. Not yet.

She heard the floor creak behind her, and she turned to face Hustle. "This was my room," she said. "I remember the window and the closet." She didn't tell him the rest. Hustle had already seen and heard enough of the dark side of humanity. He didn't need anything else to process.

"That's good," he said, but he didn't sound nearly as excited as she felt.

"What's wrong?" she asked.

"Nothing."

She shook her head. "If I'm not allowed to hedge

things with you, then why do you think you're allowed to do it to me?"

He sighed. "Look, I want you to get answers, and I want the guy who did those things to you to pay—you have no idea how much I want him to pay—but I can't help thinking sometimes that maybe you're better off not remembering. I mean, look at what those people who bought Jinx were doing. That's the most fucked-up shit I ever heard of in my life, and I've heard a lot. What if what happened to you was worse? What if it's something you can't live with?"

Shaye felt her heart break just a little. The fact that this boy, who'd been through so much, was worried about her emotional health was so touching that she wished she could do exactly that—let it all go and move on with her incredibly blessed life. But she couldn't. Any chance of moving forward and leaving the past forgotten had been blown apart when Lydia's name appeared in Clancy's journals. Knowing there was another victim out there only cemented her decision.

"I have the best support system in the world," she said. "I have my mom and Eleonore and friends like you and Jackson. None of you will let me get into a dark place. If it's too much for me to handle, you guys will help me carry the load."

Hustle shrugged. "Yeah. I guess so."

She walked over to stand in front of him. "I promise you, I will be all right. No matter what I find, not knowing is worse. Walking down the street and knowing that half the men I see could be the guy who did this to me and I don't even know is a far worse way to live. Besides, as long as he's still out there, other people are at risk. I can't live peacefully knowing that."

He studied her for a while, then finally nodded. "I get it," he said, "and I know this is the only way to get the guy, but it still sucks."

Thunder boomed overhead and they both jumped. Hustle glanced nervously out the window as the room grew dimmer.

"I'm not trying to rush you or anything," Hustle said, "but that storm sounds bad."

"Yes. It does." She pulled out her cell phone. "I'm going to take some pictures and then we should get out of here. It's getting late and with the storm, it will be dark soon. I'm going to guess that this isn't the neighborhood we need to be hanging around in after dark."

"Don't need to be hanging around here in broad daylight. Passed dealers two blocks up from here. I'm sure they'd love your car."

"Drug dealers?" Shaye frowned. "I saw two women with a stroller, but not anyone else."

Hustle raised one eyebrow. "The two women with the stroller *was* the drug dealers. They ain't got no baby in there."

"Oh!" Just when Shaye thought she'd figured a few things out, something came along and surprised her. "I'll hurry."

She took pictures and video of each room,

documenting every single square foot, even the inside of the cabinets. A lot of it probably wouldn't be useful, like the remodeled bathroom, but she was grasping on to a sliver of hope that the pictures would suffice and she wouldn't have to come back here. There was a feeling of doom in this house, like the dark cloud that currently hung over it was always there, just sometimes invisible to the naked eye.

"Let me get one more shot of the window in my bedroom," she said. "The one I took is overexposed."

They headed back down the hallway to the bedroom and she snapped several pictures of the window, both with the flash and without. "That's it," she said. "Let's get out of here."

Another clap of thunder sounded overhead, this time shaking the frail walls of the house. Shaye started to head out of the room, but Hustle grabbed her arm and put his finger to his lips, then pointed toward the front of the house. She froze and a couple seconds later, she heard boards creaking as someone walked across them.

It was impossible to tell if the footsteps came from the porch of if the intruder was already inside, but either way, they were trapped. The utility room was at the other end of the living room and there was no access from the hallway. The entire living room was easily visible from the front door. No way they could slip out without being seen.

Hustle pointed to the window and she nodded. They eased over to the window and they tugged on the old latches. For a minute, Shaye was afraid they were rusted in place and no amount of hand strength was going to get them loose, but they finally managed to get both of them open. Saying a silent prayer that the window hadn't been painted shut or nailed shut from the outside, she put her fingers under one of the decorative ridges and pulled it up.

It didn't budge.

A loud creak traveled down the hall and Shaye knew that this time, it hadn't come from outside. Someone was in the house with them. She looked over at Hustle, who tugged on the window again. His anxiety was starting to show and she knew they were in a bad situation. She grabbed the molding again and motioned to him with her head.

She whispered, "One, two, three."

On three they both pulled as hard as they could and the window flew up, crashing into the top of the frame.

"Go," she said.

Hustle threw one leg over the ledge and flipped over into the bushes. She was right on his tail as he burst out of the bushes and ran through the tall weeds that made up the backyard of her old house and into the backyard of the house behind it. They veered to the left as they rounded the corner of the other house and she tugged her keys from her pocket, unlocking and starting her SUV as they ran. She yanked open the car door and jumped inside, then shoved the key into the ignition and tore away from the curb as Hustle was slamming the passenger door shut.

He whirled around in the seat, looking behind them.

"You see anything?" she asked, peering into her

rearview mirror.

"Nothing, but someone was there. That wasn't no cat made the floor creak that way. Wasn't cops, either. They tell you who they are when they enter."

She rounded the block and turned back toward the street where her old house was. She inched up to the corner and they both looked down the street. The rain that had been threatening to fall started to come down in giant sheets, reducing visibility even more.

"I don't see anyone," she said.

"Well, if they're still inside, they're not coming out in this."

Shaye eased off the brake and pulled away, anxious to get out of the neighborhood and back to the area she knew. Most likely, someone had seen Hustle go inside and followed him. Shaye would like to think it was to make sure Hustle wasn't up to no good, but most likely, it was someone who was up to no good themselves and thought the teen might have something of value that they could take.

The drug dealers on the corner that she hadn't even noticed were stark reminders that she was out of her element here and that all kinds of danger lurked around the corner, not just the kind she was looking for. If something had happened to Hustle, she would have never forgiven herself for going inside that house.

It was stupid, and if she'd been thinking correctly, she would have known better. She liked to think she was fairly street-smart and capable of avoiding most problems but she'd been fooling herself. This might have been her life at one point, but it wasn't now. Trina Johnson probably knew the dangers of the streets. Shaye Archer had a ways to go.

"Hey," Hustle said. "Why didn't you pull out your gun?"

"If we hadn't gotten out the window, I would have. But to answer your question, my gun is a last resort. I don't want to kill anyone unless I don't have a choice, and from a professional and personal standpoint, I don't need the trouble that would go along with it."

Hustle nodded. "Makes sense. The news would be all over that—New Orleans socialite goes on shooting rampage."

"Ha. That sounds about right."

She took in a deep breath and slowly blew it out, loosening her grip on the steering wheel as she relaxed. With every inch of road she put between herself and the house, the pressure that had been squeezing her chest started to lessen until finally, it was gone.

Her cell phone signaled a text message and she lifted it to check. She'd been expecting the text but now that it came, she almost wished the timing had been different. Part of her wanted to hurry home and pore over the pictures and video she'd taken of the house. Then the practical part of her said she needed to take a break and this was the perfect way to do it.

She looked over at Hustle. "I'm starved. How about we grab a burger and shakes?"

"I can eat. What about Saul?"

"I told him we might be out for a while, and our evening just got longer. That was a text from Cora LeDoux. She and Jinx would like us to pay them a visit tonight and maybe have some chocolate chip cookies."

Hustle's eyes widened. "I'm gonna get to see Jinx?"

Shaye smiled, his excitement infectious. "If you want to."

"Shit yeah. I mean, that's great. I been talking to her some on the phone but it ain't the same. I want to meet her aunt and see where she's living. I wonder if her aunt will bring her to meet Saul sometime so Jinx can see the painting I've done."

"You can ask her tonight."

CHAPTER TWELVE

New Orleans, Louisiana, Winter 1945

It was almost midnight but he sat behind the ornate desk in his office, waiting for the arrival of the one person he'd hoped he'd never see again. As soon as he'd turned seventeen, he'd inherited all of his deceased father's holdings. He'd immediately sold the plantation. The only thing contained there was disappointment and death. His mother had gone back east to her people right after his father's death, leaving the working hands to run the plantation and an attorney to oversee the money until the boy was seventeen, the age his father's will had indicated he could inherit. The attorney had insisted he spend those five years learning how to manage his father's vast real estate holdings, but the boy had never had any interest in the plantation, and that would never change.

He learned enough to know if the hands were running things properly and spent the rest of his time learning about manufacturing. As soon as he came into the inheritance, he sold the plantation and used the money to open a plant in New Orleans, making supplies for the war. It seemed ironic that the only reason he'd avoided serving is because of a leg that had never healed properly after his father had broken it. The thing that had made him weak physically had made him strong financially. War was a lucrative business, and his father's riches quickly turned into his own wealth.

The only thing he'd kept from the plantation was the desk he sat at now.

It had belonged to his father, who'd always considered it one of his prize possessions. Once, when the boy had accidentally scratched one of the legs with his pocketknife, his father had struck him so hard that he couldn't chew for a week. He'd told the boy he was never allowed near the desk again. Nothing gave him more pleasure now than sitting behind that desk and looking at all the scratches he'd put on it that his father couldn't touch him for.

But now, the desk seemed to mock him, to remind him that no matter what he did, he couldn't escape the plantation. That somehow, things would always circle back around to that hateful place with its horrible memories.

The knock on his office door came precisely at midnight. He called out for the man to come in, one hand beneath the desk, clutching his pistol. After all, the voice on the phone could have been anyone. It sounded like the Haitian boy he'd known and the voice on the phone had known what they'd done. Only the four of them knew, and one of them was gone, a casualty of war. He didn't know about the third son. He'd gone to war as well, but his plantation had gone bankrupt while he was overseas. He'd lost track after that. Or maybe hadn't wanted to find out was a more honest explanation.

So he had to be careful. The person on the phone might not be who he claimed to be.

But the man who walked through the door looked exactly the same as he had nine years ago. His frame had thickened the way a boy's does when he becomes a man, but his face and hair looked the same. And there was no mistaking the blue eyes that almost seemed to glow against his dark skin. The man walked up to the desk and took a seat.

"It's been a long time," the Haitian said. "Do you remember your promise?"

"I remember a promise made by a scared little boy who thought you could summon the devil."

The Haitian shrugged. "What you believed isn't important. What *is* important is that I took care of your problem. I took care of all three problems."

"You poisoned my father. He wasn't killed by a demon."

"You wanted him dead. It doesn't matter how I accomplished it. Only that I kept my end of the bargain. Now you're going to keep yours."

"And if I don't?"

The Haitian smiled. "Then someone very close to you might die the same way your father did…maybe your lovely wife. And if that were to happen and an old family employee were to tell the police that you'd done this before and in the same manner, well, the police might take a harder look at everything. They might look so hard that your entire world crumbled. And for what? What I want will cost you very little compared to what you gained for my services."

Sweat rolled down his brow and he fought the urge to tug at the collar of his dress shirt, which suddenly felt constricting. "What do you want?"

"Money, of course. You have no shortage of that."

"How much?"

"A hundred thousand."

"That's ridiculous!"

"If it weren't for me, you'd have nothing, not even your life."

He knew what the Haitian said was true, but he couldn't just take a hundred thousand dollars out of the bank without people wondering. "I can't get it all at one time. Over several months, maybe."

"Six months then." The Haitian rose. "That should give you plenty of time. I'll be here next week at the same time to collect the first payment. I wouldn't be late if I were you."

As the office door closed, he reached into the desk and pulled out a bottle of whiskey, taking a huge shot right from the bottle. He had the money. It was a lot, and it would set back his expansion by at least a year, but what choice did he have? He couldn't risk his wife and everything he'd worked so hard for, all over the man taking advantage of the desperate wishes of a tortured child.

He took another drink. He'd pay the money. No other option existed.

The question was how many times he would be forced to pay again.

CHAPTER THIRTEEN

Shaye parked at the curb in front of Cora LeDoux's house and looked over at Hustle. He'd been quiet the entire drive over and now his expression was a combination of anticipation and fear.

"You're sure Jinx's aunt is okay with me visiting?" he asked.

"She wouldn't have invited you if she wasn't," Shaye assured him. "She's no pushover. Don't let her physical appearance fool you."

His shoulders relaxed a little. "Cool."

"Then let's not keep them waiting any longer," she said.

They made their way up the sidewalk to the front door, where Shaye rang the doorbell. Seconds later, the door flew open and Jinx flung her arms around Hustle.

"It's great to see you," Jinx said. "It seems like forever, and I know we talk on the phone but it's not the same. Come inside. Aunt Cora is dying to meet you and we made cookies and this awesome strawberry drink."

Jinx bounded inside, Hustle trailing behind her toward the kitchen. The girl's excitement and Hustle's smile lifted

Shaye's spirits considerably. She closed the door and gave Cora, who was standing just inside the doorway, a quick hug.

"You've gained some weight," Shaye said. "That's great."

The last time Shaye had seen Cora, she was struggling with recuperating from chemotherapy for breast cancer. In only a couple of weeks, the color was returning to her face and her body had more fullness to it. She also seemed stronger as she stood. She'd been so weak before that she hadn't been able to stand for long without shaking.

"Thanks," Cora said. "Having Jinx around has me eating more often. That girl can pack away some food. I have no idea where she puts it."

Shaye smiled. "I think it's a teenager thing. Hustle just ate two hamburgers, a huge order of fries, and a milk shake, and I'll bet he still eats half of everything you made."

Cora waved Shaye toward the living room. "Let's have a seat and chat while they catch up. Jinx will bring us something to drink."

Shaye sat on the couch as Cora sank into her recliner. Shaye noticed Cora didn't use the lift feature on the chair this time. Cora's strength really was improving. A couple seconds later, Jinx came into the room carrying a tray with two strawberry shakes and chocolate chip cookies. She flashed them a quick grin, then hurried back to the kitchen. Cora watched as she went, a big smile on her face.

"She's been such a joy," Cora said. "I can't tell you how much. As soon as she arrived, my energy level picked up, then I started eating more and my sleep improved. The doctor told me things would get better if I ate more, of course, but hearing it is a little different from having a ravenous teen pushing food at you several times a day."

"I'm so glad you're doing better. You look like you feel well."

"Haven't felt this good in a year."

"My mom said your case is almost finished. That your sister agreed to sign over parental rights."

Cora nodded. "Surprised everyone—me, your mother, my attorney—but I just gave a quick prayer of thanks and secured that signature while she was feeling charitable or guilty, whatever the case may be."

"How is Jinx doing with everything else?"

"She's enrolled in a summer school program to make up the time she missed. She should be able to join her grade in the fall." Cora shook her head. "She's such a bright girl. When I think about what could have been lost, well, it just makes me mad all over again. For her. For Hustle. For all those kids who still don't have anyone to give them the things they need to make it in this world."

Shaye nodded. "I took my mom down to the docks to talk to some of the kids there. After the kidnapping thing, they decided they can trust me, for the most part, anyway. A couple of them agreed to go into foster care and have been placed in good homes. The others are wary, and I can't really blame them. Mom and I will keep working on them."

"Your mother is a saint for the work she does," Cora

said. "I can't imagine dealing with the things she does every day and still having such a positive demeanor. I'd be one of those angry old women ready to kill everyone."

"I would too. I think people like her have a calling for the work. I can't imagine any other way that they can handle so much more than anyone else could."

"The same could be said for your work as well. You can't be in it for the money. Not taking cases for no pay." Cora smiled.

Shaye laughed. "No. I'm fortunate that money doesn't have to be one of my considerations, and that's a great thing. It allows me to help people who couldn't get help otherwise."

"Like Hustle and Jinx. But enough about them. Tell me how you're doing. I know this case must have been a tough one, and with your name all over the news because of your involvement with taking down that Clancy monster…I'm sure you'd rather maintain a low profile."

"Yeah, but I'm not foolish enough to think it's possible. Clancy would have been front-page news no matter what, but add my name to the mix and it's even juicier. It's something I've learned to live with, but not something I'll ever enjoy."

"Well, you handle it all so calmly. Are you working on a new case now?"

Shaye hesitated for a moment, but then decided that telling Cora the bare bones of what she was currently working on wouldn't be any big deal. Chances were she'd hear about it from Jinx through Hustle sooner or later.

"Actually," Shaye said, "I'm working on an old case for the first time. My own."

Cora's eyes widened. "Wow. I can't imagine how stressful that's got to be. I can't think of anything I have to offer, but if there's anything I can do, please let me know. Would you mind my asking why you decided to do this now?"

Shaye looked into the kitchen and saw Jinx and Hustle sitting at the counter, laughing and eating cookies. "You can't repeat this, but the police have deciphered some of Clancy's journals. I was one of his products."

Cora's hand flew over her mouth. "No!" She glanced into the kitchen, then leaned forward and placed her hand on Shaye's leg. "I am so sorry. I don't even have words. I knew something was bothering Corrine the last time we met—something more than the usual, but I never imagined."

"For obvious reasons, we're keeping that information to ourselves, and the police are trying to keep it confidential. I'm sure that sooner or later, it will get out, but I stand a better chance of finding out something before it becomes a media circus."

"No one will be hearing anything from me. Except God, and he's getting an earful tonight. I've prayed so much this past year he's probably tired of hearing from me."

"Well, whatever you're doing seems to be working, and I'll take all the help I can get."

"Is that detective working with you? The one who

helped find Jinx?"

Shaye nodded. "Officially when approved, unofficially when he can get away with it."

"I figured as much." Cora smiled. "I could tell by the way he looked at you at the hospital. My mama would have said he was sweet on you."

"You think so?"

"Oh, honey, I'd bet on it. The question is what are you going to do about it?"

Shaye sighed. "That's one more answer in a long list of those I don't have."

Shaye dropped Hustle off at Saul's hotel and gave him a wave before pulling away. It had been a really long day, but a good one. With Hustle's help, she'd found the home she'd lived in and more things were coming back to her. Hopefully, it was only the beginning and her memory would progress forward so that she could pin down something that would help lead them to her captor.

That would help save the girl he had now.

She smiled as Hustle bounded into the front entrance of the hotel. He hadn't stopped talking since they'd left Cora's house. His visit with Jinx had been a really good thing. No matter how well Shaye and Jinx spoke about Jinx's situation with her aunt and how great Cora was, Shaye knew Hustle had to see it firsthand before he let go of that last thread of worry that he carried around. After everything Jinx had been through, his worry was warranted, but Cora and Corrine had assured Shaye that Jinx was in counseling and talking openly about her abduction and escape. Even though she was only fifteen, Jinx had a practical mind and a mature perspective on everything. Corrine said Jinx reminded her of Shaye in that regard.

It was also clear to Shaye that Jinx had done a fair amount of worrying about Hustle. She'd been asking Hustle a lot of questions during their phone calls and asking Cora to check up on him and make sure everything was as he'd presented. Shaye suggested to Cora that she bring Jinx to visit Hustle at the hotel for their next get-together. That way, she too could see firsthand how her friend was living. It would be one less thing on the girl's mind. Cora had been excited at the idea and said she'd call Saul and arrange for a visit.

Shaye turned her SUV back toward the French Quarter and glanced at the clock on the dashboard. It was only 10:00 p.m. but she felt as if she'd been up for days. Her sleep had been as disrupted as her eating and exercise schedule, and she was paying for all of it. Everything was up in the air right now, but she needed to get things back to some sort of normalcy soon. She couldn't afford for her strength to lapse or for her mental acuity to lessen in any way. Staying focused and physically strong was necessary for survival. After nine long years of practically nothing, now things were racing forward, sometimes at lightning speed.

She glanced in the rearview mirror and made a note of

the shape and light intensity of the headlamps on the vehicle behind her. It had been going the same direction for the past four blocks, staying about a block behind. That wasn't necessarily unusual. After all, a lot of people lived in and visited the French Quarter, but Shaye had learned long ago that too much caution was rarely a bad thing, especially in her line of work.

The most direct route to her house kept her straight for another two blocks and then turning right, but instead, she made a right turn at the next stop sign, then stomped on the gas and made a hard right turn into a parking garage, turning off her headlights as she went inside. She circled around the lower level, giving her a clear view of the street, but didn't pull into a parking space. Instead, she stopped in the middle of a big empty area and pulled her binoculars out of her glove compartment.

A couple seconds later, the car she'd spotted passed the garage at a much slower speed than it had been traveling behind her. Training her binoculars on the car, she hoped to make out the driver and was momentarily surprised when she saw two figures in the front seat, rather than just one.

Maybe you aren't being followed.

That would be the most logical explanation. If one person had been in the car, it would have fit better for following her theory. Two meant a bad guy and an accomplice, and stalkers usually worked alone. Still, something about it didn't feel right and she knew better than to ignore those feelings.

What if it's him?

It had crossed her mind as she and Hustle fled the house earlier that day. Only for a second, but it was still something she had to consider. With Clancy being headline news, her abductor might feel threatened and make a move. Maybe he'd been following her for a while. She didn't think that was the case, but she couldn't be certain. If it was her abductor, maintaining her safety and that of anyone around her had just gotten more complex.

Zeroing in on the back of the car, she tried to read the license plate, but only got a partial. Still, a partial and the make and model of the car—a black Mercedes S-Class—might be enough to get some information on the occupants. A starting point at least.

She watched as the car crept by and waited until it had been gone for at least a minute before inching forward to the exit. The street was clear as far as she could see so she pulled out and turned her lights back on, then made a left turn and took a circuitous route to her apartment, constantly checking her mirrors for any sign of the black sedan.

No other cars stayed in line with her for more than a couple blocks, so she circled around once and then parked in front of her apartment. She pulled out her nine-millimeter as she scanned the streets for any sign of movement, but not even a piece of paper stirred in the dead night air. She climbed out of her car and headed for her apartment, quickly unlocking the front door and stepping inside. It took only a couple seconds to disarm the alarm, then she bolted the door back down, reset the alarm, and pulled back the blinds on the front window to peer outside.

She sucked in a breath.

The car had just turned the corner and had pulled to the curb a block away from her apartment. At least, it looked like the car and the headlamps were the same, but without her binoculars, she couldn't be sure, and she'd left them in her SUV. She waited several minutes for someone to get out, but no one ever emerged. She tapped her fingers on the windowsill. The service she used for tracking license plates was closed, so either she waited until tomorrow or she called in a favor. Reaching into her pocket, she grabbed her cell phone and called Jackson.

"I think a car was following me," she said when he answered.

"What? When? Did you get a good look?"

"About ten minutes ago, a black Mercedes S-Class, and I got a partial plate."

"Give it to me."

She recited what she had of the license plate number. "I think the same car might be sitting a block away from my house. The headlights and shape and color of the car are the same. I just can't see enough to be certain."

"Did anyone get out of the car?"

"No."

"Okay. Do not go outside your house, and make sure your alarm is on. You've got your pistol, right? Keep an eye on that car and if anyone gets out and moves toward your house, call 911. I'm going to call this plate in and I'm headed over there right now."

Jackson disconnected the call and Shaye placed her cell phone on the windowsill, not taking her eyes off the car. There was still no movement from inside, and the longer they sat there, the more strange it seemed. The area the car was parked in front of contained a couple of businesses that had closed hours ago, leaving no reason for anyone to be parked there at this time of night.

A couple minutes later, Jackson called her back.

"Got it," he said. "We lucked out. There's only one black Mercedes S-Class with that combination on the plate. The car is registered to a Wayne Moody. Lives in the Garden District."

A flush of anger rose from Shaye's chest and onto her face. She knew exactly who Wayne Moody was and exactly why he was sitting outside her home. "He's a private investigator," she told Jackson, "and he works for my grandfather. I'm going back on my word. I need to step outside for a minute."

"Wait—"

She hung up before Jackson could argue and left the phone on her windowsill. She hurried into the kitchen, turned off the alarm, and slipped out the side door into the courtyard, locking it behind her. She headed to the back wall of the courtyard, pulled the small bistro table over to the brick wall that closed off the courtyard to the street behind it, and used the table to vault herself over the wall and into the parking area behind her apartment.

She jogged down the street for two blocks, then went

over a block, crossing the street at the same time as a car, ducking down behind it as it went. The other side of the street had a long hedge that covered half of the block, so she slipped behind it and headed toward the Mercedes. When she got to the end of the hedge, she peered out and could see the two figures still sitting inside. The passenger's window was rolled down and a man's arm was propped on the door.

She clutched her pistol and crept out of the hedge, then covered the ten yards to the car as quickly and quietly as possible. When she stepped up to the window and lowered her pistol at the men, they both jumped.

"What the hell, you crazy bitch!" the man on the passenger's side yelled at her.

Shaye stared down at him, but she'd never seen him before. She leaned down and looked at the driver. Wayne Moody. "You wanna tell your partner who he just called a crazy bitch?"

Moody's eyes widened. "Shaye? What are you doing here?"

"I live here, which I'm sure you already know. Now I'm going to ask you the same thing."

Moody puffed up his chest. Now that his initial shock had worn off, he was going to get belligerent, his usual stance. "If you must know, we're on a case, and I don't appreciate this interference."

His partner stared back and forth between the two of them, clearly having no idea how to handle the situation. Shaye shook her head. "You're on a case all right," she said, "and I'll interfere all I want when that case is me. This isn't going to happen, Moody. Not by you or anyone else Pierce pays. You can either start your car, go home, and tell my grandfather this ludicrous plan of his won't work, or I'll report you for stalking to the detective who's on his way here now."

Moody flushed and he straightened up in his seat. "Stalking? You can't do that."

"You want to try me?"

Moody stared at her for several seconds, and Shaye knew he was weighing Pierce's anger over the prospect of being arrested. Not a good look for private detectives, and it usually didn't buy you any friends down at the police department. Pierce's anger or money must not have been enough to trump potential long-term career problems, because he shot her a disgusted look and pulled away from the curb, tires squealing as he left.

Shaye was halfway back to her apartment when Jackson's truck pulled up beside her. "He left?" Jackson asked, glancing up and down the street.

"I offered him the option to leave or be arrested for stalking."

Jackson laughed. "I bet that pissed him off plenty."

"It's going to piss him off more when Pierce gets a hold of him. I'm sorry you came all the way over here for my family drama."

"I needed to be sure. Besides, it's not that far and I'm not sleepy. Anyway, I got a laugh out of it, and those are getting harder to come by these days."

"So true. Well, since my blood pressure is through the roof, I'm going to make a root beer float and try to calm down enough to sleep. I'd be glad to fix one for you. After all, you ran a plate and attempted to come to my rescue after hours. It's the least I can do."

Jackson smiled. "A root beer float sounds great, but I won't stay long. I know it's hard, but you need to get some rest. So do I."

"You might change your mind about that when you hear about my day."

"You found out something?"

"I found out a lot of somethings. Not enough to launch us forward, but it's a start. A really good start."

"I like the sound of that."

"Come in then. Moonlight's wasting."

CHAPTER FOURTEEN

Monday, July 27, 2015

At 10:00 a.m., Shaye punched in the code to open the gate to her mother's home and drove through the tall iron spires as it swung open. Pierce's car was already parked in the circular drive, so she pulled in behind him and made her way inside. Her mother's and grandfather's voices carried from the kitchen to the front entry, and she could tell by the elevated levels of both volume and pitch that the conversation wasn't an agreeable one.

She shut the front door a bit loudly and all talking ceased. When she walked into the kitchen, they were both standing on the other side of the counter, their bodies squared off at each other. They looked at her and smiled, but Shaye could tell that both were forcing it. "Problems in paradise?" she asked.

"No, of course not," Corrine said, but the tone of her voice said differently.

Whatever was going on between the two of them, Shaye didn't even want to know, especially as they were probably arguing over her. She was definitely here to raise some hell, but it was going to be on her terms.

"You said you needed to talk to us?" Pierce asked her. "Is there something we can help you with?"

Shaye grabbed a cookie off the plate on the counter and took a seat at the counter. "Yeah, you can help me by calling off Wayne Moody and any other of your monkeys you were thinking of sending to follow me."

Shaye watched Corrine's face, certain she'd be able to tell by her mother's reaction whether or not she knew about the tail Pierce had put on Shaye. Her dismay as she whipped around to glare at her father was unmistakable.

"You didn't," Corrine said.

Pierce pulled his shoulders back and Shaye could almost see him digging the heels of his dress shoes into the tile floor. "I did what was necessary," he said.

"You invaded my privacy," Shaye said, "and disrespected my wishes. And you almost got Moody arrested for stalking. I won't let the next one go that easily. And just so you know, when I leave here, I'm going to the police station and Detective Lamotte is going to have his forensics team sweep my car for tracking devices. I'd hate to tell them who's responsible for anything we find, so you're on notice for that one too."

Corrine shook her head at her father. "You should have stuck with that whole castle idea instead."

Shaye frowned. "What castle idea?"

"Your grandfather thought he could tempt us out of the country by buying a castle."

Shaye nodded. "I agree. You should have gone with

the castle plan."

Pierce perked up. "You would have gone?"

"No," Shaye said, "but I wouldn't be mad at you, either."

Pierce looked from Corrine to Shaye and sighed. "You've got to be reasonable. I'm not the kind of man who sits around waiting for things to happen, especially when those things involve the safety of my daughter and granddaughter." He narrowed his eyes at Corrine. "I would expect a bit more sympathy from you of all people."

"Oh, I have plenty of sympathy for your position," Corrine said. "I just don't condone your actions."

Pierce threw his hands in the air, clearly exasperated. "How can you say that? How can you sit here knowing Shaye is running around the city, looking into things best left forgotten?"

"Best for whom?" Shaye asked.

Pierce appeared momentarily taken aback. "Well, for you, of course. You've already been through enough. I don't want you to suffer anything you don't have to."

"Not knowing *is* suffering," Shaye said quietly.

"Damn it." Pierce ran his hand through his hair. "What do you want me to say—that if I could find the guy who did those things to you, I'd kill him with my bare hands? I would. I tried, Shaye. Back when you first came to live with Corrine, I hired every private investigator in New Orleans. I flew a couple in from other states who were supposed to be experts in this sort of crime. Whatever the hell 'this sort of crime' is supposed to imply. They couldn't find anything. So I let it go. I didn't have another choice."

"You didn't have another choice then," Shaye said, "but things are different now. We know who my biological mother is and that Clancy sold me to that animal."

"But that doesn't tell us anything about him," Pierce said. "And this morning I find out he has another girl."

He slumped onto a stool, and Shaye felt a twinge of guilt at his helpless expression. She knew he meant well, but Pierce Archer wasn't used to problems that couldn't be solved with money. He also wasn't used to losing, and Shaye knew he saw this as exactly that—a loss on his record.

"Yesterday, I found the house I lived in with Lydia," Shaye said.

Corrine clutched the counter and stared at Shaye. "Oh my God. How?"

"I had a little help from Hustle," Shaye said. "A lady at Lydia's old apartment complex was willing to talk to him. She wouldn't even admit to me that she knew who Lydia was."

Corrine nodded. "It's hard to get information. There's so much fear of law enforcement and government agencies. Where is the house?"

"In the Ninth Ward. It's abandoned and needs to be bulldozed, but at least it was still standing." Shaye looked from Pierce to Corrine. "I remember it."

Corrine's hand flew over her mouth and Pierce'e eyes widened.

"You remember?" Corrine said. "Oh, Shaye. Are you

okay?"

Shaye nodded. "It was only flashes of memory—things like wallpaper, a closet, and a window, but it's a start. Don't you see, if I can remember that night, then I'll know where I escaped from. We can finally catch him."

Corrine moved around the counter and hugged Shaye tightly. "If there was any way I could take this burden from you, I would."

Shaye's hugged her mother and kissed her cheek. "I know you would."

Corrine released Shaye and moved back enough so that she could look at her. Tears pooled in the corners of her eyes, threatening to fall over. "I'm so afraid for you," Corrine said. "I want this to be over, but I don't want you to hurt anymore."

Shaye reached out and took her mother's hands in hers. "I won't tell you not to worry because there's no point, but when you start worrying, remember that I have you and grandfather and Eleonore. No matter what happens, I'm going to be fine. You won't let me be any other way."

Corrine managed a small smile. "I *can* be a bit bossy."

Shaye raised one eyebrow. "A bit?"

"Just a scootch." Corrine glanced over at Pierce. "And while I don't condone what your grandfather did, hearing that you're traipsing around the Ninth Ward with only a 15-year-old boy as backup is something I'm not going to let slide. You can't take those kinds of chances. With Clancy all over the news, we have to assume that monster knows about the journals. He's left you alone all this time, but this could be the thing that puts him on alert. Promise me you won't go anywhere unsafe without proper backup."

Shaye looked over her mother's shoulder and into the backyard. Corrine had hit on the one thing Shaye had as well. That Clancy's exposure might prompt her captor to make a move. Going to the house yesterday with Hustle had been a serious miscalculation on her part. She wasn't going to make that mistake again.

"I'd be happy to furnish a bodyguard," Pierce said. "Someone entirely at your disposal. If you need him, you use him. If not, he can sit and wait until he's needed."

"No," Shaye said. "I appreciate the offer, but I wouldn't be able to think straight with some stranger hulking around behind me. If I return to the house or go anywhere else sketchy, I'll have Jackson go with me. Will that work?"

Pierce frowned. "So it's 'Jackson' now, not Detective Lamotte? Is there anything you'd like to tell me about that?"

"He's a friend and I trust him," Shaye said. "That's all there is to it."

It wasn't exactly a lie. The part beyond friends was only in the contemplating stage. It was serious contemplation, but none of that was something her grandfather needed to know. Corrine already had her suspicions, but she'd been smart enough to remain relatively silent on the subject.

"Well, at least give me the address for the house,"

Pierce said. "I'll find out who the owner is and buy the damned thing before it's torn down."

Shaye gave him the address and he made a note on his phone.

"I'll have my attorney get right on this," Pierce said. "In fact, I'm going to text him now."

He looked so pleased to finally be doing something that Shaye couldn't help but smile. She really did have the best of everything. Her start in this world might have been a really crappy one, but her finish was going to be amazing.

He watched as they entered the hotel and waited a while before following them inside, where he headed for the bar. He'd been here once before and knew the bar offered a decent view of the restaurant. Without the mask, he felt naked, but even with the oddities of New Orleans, it wasn't the sort of thing you wore into the Ritz-Carlton. He stepped up to the bar and ordered a club soda. No alcohol for him. Impurities clogged your mind and spirit. The One liked pure vessels with which to operate. That's why the girls had to be young, still innocent. Ruining innocence was the One's purpose on earth and as his facilitator, the man did everything possible to see that the One was never disappointed.

The bartender slid the glass in front of him, and he took it and walked around the tables of people and the couches. It was fairly crowded, which made it easier for him to disappear. As he walked, he snatched glimpses of the restaurant, searching the patrons for Shaye and her date, Detective Jackson Lamotte. The man frowned. Lamotte hadn't been around when Shaye escaped, so he could offer no contribution to her past. Not firsthand, anyway. But the detective was becoming a problem.

Lamotte was clever and he was clearly enamored of the girl. That gave her the backup she needed to pursue her past without hesitating and with access to things she wouldn't have otherwise—like Clancy's journals. The news reports claimed Clancy had used code for the journals, but if the cops broke that code, they might be able to locate him. They might also know about his recent purchase. And if the cops found out that Shaye was one of Clancy's products, then he had no doubt Lamotte would provide her with that information.

Detective Lamotte needed to go along with the others.

He walked along the far end of the bar and glanced over at the restaurant again, and that's when he caught sight of them. She was wearing a blue dress and her hair was on top of her head—one of those fancy styles that wealthy women seemed to like. The dress, fancy hairdo, and makeup weren't her norm, nor was the suit Lamotte wore normal for him. It was clear by the chairs slid closely together and the intimate looks they shared with each other that tonight wasn't about work.

He'd suspected the two would progress to something deeper than friendship, and that it would ultimately be a problem for him, but now he had proof. Lamotte leaned over and whispered something to Shaye and she smiled. He picked something off the table and handed it to her and when she took it, the man realized it was a room card.

So tonight was all about romance.

He set his glass on the nearest table and headed out of the hotel. The security at the Ritz was excellent and there were cameras everywhere, leaving him no opportunity to act and escape without being recorded, assuming he could bypass all the security checkpoints in the first place. No, this was not the time or place. It was too difficult and too risky. He'd wait until they were vulnerable. Shaye's apartment was secure and her mother's estate was a fortress, but both Shaye and Jackson left their homes, sometimes working in questionable areas.

Staging a carjacking on Shaye would be a simple enough matter. The cop was harder. A single bullet from a distance was the safest option, but not the choice of killing for the One. Perhaps an exception could be made. Maybe penance would be enough. He wasn't necessarily worried about suspicion falling on him. After all, cops got killed all the time and their enemies were too many to list. But killing the cop and the girl at the same time would definitely raise more red flags, which he was trying to avoid. So tonight, they were safe, but the night wouldn't be a total loss. He had other liabilities to eliminate.

He walked out of the hotel and around the corner where he'd parked. Tonight wasn't the night for Shaye, but it had to be soon.

Before she remembered.

Shaye gave Jackson a smile that she hoped looked sexy and held the room key in her hand for a couple seconds before slipping it into her purse. If anyone was watching, Shaye needed them to think this was a romantic rendezvous. The Ritz was an excellent choice because the restaurant was top-notch, and if they were being followed, then whoever was watching would think they were having a nice meal as a prelude to an even nicer dessert.

A flush crept up Shaye's neck as all those thoughts ran through her mind. It was a solid plan except for the piece where part of her wished it wasn't all staged. The rest of her, however, froze at the thought of being so intimate with Jackson. She was willing to admit that her feelings for him had moved beyond friendship, but she wasn't quite ready to consider all the ramifications of a romantic entanglement. Still, her body responded to him in a way it never had another man, and that was such a big step. A potentially life-changing step. At least for her.

Jackson leaned over and whispered, "You're doing great. Now, we just have to maintain this casual appearance through dinner."

She relaxed a bit with his compliment. The dress, makeup, and upswept hair were things she forced herself to do for charity events. This was the first time she'd taken so much care for dinner with a man. It felt too much as if she was playing a role, and she supposed that's exactly what she was doing. Except for the part where Jackson was the only man she'd want to be with under any circumstances.

"Have you eaten here before?" she asked.

He shook his head. "I haven't had the pleasure."

"Well, it won't be hard to look happy through the meal. The food is fantastic."

He grinned. "I am definitely a man who appreciates good food. Add to it that the company isn't so bad, and the night is looking up. In fact, work has never been this fun. Or offered such a great view. You look beautiful."

The flush that had remained on her chest and neck earlier crept all the way up her cheeks. "Thank you. You look pretty hot yourself."

In his black suit, white shirt, and black-and-silver tie, Jackson looked as if he'd stepped off the cover of a fashion magazine. He never stopped surprising her. His taste in high-end clothes was excellent. She was certain the suit had been tailored. Off the rack never fit quite right. She'd learned all about high-end clothes from her mother and grandfather. Much to Corrine's dismay, Shaye had never taken much of an interest. Unless it was time to rotate to a new dress for those awful charity events, Shaye wasn't much for shopping. Everything she wore daily could be ordered on Amazon and delivered to her doorstep.

Jackson looked pleased and a tiny bit embarrassed with her compliment, and she felt her heart flutter. He was into her, right? She wasn't misreading him helping her as romantic interest? No one else seemed to think so. Eleonore, Corrine, Cora, and even Hustle had immediately suggested that Jackson had his eye on her for far more than her caseload. But since she'd never let her guard down with another man, she had no experience to draw on. It seemed that he wanted more than friendship, but that tiny doubt niggling at the back of her mind always kept her from crossing the friendship line. Unfortunately, one thing she was fairly certain of was that she would have to make the first move. Jackson had too much respect for her to do it, and she knew he worried about and was very protective of her emotional state. He wouldn't risk setting her back.

Jackson leaned in again. "Beaumont didn't give you any clue as to what he wanted to tell you?"

"No. He said he needed to see me in person. He gave me the hotel and room number and said I needed to make it look like a rendezvous because there was a good chance I was being watched." She frowned. "He specifically said to bring you as my date. He moved away after he retired. How does he even know about us?"

"Beaumont was a great cop who served a lot of years. I have no doubt he's got eyes and ears in the department."

"You think someone is feeding him information about us?"

"I'd bet on it and I have a really good guess who it is—the desk sergeant."

"Why him?"

"He and Beaumont were partners for a lot of years until the sergeant's physical health wasn't good enough for street work. If someone in the department is feeding Beaumont information, the sergeant is my pick."

The server stepped up to their table and Jackson straightened in his chair. As the heavenly smells of the food wafted toward Shaye, she realized how hungry she was.

"Can I provide you with anything else?" the server asked.

"No, thank you," she said. "This looks perfect."

Jackson shook his head and the server moved away. "We have an hour to kill before we meet Beaumont. If the dessert tastes anything like this looks, it might be the best hour I've had in years."

Shaye smiled. "Prepare for an hour that you'll remember forever."

Corrine removed her hand from her mouse and leaned back in the stool, lifting her arms above her head to stretch. She closed her eyes and sighed as the burning sensation began to dissipate.

"You should take a break," Eleonore said. "You've been at this for ten hours already."

"So have you," Corrine said.

"Yeah, but I spend every day sitting on my ass, and staring at either a computer or someone in my chair. You're used to moving around more."

"Are you admitting that my ass is smaller than yours?"

"Honey, that was never in question. Seriously, get off that stool and let's take a lap around your backyard before your muscles start to atrophy."

Corrine slid off the stool and headed for the patio. The heat and humidity were overwhelming, even though the sun disappeared over the tree line an hour ago. She looked over at Eleonore, who was already fanning herself with her hand, and shook her head.

"This is not refreshing," Corrine said. "All this is doing is making me sweaty and more irritable."

"Jesus, how much more irritable can you get? You flew right past unbearable this afternoon. If you take it up another notch, I'm going to tranquilize you."

"That's what friends are for."

"You're really pushing the friendship envelope."

Corrine rolled her eyes. "Let's get back inside in the AC before I melt. I'm not good with heat."

"Please. Talk to me when your ovaries call it quits. Last week, I emptied my entire deep freezer and sat inside. Half of my shrimp thawed out and I spent the rest of the night cooking it all. I've given casseroles to half the neighborhood, and I don't even like casserole. *Or* my neighbors."

Corrine crossed the kitchen and opened the refrigerator door. She stood there for a while. "Hey, this works," she said. "I bet the freezer was even better."

"If this crap doesn't go away soon, I'm going to look into buying one of those cryo tanks. I could probably fund my retirement renting it out to the neighborhood wives. If you ever come out of there, will you bring me a Diet Coke?"

Corrine grabbed two Diet Cokes and closed the

refrigerator. She plopped back onto her stool and slid one of the cans across the bar to Eleonore. "What are we doing?" she asked.

Eleonore rubbed the can across her forehead. "What do you mean? We're trying to figure out who this girl is that Clancy sold."

"But does it really matter?"

Eleonore frowned and lowered the bottle. "That seems a really strange question, especially coming from you."

"That's not what I meant." Corrine blew out a breath, frustration getting the better of her. "Of course the girl matters, but knowing who she is won't tell us *where* she is now. Even if someone saw Clancy take her, it doesn't help us. We already know that Clancy had her."

"Her parents need to know."

"Even though they're the likely reason she was on the street in the first place?"

"You already know the answer to that."

"Well, the answer sucks."

Eleonore nodded. "What if someone saw the girl after Clancy sold her? It's a long shot, but maybe someone saw her in a car, thinking she was asleep. Or maybe the guy checked into a hotel, or ran a stop sign. Yeah, it's so thin, it's practically invisible, but if we can identify her, and the police release her information, then someone might report seeing her."

"If her face is plastered all over the news, he'll just kill her sooner."

"Maybe that would be better than the alternative,"

Eleonore said quietly.

Corrine didn't want to think about the alternative. It was far too close to home. "Shaye came to see you today, right?"

"Yes."

"I assume she told you about finding the house and remembering?"

"She did."

Corrine looked across the bar at her friend. "I'm scared. Scared to death for her. What if she remembers everything and can't handle it? What if she figures out where she was held captive, but he's no longer there? What if he gets away? How will she live with that? Everything rushing back in and knowing he's still out there?"

"I don't suppose it's going to help you any for me to say I'm worried too."

"Actually, it does. I've been feeling kinda crazy."

"You're not crazy and you're not being overprotective. You have valid reasons for your concerns—all of them. Stop beating yourself up over this. There's nothing you can do except what you're already doing. We all wish we could do more, but the reality is, our hands are tied. Either the police catch a break or Shaye remembers. Those are the only two ways I see this resolving."

"Either way, Shaye will end up reliving it. Even if the police beat her to it, the fact that she's remembering her time with her mother means it's all likely to come back."

"That woman was not her mother," Eleonore said. "You are, and you're a damned fine one."

Corrine forced a smile. "Will you marry me, Eleonore?"

"Where's the ring? Never mind, I don't need a ring. You're the best offer I've had in a while. But I'm keeping my last name and I won't pick out china with you. You have horrible taste in dinnerware."

Now Corrine smiled for real. "We're going to get through this, right?"

"Count on it."

CHAPTER FIFTEEN

Shaye watched as Jackson activated the elevator with his room card. The meal had been great but with every bite, her anxiety had increased a tiny bit more. Whatever Detective Beaumont had to tell her was serious enough that he'd insisted on this level of secrecy. That worried her on so many levels. Beaumont was a highly experienced and decorated cop. He was hardly the type to be an alarmist.

The floors seemed to creep by, but finally the elevator stopped on Beaumont's floor. They got out and headed for his room. As they walked, Jackson kept glancing over at her. She knew he was worried about why Beaumont had wanted to meet with them and under strange circumstances, but he'd tried really hard to keep things casual during their meal, practically carrying the conversation at some points.

They located the room and Jackson looked at her, as if to ask "are you ready?" She nodded and he rapped on the door. A second later, the door swung open and Detective Beaumont motioned them inside.

He had more silver than before. In fact, he was almost entirely silver now, but he hadn't let himself go in retirement. His forearms still rippled with muscle and the pot belly that so many men his age developed was nowhere in sight. He stared at Shaye for several seconds, then shook his head.

"You're even more lovely in person than on television," he said. "And tough to boot. Private investigator. You're going to need all that tough and those smarts."

"It's good to see you again, Detective Beaumont," Shaye said and gave him a quick hug.

He looked both pleased and slightly uncomfortable with the hug. "Call me Harold. I'm out of the detective business, at least when it comes to payroll. Can't take the cop out of the man, though."

Harold looked over at Jackson and extended his hand. "It's a pleasure to meet you. I've heard a lot of good things about your work. You're making a name for yourself down at the department."

"Thank you, sir," Jackson said. "That's a huge compliment coming from someone with your record."

"Well, now that the mutual lovefest is over," Harold said, "let's get down to business. I had an extra chair brought up here."

He stepped out of the entry and into the sleeping area. Three chairs were on the far side of the room next to a window that had the drapes drawn. A bottle of whiskey sat on a small table nearby. "Anyone want a drink?" Harold asked.

Shaye and Jackson both shook their heads.

"If you don't mind," Harold said, "I'm going to pour one for myself. The last several days have been strange and more than a little hectic."

"I imagine they must have been, given all the precautions for this meeting," Shaye said.

Harold poured himself a drink, sat, and took a big sip of the whiskey. "I'll give you a little background, then I'll get to the reason I'm here. First off, I've been following the Clancy case and I probably don't have to tell either of you that I have some friends in the department who fill me in on some of the things that the news doesn't carry."

He looked at Shaye. "I know about them finding your biological mother, and I know she sold you to Clancy." He shook his head, clearly disgusted. "I can't begin to tell you how sorry I am about that. I knew nothing good was buried in your past, but I never imagined something this evil. I don't use that word lightly, but this Clancy situation trumps anything I've seen in decades of police work. It made me sick to find out that you were a part of it."

"Thank you," Shaye said quietly.

"I know about the girl Clancy sold to that monster last month, too," Harold said. "So the many layers of urgency in this case are really clear to me." He looked at Jackson. "I understand you're working on that with Grayson?"

"As much as we can work on it with nothing to go on," Jackson said.

"Well, I don't know how much help I can be," Harold said, "but I'll be damned if I'm not going to give you anything I can."

"I appreciate any help you can offer," Jackson said.

Harold nodded. "First, I need to explain why I'm here. To do that I need to take you back a bit, so you understand what happened this week."

He took another drink and sat silent for several seconds, then started speaking again. "That night we found Shaye was one of the worst of my career. And you can bet, I did everything I could to figure out where you'd been held and by whom, but we had practically nothing to go on."

"I've read the files many times," Jackson said. "You pursued every line of investigation that was available and many that weren't. If there was something you could have done and didn't, I haven't put my finger on it."

Harold nodded. "We did everything we could, but eventually, time passed and with no leads, the case went cold and after a couple months, it was shoved into a box and sent to the warehouse for storage with all the others. About a year later, when they started scanning the old documents, I pulled the file up again. I figured a bit of time had passed and maybe something would jump out at me that hadn't back then."

"Makes sense," Jackson said.

Harold leaned toward them. "And that's when I discovered parts of the file were missing."

Jackson's eyes widened as Shaye sat upright. "What?" she asked.

Harold nodded. "I went down to the warehouse and asked about it. They said some of the paperwork stored had been damaged by a sprinkler malfunction before it could be scanned. That explanation would have worked if the entire file was destroyed, but explain to me how a sprinkler could ruin some of the paperwork in a box and not the rest of it?"

"That doesn't make sense," Jackson said.

"So I asked to see the original files," Harold said. "I thought maybe they did a poor job scanning and missed some items. They looked for a while and couldn't find the box. Finally, they decided that it might have been misplaced or accidentally destroyed along with old administrative paperwork that they no longer needed to keep."

"That's a pretty big screwup," Jackson said.

Harold nodded. "Monumental."

"What was missing from the scanned files?" Jackson asked.

"Some pictures taken at the hospital for one," Harold said. "Specifically, a picture of the pentagram on Shaye's back. And the statement I gave the night we found Shaye, plus some personal notes I made while we were investigating. My official reports were still there, but you know how you sometimes add your thoughts or feelings on things."

"You just don't put those thoughts in the official report," Jackson said.

"Exactly," Harold said. "Hunches were always considered a positive thing in police work by other cops, but administration frowned on having those type of things in official records. They didn't want people to think we were running willy-nilly or something. Stupid, if you ask me, because a hunch has been the catalyst for cops breaking some of their biggest cases, but you know how it is with people who never did the job."

"Did you report the missing information?" Shaye asked.

"Told Bernard about it as soon as I discovered it. He poked around a bit and came back to me with the same stories I'd heard from the others. Since there didn't seem to be any good reason for it other than the story he was told, he dismissed it."

"And you're sure it couldn't have been just like they said—a sprinkler leak and an accidental destruction?" Jackson asked. "It would be highly coincidental but it wouldn't be the first time something that strange has happened without an undercurrent pushing it through."

"I suppose I thought it was possible at the time," Harold said, "or I dismissed it since there wasn't anything I could do about it. But it never sat right with me, and when things don't sit right with me, there's always been a reason. Still, I had no proof of wrongdoing and no way of getting any, so I let it go. Then I heard about Clancy and the journals. I had a feeling the dam was about to burst. That's when it started."

"What started?" Shaye asked.

"Someone has been watching me," Harold said. "I never saw him, mind you, but I could feel him there, somewhere in the woods near my house. Felt it twice, once during the day and once at night. After the second time, I knew something was wrong. I found his footprints where he'd stood in the bushes across the road from my place. Only one reason to stand there and that's to watch my house."

"And you think it's because of me?" Shaye asked.

"I'm sorry to say it," Harold said, "but that's the first thought that hit me, and the longer I chewed on it the more it bothered me." Harold leaned forward in his chair. "Think about it. The guy who took you has gotten away clean for nine years. Then Clancy goes down and the journals are big news. But the news is also clearly stating that they're in code."

"So as far as he knows, he's still safe," Jackson said.

Harold nodded. "So why risk making a move now, right? But there was that feeling—you know the one that good cops get? I knew something was coming and it wasn't anything I wanted to be there for. So I planned my getaway. And I was just in time. He struck that night."

Harold told Shaye and Jackson about his plan with Old Joe and how he'd disappeared in plain sight. Shaye sat fixated on Harold's face the entire time, floored by the man's survival instincts and thankful that he hadn't ignored the feeling that he needed to leave.

"You said you had security cameras?" Shaye asked, her excitement growing.

"Yeah, but it didn't do any good," Harold said. "Can't see his face."

Shaye slumped in her chair, trying to stop the wave of disappointment that rolled over her, but it was hard. Every time she thought they were getting closer to an answer, they just found more questions.

Jackson, who'd been silent the entire time Harold told his story, shook his head. "I would never question your intuition and clearly, you were right in your assessment that someone was watching you, but how can you be certain it's about Shaye and Clancy? Like you said, he's been in the clear for nine years. Why mess that up by attempting to kill a retired cop in his own home? He's exposing himself when he doesn't have to."

Harold raised one eyebrow. "Is he? He's in the clear for the moment, but the police have broken part of the code, and they know not only that Shaye was one of Clancy's victims but that he sold another girl to the same man just a month ago."

"But that information hasn't been released," Jackson said, "and isn't going to be."

"And yet," Harold said, "I know about it."

Jackson's eyes widened. "You think he has someone inside the police department?"

Harold nodded. "I can't prove it, but yeah, that's exactly what I think. And once I worked my way around to that line of reasoning, I started thinking about that incomplete file again. What if it wasn't an accident or sloppy work?"

"You think someone deliberately removed certain documents from the file?" Jackson asked.

"Think about it," Harold said. "Why remove a picture when Shaye is walking around with the image on her body? Why remove my notes when I still worked for the department?"

Jackson frowned. "Because those things were more relevant than the other information in the files?"

Harold nodded. "I just don't know why. Then there's the issue of him knowing where I lived. Now, I'm not claiming I changed my identity and disappeared or nothing like that, but I bought the house through an attorney using one of them estate things that's supposed to keep people from paying tax on inheritance. My name's not attached to the house in any way, I don't have a home phone, and I get all my mail at a post office box in Pensacola."

"But the department would have your forwarding address because of retirement." Jackson blew out a breath. "I didn't see this coming."

Shaye's mind whirled as she tried to absorb everything that Harold had said. If he was right, it changed everything. "If someone in the police department is protecting this man," Shaye said, "then won't they attempt to mislead or misdirect the investigation away from me?"

"Probably," Harold said. "I'm going to assume, although I hate the word and the action, that whoever altered the files is the only person who'd have a firsthand interest in doing it now. That takes out the newer people who weren't around at that time."

"But it leaves a bunch of others," Jackson said. "There's a lot of people with a decade or more in with the department. And we can't assume it's only cops. It could be anyone with access to the physical records or the database, which includes some of the administration staff as well."

"But not the staff who weren't there the night Harold found me, right?" Shaye asked.

"Probably not," Harold said, "but someone could manipulate or outright coerce another employee to help them, if they had the right leverage."

Jackson nodded. "Power or knowledge. Either he controls their job or has something on them."

Harold nodded and looked directly at Jackson. "The bottom line is that at this point, there's only two people in the department I trust completely—my inside source and you. As much as it kills me to say, everyone else is a suspect."

Jackson blew out a breath. "Wow. Okay, well, the first thing is, I won't be sharing anything about Shaye and her investigation with anyone in the department."

"Not even Grayson?" Shaye asked.

"Not until we know for sure if there's a leak and who it's coming from," Jackson said.

"I agree," Harold said, and reached for his cell phone. "Let me show you that video footage."

"I thought you said we couldn't see his face?" Shaye said.

"No," Harold said, "but you can get an idea of his size, and make note of the way he walks and moves. It might be enough for you to zero in on him, if he gets too close. And there's something else…I would try to explain but it's better if you see it for yourself."

Harold handed the phone to Jackson, and he held the phone between him and Shaye. She leaned in and forward and focused on the small screen. The clip started and she saw a figure creeping down the hallway in Harold's house. He was lean and tall, and his physique and movement looked like that of a man. She watched as he moved into the kitchen and the footage shifted from one camera to another as he entered the garage. Several seconds later, he walked back into the house and the camera caught him from the front for the first time. He lifted his head and the hoodie no longer covered his face.

And that's when she saw it.

She gasped and pushed herself backward in the chair, trying to put some distance between herself and the horror displayed on the screen.

"What's wrong?" Harold asked.

"The mask," she whispered. "It's him. The man who tortured me."

Harold's eyes widened. "You're remembering? Holy shit, things just got more real."

Clara Mandeville slipped into the hospital room, stepped up to the bed, and gave a critical eye to the man lying there. She'd worked with Dr. Thompson in the ER for almost twenty years before he'd retired. Seeing him lying there as a patient felt wrong. The entire reason he was lying there felt wrong.

The police said the doctor had called 911 and reported an intruder in his house. A window on the front had been forced open, so his story checked out. But when the police arrived, all they found was an empty house and Dr. Thompson lying on the floor next to his bed. One of the officers started CPR and not a minute too soon. Now it was touch and go as to whether he'd make it or not. And even if he regained consciousness, there was no telling what kind of damage the heart attack might have caused.

She tucked the covers in around him and said a quick prayer before leaving the room. This was the fifth time she'd made her way around to his room the past hour, even though her regular schedule called for a quarter that amount. But she couldn't shake the feeling that something was wrong. The police had been cagey, as they always were, but she'd managed to get out of them that it didn't look as if anything was stolen, at least not the things a thief was usually after. Dr. Thompson's wallet and his Rolex had been sitting on the kitchen counter, and the wallet had money in it. The cops didn't tell her how much, but a garden-variety thief would have helped himself to any amount and definitely would have taken the watch.

At first, Clara thought maybe she was just on edge because of all the things that had happened. Her former coworker Emma Frederick and that horrible stalker and then that evil John Clancy and all that terror he inflicted on those street kids and God only knew who else. It was enough to make you think twice about most everything you did, especially when you were a woman living alone. Granted, Clara lived in a nice area and had a first-rate security system, but Dr. Thompson hadn't exactly lived in the ghetto and someone had managed to get inside his home.

And for what?

Which brought her right back around to the thing that had been bothering her from the very start. Unless Dr. Thompson had a Van Gogh or other valuable item in his home, why had someone broken in but yet not taken cash or an expensive watch that were both right in the open? She headed back for the front desk and logged on to the computer to clock out.

"Missy," she called out to the nurse who'd just come on shift. "Would you do me a favor and check in on Dr. Thompson more than normal?"

"Of course, Ms. Clara," Missy said. "It's just terrible what happened. I'll make sure he's comfortable. Do you want me to give you a call if anything changes?"

"I would appreciate that." She gave Missy's shoulder a squeeze and headed for the locker room. She hated leaving, but the hospital had strict rules about work hours and about being on the floor when you weren't on the clock. Clara figured it was all about liability and such. Lawyers seemed to make everything more complicated and cumbersome than it needed to be, especially when death was involved.

Still, Clara knew Missy would take good care of Dr. Thompson. She was a new nurse, only a year out of school, and young for the ER. But she was bright and had the kind of perception that made her an asset now and would make her irreplaceable years from now. Aside from Clara herself,

Dr. Thompson was probably being looked after by the best hands on the ward.

She grabbed her purse from her locker and pulled out her car keys, then headed back down the hall and out of the hospital. The parking garage was across a walkway from the hospital building and was one of those multistory jobs. Clara was halfway across the first level of the garage when she felt the back of her neck prickle. Chastising herself for not asking the night guard to walk her to her car, Clara kept moving, her eyes glancing as far as they could without turning her head, trying to determine what direction the threat came from.

If someone was following her, looking for a random victim, they'd be behind her. If someone wanted her specifically, they'd be waiting at her car. She slowed and opened her purse, making it look like she'd forgotten something, but she tucked a small bottle of Mace in her hand before removing it from the bag. She shook her head and turned around, then headed back for the hospital. If she could get close enough to the entrance, they might be able to hear her scream.

The cars that had filled the lot when she'd come on shift were mostly gone, leaving only a few random vehicles scattered up and down the two rows she had to cross to get back to the entrance to the garage. The first row of the garage held most of the third-shift staff—where Clara would have parked if she hadn't gotten to work early to talk to the on-staff doctor about Dr. Thompson's condition. Visiting hours were still going on then, and visitors' cars had filled the lower level.

She cleared one row and veered slightly to the left to avoid an SUV parked nearby. It was too easy for someone to launch from behind a parked vehicle and tackle her. When he made his move, Clara wanted to make sure she saw him coming. Then she was going to give him a face full of burning spray.

Something moved behind the SUV, causing the shadow of the car to shift slightly in shape. She clenched the Mace and picked up speed, her gaze locked on the vehicle. Her pulse shot up, sending her heart fluttering so hard she could feel it in her chest and her temples. The shadow shifted again and her breath caught in her throat. This was it. He was going to attack.

The footsteps pounding behind her gave her only a split second to realize she'd been wrong. He wasn't lurking on the other side of the SUV. He had been behind her, probably slinking around one of the huge columns, making sure he kept out of her line of sight. She'd been fooled and it was going to cost her.

He hit her square in the middle of the back and sent her flying. She screamed and put her hands out to break her fall, dropping the can of Mace as she went down. Her knees hit the concrete first and pain shot through her right leg. Her hands hit a millisecond later, the rough surface tearing the skin on her palms as she tried to break her fall. She scrambled to get up, but the man was on top of her before she could get her legs underneath her. She swung her right arm back as hard as she could and struck him with her elbow. It was enough to cause him to loosen his grip and instead of trying to get up, she switched tactics and flipped over, using one of the moves she'd learned in self-defense class.

When she saw the mask, she screamed again, this time involuntarily. Her right leg throbbed in pain but it was also her strongest, so she drew it up as quickly as possible between his legs, hoping for a strike that would free her, but he shifted and she hit his thigh instead. He punched her once in the jaw, and her vision blurred as a wave of nausea passed over her. She held her arms up to block the next blow and he struck her wrist, sending shock waves of pain up her arm and into her shoulder. He clutched her throat with his left hand and slammed her head into the ground, squeezing her neck until she started choking.

She grabbed his hand, trying to pry his fingers from her neck, but he was too strong and she was losing oxygen too quickly. Her strength was failing and she struggled to keep focus as her body tried to slip into unconsciousness. Something flashed in front of her and her vision cleared enough to see the knife raised above her.

In a last bid of desperation, she used every ounce of strength left in her body to grab the man's left arm and fling her head upward, biting into the soft flesh of his forearm. He howled and let go of her neck. She rallied a second time and popped upright, shoving the palm of her hand at what she hoped was his nose. She felt the slash of the blade on her left arm and screamed again as the burning pain flashed through her again.

She managed to pull her left leg out from under him and kicked him directly in the chest, knocking him backward. He didn't fall over completely, but it was enough for her to leap to her feet and run for the front entrance, yelling for help as she ran. She was almost to the crosswalk when Jeremy, the security guard, ran outside, his gun drawn.

She ran another two steps and collapsed at his feet. "Behind me. Shoot him," she managed.

Jeremy stood above her, gun in firing position, his head moving back and forth. "There's no one there."

Two nurses ran outside and one yelled back for a stretcher. The other dropped to the ground next to Clara. "Can you hear me?" the nurse asked. "What happened?"

"Attacked," Clara said.

She heard footsteps pounding behind her and Clara looked over to see Jeremy running up. "There's no sign of him," Jeremy said. "The police are on their way. Did you get a look at him?"

Clara started to shake her head, but it hurt too bad to move. "No. Mask."

She lifted her hand up and opened her clenched fist. "But I got a piece of him," she said and dropped the bit of forearm skin in Jeremy's hand. The last thing she remembered was whispering Shaye's name, and then everything went dark.

CHAPTER SIXTEEN

It was long after midnight by the time Shaye and Jackson finished up with Harold. For every question that was answered, Jackson came up with ten more that weren't. It was the most frustrated he'd ever been since he started his career.

It's personal.

He held in a sigh. Like he didn't know that without his mind constantly pushing it on him. His involvement in this went far beyond a professional capacity, but that couldn't possibly be a bad thing. A horrible man was out there doing God knows what to another girl and he was stalking the detective who'd found Shaye that night nine years ago. Jackson could think of only one reason to break into Harold's house and it wasn't to have a beer and watch the game.

When it was clear they were all out of answers or ideas, Harold suggested they call it a night. They all pushed themselves up from their chairs, and Jackson watched Shaye closely. The conversation had taken a toll on her, especially the video footage, then explaining to Harold the things she'd started to remember. Harold had been properly empathetic to the strain it had put on Shaye, but Jackson could tell he was also excited about the prospects that Shaye's returning memory might bring. If they could catch this guy, so many people would be able to close a horrifying chapter in their lives that had remained open for a very long time.

Harold walked them to the door. "The number I called you on is a disposable phone. Use it to reach me."

"How long will you be in New Orleans?" Shaye asked.

"Until this is over," Harold said. "But I'm going to try to keep things on the down low. I don't want him to know I'm here. Not unless we need to use me as bait."

Shaye shook her head. "That's not an option."

"It's an option if I say it is," Harold said. "I know this is far more important to you, but that man was in my house. My life stands still until he's caught or dead. I'll be the first to admit, I'm hoping for the latter."

"I think we all are," Jackson said.

Harold nodded. "Anything I find, I'll let you know, and please do the same. I'm making notes about everything I can remember from the investigation—my own file that no one can conveniently destroy. Anything you want added, you get it to me. I'm registered here under Bart Phillips, an old alias I used for undercover work. Somehow, I forgot to turn in my ID when I retired."

Jackson smiled. "Imagine that."

"You got a room here like I told you, right?" Harold asked.

"Yes," Jackson said. "Shaye and I were both at the

desk for check-in and I gave her a room card in the restaurant. If he was watching, he would have seen it."

"Good. Then I suggest you head to your room and try to get some sleep. We have a lot of work ahead of us."

Shaye's eyes widened. "But…we weren't planning on staying."

"You brought clothes like I told you, didn't you?" Harold asked. "I didn't give those instructions just so it would look more real when you checked in. You can't leave until morning. He might be watching."

Jackson knew Harold was right, but the entire situation was uncomfortable. "I'm sorry," he said to Shaye. "I didn't think or I would have gotten two rooms."

"No, you wouldn't have," Harold said. "What if he calls and asks for your room? If you're staying in two different suites, your cover is blown and so is mine. I know it might not be the most appropriate arrangement for you two, but no one cares once they're asleep. Exiting this hotel is asking for potential trouble, and he's got the cover of night to help protect him."

"And the mask," Shaye said.

Harold nodded. "And the mask."

"It's not a big deal," Shaye said to Jackson. "Leaving tomorrow morning will look normal. The last thing we want to do is tip our hand."

"Listen to the woman," Harold said. "Rent a movie. Get room service. I highly recommend the beignets here."

Jackson's unease lessened a bit. "You're sure? I can sleep on the floor."

"We can worry about that later," Shaye said. She hugged Harold. "Thank you so much for coming, and I'm sorry you're stuck in this mess."

"I'm not sorry," Harold said. "I've been waiting to close this case for nine years."

They headed for the elevators and located their room. Jackson opened the door and held it for Shaye to enter. The two bags they'd brought when checking in were sitting on luggage racks at the foot of the bed. The covers on the bed had been turned down and a single mint had been placed on each pillow.

Shaye pulled off the heels she'd been wearing and dropped them next to her luggage. She unzipped the bag and pulled out yoga pants and a T-shirt. "I'm going to take a hot soak, if you don't mind," she said.

"No. Enjoy. I'm going to get out of this suit and make some notes."

She nodded and shuffled into the bathroom. A couple seconds later, he heard water running in the tub, and he pulled off his jacket and started unbuttoning his dress shirt. His body felt more comfortable once it was free from the restricting garment but his mind wasn't at ease at all. Harold had thrown them some curveballs that Jackson still hadn't completely processed, starting with the potential traitor in the police department. It was a hard pill to swallow, but given the circumstances, it was a consideration Jackson couldn't afford to ignore.

With an inside contact, the man who'd purchased Shaye would know about Clancy's files and the progress on deciphering them. He'd also know about Shaye's biological mother. Given that the man had recently purchased another girl, he must be panicking. And maybe that panic had put him in cleanup mode. That would explain why he went after Harold. Following that same train of thought, that also meant anyone with a connection to Shaye was at risk. First thing tomorrow, they needed to warn everyone on the list they'd put together with Harold and think again about anyone they might have left off.

He slumped back in his chair. That was the business end of things, but the elephant in the room kept creeping back into his thoughts. If Jackson was being honest, he'd had more than one passing thought about spending the night with Shaye, but this wasn't the romantic image his mind had drummed up. Shaye had seemed okay with the situation, and it wasn't like he hadn't spent the night with her before. After they're rescued Jinx, they'd both crashed on her couch. But that hadn't been planned.

Neither was this.

Okay, so that was sorta true. Neither one of them had really expected to stay the night. They'd both brought a change of clothes because Harold had instructed them to. Without knowing what Harold had in store for them, it seemed smart to have something besides evening wear. He'd packed a T-shirt, jeans, and sweats, but hadn't planned on sleeping in them. Then, he also hadn't planned on sleeping somewhere other than his own bed.

The water in the bathroom shut off, and he shook himself out of his stupor and ordered himself to stop being stupid. If anyone was making this awkward, he was doing it to himself. If Shaye didn't have a problem with it, then he shouldn't worry about it. He pulled his laptop out of his bag and started making notes. One of the most damning things that Harold had said was his suspicion of a mole in the department. Jackson didn't want to think about any cops or other employees he knew being a part of something so horrid, but Harold had made a compelling case for an insider, and Jackson had every intention of taking that seriously.

When Jackson had first met Shaye and reviewed her file, he'd also reviewed some of Harold's cases, trying to get a feel for the man and his investigative process. What Jackson had found was that Harold was damned good at his job. Sometimes he'd made leaps from A to C with no B in sight, but every time he'd done so, he'd apprehended the suspect. His close rate was far higher than department average, there was not a single mar on his record, and he'd received several commendations. Added to that, no one at the department ever had anything bad to say about the man, and several of the tougher detectives actually dealt out compliments about Harold's perception on some of the more complicated cases he'd solved.

Bottom line—if Harold thought there was a problem in the department, then there was a really good chance he was right.

The interesting part of that, though, was that Harold himself hadn't been able to offer any theories as to who the traitor might be. Which meant that either the insider was clever enough to avoid detection, or he was someone so close to Harold that he'd overlooked the signs. Jackson hoped to hell it wasn't option number two because that put Bob, the desk sergeant, in the slot as the number one suspect. Bob was the closest friend Harold had left at the department. On the other hand, Jackson would also bet money that Bob was Harold's source for information. If Bob was the traitor, it wouldn't make sense for him to provide Harold with the very information that saved his life, but that didn't mean Bob was off Jackson's list to take a harder look at.

Starting tomorrow, Jackson was going to take a closer look at everyone with access to case information and anyone who was around the night Harold found Shaye or hired soon after. It could be that Shaye's abductor didn't have a man in place at the time but managed to get someone in afterward. That was a theory he'd pitched to Harold, and he agreed that it had merit.

He heard the water in the tub draining and a few minutes later, Shaye emerged from the bathroom wearing yoga pants and T-shirt, with her hair pulled back in a ponytail. It was a far different look from the one she'd had at dinner, but Jackson preferred this one. The casual, no-makeup Shaye was still the most beautiful woman he'd ever met.

"How was the bath?" he asked, then chided himself for the stupid question.

"Great. It loosened up some of the worst of my back and neck. I think it would take a horse tranquilizer to completely work the knots out."

"I'm not sure room service has those, but we could ask."

Shaye smiled. "I think wine from the minibar will have to do. Can I get you something?"

"Do they have a beer in there? I'll drink most anything."

Shaye opened the fridge and looked inside. "You're in luck." She handed Jackson the beer and poured the small bottle of wine into a glass, then took a seat in the chair across the table from him. "So, where do we start?"

"I've been thinking about what Harold said—about the items missing from your case file."

Shaye frowned. "Yeah, that one was hard for me to swallow. You said you thought Harold's source was the desk sergeant, right?"

Jackson nodded.

"But the sergeant isn't working on the Clancy files and he wasn't privy to the meeting about my biological mother, so how would he have gotten that information to share with Harold?"

"Because a cop who had the information shared it with Bob. You have to understand, Bob's part of the old guard. There's nothing he hasn't seen or heard, so all the guys bounce things off of him, especially if they're stuck on a case."

"And Bob has never repeated the things cops tell him?"

"Everyone says telling Bob something is like storing it

in Fort Knox. Clearly, if he's Harold's source, then he's repeating the information in this case, but given Bob and Harold's history, I can't blame him. Even Chief Bernard gets advice from Bob."

She shook her head. "I can't imagine how you must feel, knowing someone you work with might be involved in this."

"I feel sick about it but pissed off more than anything. Trust me when I say, if Harold is right, I'm going to find that person and make them pay, dearly, but suitable punishment is a whole other topic for discussion. I wanted to get your take on the items that were missing from the file. I keep wondering, why those things? If we make the leap that someone deliberately removed them, then they must have some importance that no one recognized."

"I agree that if the items were taken on purpose they were important to someone, but I don't see why. Like Harold said, I'm wearing the brand and he was still available at the department for questioning until he retired."

Jackson opened his mouth to speak, then hesitated, not wanting to bring up the subject, even though he needed to.

"You're hesitating," Shaye said. "Don't do that. I want to hear whatever you have to say. You're closer to this than anyone else but me. If I didn't value your opinion, you wouldn't be here."

The compliment not only pleased him but offered him a bit of relief given the topic he was about to broach. "Okay. Have you ever done any research on the brand itself? Is it unique or a common rendering?"

She frowned. "I don't know. I've never pursued my past as I would another investigation, so I never thought about it as evidence. To me, it was just another scar. I spent a lot of time and money trying to remove it from my skin but there's only so much that lasers can manage. The same with the cuts. The ones on my arms are faint now, but the deeper ones on my stomach and chest didn't lighten as well."

He felt a surge of anger course through him all over again. The same one that he'd had the first time he read Shaye's file and every time he'd thought about it since. "Since the picture was removed from the file, do you mind if I take another one? If it makes you uncomfortable, I understand."

"It's fine. I should have thought of looking into it before, especially since I believe the occult has something to do with all of it." She stood up and turned around, then lifted her shirt until the pentagram was exposed. "Can you get a couple with my phone as well?"

Jackson closed in on the brand as well as he could with his cell phone and took several pictures, then grabbed Shaye's from the table and took a couple more. "All done," he said, and Shaye dropped her shirt and sat down again.

He accessed one of the images on his phone and enlarged it, scanning every square inch. "What is this?" He pointed to what looked like small lettering in between two points of the pentagram.

"Initials, I think. At least, that's what it looked like but they were so small I could never be certain. It looked like 'JD.'"

"Maybe that's the initials of goat man."

"Or the guy who made the brand. Either way, it's not like we can hunt down everyone in Louisiana with those initials. Can you run the images through the police database?"

He nodded. "I'll do it first thing in the morning."

"Good. I'll approach it from another angle."

Before he even asked the question, he was afraid he already knew the answer. "What angle is that?"

"I'm going to run it by some shops…the kind that specialize in this sort of thing."

He knew it was no use telling her not to do it, but he couldn't help giving her a warning. "If this is occult related, then someone who owns one of those shops could be the guy or one of his cult members. He came after Harold in his home in another state. We have to believe that he's watching you as well."

"I'll go during the day, when all the tourists are out and about."

He knew Shaye wasn't foolish, but his biggest fear was that being careful wasn't going to be enough. And with a full day of work ahead of him, there was no way he could go with her, not without explaining to Grayson why he needed the time. And since they'd already agreed that Jackson wouldn't share anything about Shaye at the department, that option was off the table.

"Will you humor me with something?" Jackson asked.

"What?"

"Will you text me your location before you go in somewhere, then let me know when you're leaving?" He didn't want to say out loud that at least if something happened, he'd know where to start looking, but he was sure he didn't have to. Shaye knew the score better than anyone.

"I can do that, and I can do you one better. Let's set you up to track my iPhone location."

"You'd do that?"

"For you, yes. Look, I know the stakes, and I want as much backup as I can get from qualified people. Now, my mother is a completely different story. She'd spend her entire day tracking my phone, then calling to see what I was doing."

Shaye gave him her password and they set up Jackson's phone to track hers. It wasn't bulletproof, but it made him feel a little better about Shaye investigating alone. When they were done with the phones, she rose from the chair and stretched.

"If you don't mind, I'm going to call it a night," she said. "It's been a long couple days and I don't see an end."

"Of course. Let me call room service and get some extra blankets."

"Don't bother. It's a big bed. We're both adults and besides, it's not like we haven't slept together before." She smiled. "I'm setting my phone alarm for six a.m."

"Works for me. I'm going to make a few more notes first," he said, and watched as she headed to the far side of the bed, tossed the covers back, and crawled under them. He tapped on his laptop for a couple minutes, casting side glances at her as he jotted down some notes. When her breathing shifted, he rose and turned off the bedroom light, leaving the light in the entry on. Total darkness wasn't a good call in a strange place, and it definitely wasn't a good call with Shaye.

He moved to the other side of the bed and lay down on top of the comforter, not wanting the heavy cover on top of him. It was a humid night and even though the air-conditioning was running at top speed, he still felt the stickiness of the night air all over his body. But he couldn't blame the weather for the overwhelming feeling of dread.

Something was coming. Something dark and decades old.

The man slammed his hand onto the kitchen table and cursed. How had the old nurse gotten the better of him? His plan should have worked. He'd done all the preparations, the prayers, the blessing of the knife, only to be thwarted by an aged, overweight woman. First the cop, now this. Even the doctor hadn't been a complete success. He'd thought the man was dead when he saw him lying there on the floor next to the bed, but he was still clinging to life in the hospital, making it next to impossible to get to him.

He cursed again and sat down at the table, trying to

figure out where he'd gone wrong. The hospital garage lot had been the perfect choice, or so he'd thought. The nurse worked the night shift so approaching her house during the day wasn't optimum. She lived in one of those neighborhoods full of busybodies—always weeding lawns and planting flowers as an excuse to mind someone else's business. Added to that, she had a top-rate security system, and the alarm was always set.

The hospital garage was the best option. It was still dark when she got off work and the garage was too far from the hospital for anyone inside to help her even if they heard her scream. He certainly wasn't worried about the crap security cameras. Even if they caught him on the screen, the security guard was inside the hospital and too far away to help her. It should have taken only seconds for him to slice her throat and disappear.

Not only had she gotten away, she'd left a mark on him.

He looked down at his forearm. Blood was already seeping through the flimsy bandage he'd wrapped around it, and the sight of the red stain made him even angrier. He could still handle this. It hadn't gotten away from him yet, but the cop and the nurse had been stark reminders that the enemy was real and strong. He'd been vain to assume taking them would be easy. If simple actions were all that the One required, then anyone could be his servant. He was not anyone. He was chosen.

And if he decided it was too dangerous for him to continue, then he would play his trump card.

CHAPTER SEVENTEEN

Tuesday, July 28, 2015

Shaye looked down at Jackson as he slept. She felt bad about having to wake him because she knew he'd been up most of the night. She was certain of it because she hadn't slept much herself. She squeezed his shoulder. "Jackson, wake up," she said.

He opened one eye and then the other. "It's morning? I swear I just fell asleep."

"Me too, but I've got to get moving. Change of plans for this morning. There's an emergency at the hospital."

Jackson sat upright, the previous drowsiness disappearing completely. "Is something wrong with Corrine?"

"Corrine is fine. It's Clara—the nurse who cared for me after I was found."

Jackson nodded. He knew exactly who Clara Mandeville was. "What's happened?"

"She was attacked in the hospital parking lot early this morning. By a man wearing a mask."

Jackson's eyes widened. "The goat mask?"

"She didn't say, and she passed out before they could get more information. Jeremy, the security guard, called me. He said she managed to fight off her attacker, but he got away."

"Is she going to be all right?"

"The doctor thinks so. She has a concussion, though. I hope it doesn't affect her memory. The last thing she said before she passed out was my name. I have to get to the hospital. I need to be there when she wakes up."

"You don't have your car."

"I'll Uber there and back to my apartment when I'm done."

"That's not necessary." Jackson jumped out of bed. "I'm going with you."

"I appreciate it, but you have a job to do."

"Yeah, and my job is finding the psycho who bought that girl. Clara was one of the names on our list. If Harold's theory is correct—and I think it is—that man attacked Clara."

"What about Grayson?"

"Don't worry. I'll figure out something."

She nodded. "You're sure?"

"Positive."

He grabbed his jeans and headed for the bathroom. Shaye had gotten ready before she woke him so she shoved her laptop into her bag and zipped it up, anxious to get to the hospital. Jackson was ready a couple minutes later and they headed out.

They were both quiet on the ride to the hospital. Shaye

was consumed with her thoughts about Clara and hoping she would be all right, and then with anger over the attack, launched against a woman for no good reason. If Clara had known anything that would have helped the police find her captor, she would have told them years ago. Why go after her now when she was no threat at all? First Harold, now Clara. None of it made sense.

When they arrived, Shaye rushed into the emergency room and the nurse at the desk jumped up from her chair the moment she saw her. "Ms. Archer! I was just about to call you. Clara woke up a short while ago and she's been giving the doctor heck. He wants to run tests, but she's refusing, insisting that she speak to you first. Come with me."

They followed the nurse down the hall and she spoke as they went. "The police were here as well, trying to get a statement, and she refused to talk to them too." The nurse gave them a worried look. "I've never seen Clara like this. She's in a real twist."

"But she's okay?" Shaye asked.

"Seems to be, but until they can run tests, we won't know for certain."

"Don't worry," Shaye assured the nurse, "I'll keep it as brief as possible and get her off for testing."

The nurse looked relieved. "Thank you. We're all really worried about her. Clara's like a mother to everyone who works the ER."

"I'm worried about her too," Shaye said, "and I'm going to make sure she's all right from now on."

The nurse nodded and pointed to a door. "That's her room."

"Thank you," Shaye said before pushing the door open and rushing inside.

Clara sat propped up in the bed with bandages on her hands and right knee. She looked tired, but the fire in her eyes burned strong. Clara might be hurt, but she was more angry than anything else. As Shaye stepped up to the bed, she saw the bruises on Clara's neck and face and knew immediately how they'd gotten there. Anger coursed through her and she clenched her hands, wishing she could lock them around the bastard's throat as he'd done to Clara.

"Are you all right?" Shaye asked.

"I'm a little banged up and a whole lot pissed off," Clara said. "But I'm even more worried. I wasn't a chance victim. That man was waiting for me."

Shaye glanced at Jackson, then looked back at Clara. "What makes you think that?"

"It started with Dr. Thompson," Clara said.

Shaye stared. "What about Dr. Thompson? Did something happen to him?"

Clara nodded. "They brought him in last Friday night. Heart attack. He'd called 911 and said someone was in his house. The police found signs of a break-in, but his wallet and his Rolex were on the kitchen counter. Dr. Thompson was on the floor on the side of his bed."

Shaye drew in a breath, trying to process this unexpected piece of bad news. "Is he going to be all right?"

"Hard to say," Clara said. "He's stable but still

unconscious. We won't know how much damage there is, if any, until he wakes up."

"But he's going to wake up?" Shaye asked.

"I'm praying hard for it," Clara said, "but I can't make any promises. I've seen patients in his condition go both ways."

Shaye nodded and glanced over at Jackson. She could tell by his worried expression that he understood the significance of what Clara was saying. Dr. Thompson was one of the names on the list they'd created with Harold. So was Clara. They now had two more reasons to believe Harold's theory was right.

"Can you tell us what happened last night?" Jackson asked.

Clara nodded. "I was on my way to my car when I just felt wrong. You know? So I opened my purse and pretended I had forgotten something, but really, I took out my Mace. Then I turned around and headed back for the hospital. I figured if he thought I was going to get something I forgot and come right back, then I had a chance of getting back into the hospital."

"Smart," Jackson said.

"Would have been smarter if it had worked," Clara said. "I hoped he was hiding near my car, which was parked on the back row, and that I had a half a garage advantage on him. But he fooled me."

"How is that?"

"He must have been hiding behind one of the columns in the parking lot, circling around it to stay out of sight as I walked. He was closer to the entrance than my car." Clara's voice hitched up a notch. "I saw something move behind an SUV. I thought it was him, but he was already behind me. He hit me from behind and knocked me down. I swung my elbow and got a solid hit on him, then I managed to flip over and tried to get him with my knee."

Clara swallowed and shook her head. "I admit, the mask made me hesitate. It was only for a second, but it was probably enough to keep me from kneeing him in his privates."

Shaye's pulse quickened. "You got a good look at the mask?"

"Was only a foot in front of me, and it's something I won't ever forget. It was a goat's head. One of those like you see in those horror movies." She shivered slightly. "That was the first time in my life I ever thought I was going to die, and if you knew where I grew up, you'd know what a big statement that is."

Shaye reached over and placed her hand on Clara's arm. "I am so sorry. If you hadn't gotten away—"

"Don't you even start," Clara interrupted. "This isn't your fault. Neither is what happened to Dr. Thompson. But there's something else I need to tell you. Do you remember Nadine, your physical therapist?"

"Of course," Shaye said, then her breath caught in her throat. "Did something happen to her?"

Clara nodded. "One of the other nurses told me yesterday that she was killed in the parking lot after teaching class at the community center."

"Carjacking?" Jackson asked.

"Not unless the thieves have started slitting throats and leaving the car behind," Clara said.

"Jesus," Jackson said.

Shaye covered her mouth with her hand, horrified by Clara's words.

"That's me, Dr. Thompson, and Nadine, in a matter of days. I suppose it could be coincidence, but I've never been a big fan of the concept."

"Me either," Shaye said.

"I already didn't feel right about Dr. Thompson," Clara said, "and then when I heard about Nadine, it only strengthened my conviction that something was wrong. I was planning on calling you today and letting you know, just in case something was going on more than what the police could see and I could understand. Then that man attacked me, and I knew I was right about the others. That's why I asked for you as soon as I woke up."

Shaye looked down at the floor, still trying to process that Nadine was dead, Dr. Thompson was clinging to life, and Clara was battered and bruised all because of her.

"You didn't cause this, child," Clara said, clearly cluing in to her guilt. "Don't ever allow him that kind of power of you. Only one man is responsible for this."

"She's right," Jackson said. "I'm really sorry that this happened to you, Ms. Mandeville, and I can't tell you how glad I am that you got away. You, Dr. Thompson, and Nadine are on a list of people Shaye and I intended to contact today and warn that you might be at risk."

"So you think I'm right?" Clara said.

Jackson nodded. "Too many things have happened for me to think otherwise. There was an attempt made on someone else related to Shaye's case, but he got a bad feeling and went into hiding before the man broke into his house. The security cameras got him, though. He was wearing a goat mask."

Clara looked at Shaye. "It's the man who took you, isn't it?"

"I think so," Shaye said.

Clara studied her for several seconds, her indecision clear. Finally she asked, "Are you remembering?"

Shaye glanced at Jackson, then looked back at Clara. "Yes," she said, her voice barely a whisper.

Clara nodded. "Then I'm going to tell you something I never told the police. What I knew wasn't going to help the police any with their investigation. But I knew that one day you'd want to read those reports, and those words would have only done more harm. But if you're starting to remember, then it's time I break my silence."

"What is it?" Shaye asked.

"You woke up during the X-rays and starting screaming," Clara said. "You said 'Mama, don't make me go. You know he scares me.' Then you passed out again."

Shaye knew something like this was coming, but to hear Clara confirm what she already knew made her angry and sad all over again.

Clara stared at Shaye, studying her as she would a patient, then her eyes widened. "You already knew."

Shaye nodded. "My biological mother sold me to John Clancy."

"Oh my God!" Clara moved her bandaged hand on top of Shaye's and squeezed. "When will it all end for you? It's so unfair."

"Now that I'm remembering," Shaye said, "it could end soon. The question is what the end will be and how many people will be hurt before it's over."

"Might be sooner and better than you expect," Clara said. She sat up straighter and leaned toward them. "I got a piece of him when I bit him. Gave it to Jeremy before I passed out."

"A piece of him?" Shaye knew she had heard Clara correctly, but she had to make sure.

Clara nodded. "From when I bit him. A good-sized piece of skin it was. If he's in the police database, this could all be over soon."

Jackson pulled out his cell phone. "I'll call the station," he said, and left the room.

Clara waited until the door closed. "He cares about you," she said. "I can see it in the way he looks at you. Even in the way he stands. He's protective. That's a good thing to have in a man."

Clara squeezed her hand again. "And you deserve something good."

Jackson stepped into the hall, calling Grayson as he

walked. Despite the early hour, the detective answered on the first ring.

"I was just about to call you," Grayson said. "I guess you heard about Clara Mandeville."

"I'm at the hospital with Shaye right now."

"Good. Reynolds wanted me to get in touch with you so you'd get in touch with Shaye and let her know that Ms. Mandeville was asking for her."

"What can you tell me?"

"Reynolds got the call but Ms. Mandeville was unconscious when they arrived. A nurse said she called out Shaye's name before she passed out and when she woke up, she refused to speak to Reynolds, insisting she talk to Shaye first. What the hell is going on, Lamotte?"

Jackson hesitated for a second, but then figured there was no point in trying to keep information from Grayson. Clara would give her statement to Reynolds, so the goat mask would be on record. And sharing Clara's information about Dr. Thompson and Nadine would only get Grayson involved in helping notify the other potential victims. Jackson could leave Harold Beaumont and Shaye's returning memory out of his explanation entirely and their side investigation wouldn't be at risk.

"I think we have a huge problem," Jackson said and filled Grayson in on Dr. Thompson and Nadine. "That makes three people connected directly to Shaye who have met with foul play in less than a week."

"I don't like it."

"Neither do I."

"Did Ms. Mandeville talk to Shaye?"

"Yeah, she talked all right." Jackson told Grayson about Clara's attack.

"A goat mask?" Grayson asked when he finished. "Like with horns? Jesus Christ. What kind of psycho is this guy?"

"I know. Just when I think we've seen it all, something else comes along that blows that thought right out of the water. Clara said the hospital security guard took the piece of skin she bit off her attacker. Do you know anything about that?"

"The lab is processing the sample now. I asked Reynolds to keep me in the loop on the test. We should know soon if there's a match."

"I'd love to think this is it, but I have trouble believing it's going to be this easy."

"As little as we've had to go on for all these years, so do I, but they all screw up eventually. That's why we catch them."

"This would be the screwup of the century."

"Yeah. The whole thing is weird. I can't figure out why this guy didn't shoot her. Why risk a hands-on attack?"

"I have no idea. I mean I get wearing a mask. Not *that* mask necessarily, but I understand wanting to hide your face. But a knife over a gun? I don't know."

Jackson hoped the lie sounded legitimate, because the truth was he had an idea about the knife. The marks on Shaye's body were indicative of torture but could have also been used for bloodletting. The pentagram on her back and the horned goat mask all pointed to the same sort of ritualistic behavior. Clara said the knife was ornate with a red jewel in the hilt. The description was that of a ceremonial knife, not something used for hunting or in the kitchen.

The killer had a knife when he broke into Harold's house as well, and that was an even riskier move. Entering the house of a retired cop armed with a knife rather than an arsenal? And Nadine's throat had been slit. Everything came back around to the knife except Dr. Thompson, but the killer might have assumed he died when he had the heart attack.

"Well, I bet he's changing his tune on weaponry after losing a piece of his arm," Grayson said. There was a pause, then Grayson said, "It's Reynolds. Hold on a sec."

Jackson heard muffled talking but couldn't make out what was being said. A minute later, he heard Grayson curse and he came back on the line.

"No match."

CHAPTER EIGHTEEN

Shaye parked in front of the tiny shop and assessed the neighborhood. It was run-down and not as populated as she would have liked, but it wasn't a ghost town, either. She grabbed her phone and texted Jackson the cross streets and name of the store. She scanned the street one last time, then climbed out of her SUV and headed into the shop.

The storefront that had looked tiny from the outside felt practically claustrophobic inside. Shelves ran the length of both walls and down the center of the room, floor to ceiling, and stuffed with merchandise. Dolls, stones, sticks, and bottles of herbs that she didn't recognize the names of lined the shelves. The overhead lighting wasn't great, and the bookshelves prevented some of it from filtering between the rows. Added to that, the shop faced west so the morning sun couldn't reach inside and help illuminate the space.

Shaye glanced down one of the rows and saw the end of a counter at the back of the store. She glanced once out the front window, then walked down one of the rows to the counter in the back. An old black woman, probably in her eighties, sat in a chair behind the counter. She rose as

Shaye approached and placed the doll she'd been stitching on the table next to her.

"Ain't got no potions for boyfriends and the like," she said. "We're serious about our beliefs. Don't play into that Hollywood crap."

"No, ma'am," Shaye said. "I'm not here for anything like that." She pulled out her wallet and showed the woman her identification. "I'm a private investigator. I have a client who was attacked by a man with very particular taste."

"What kind of taste? We don't go in for that weird sex stuff, either."

Shaye pulled out her phone and accessed the image she had of the goat mask that she'd gotten from Harold. "This is a security photo of the man. Do you know where I can find a mask like this?"

She turned the phone around and showed it to the woman. Her eyes widened slightly, but her expression didn't change. If Shaye hadn't been watching closely, she wouldn't have seen the reaction at all.

"Ain't never seen it before," the woman said.

Shaye knew she was lying and any more conversation was probably pointless, but she scrolled to the picture of the pentagram and showed it to the woman. "What about this?"

"It's a pentagram," the woman said.

"Yes, but I haven't seen one exactly like this. These letters at the bottom—JD—do they mean anything?"

The woman didn't even look at the image again before shaking her head. "Don't know anything about no letters."

A curtain behind the counter swung back and a younger black woman, probably in her fifties, stepped out. The old woman turned around and glanced at her. "Don't need any help," she said.

Shaye recognized a dismissal when she saw it, and based on the younger woman's expression of surprise, it wasn't a typical occurrence. The younger woman looked at Shaye, then glanced down at the cell phone. She looked back at the older woman and nodded. "Okay. I'm going out to pick up some supplies. I should be back in an hour."

The younger woman exited through the curtain and the old woman lifted the doll from the counter and sat back in her chair. Shaye assumed that meant the conversation was over. Not seeing any other alternative, she headed out of the store. As she stepped onto the sidewalk and pulled out her car keys, she heard someone calling.

"You. Lady."

Shaye looked in the direction of the voice and saw the other woman from the shop beckoning to her from an alley in between two buildings. She unlocked her vehicle, just in case she needed to get into it quickly, and headed up the sidewalk to where the woman had disappeared. The space between the buildings was maybe five feet wide, and the woman stood several feet back from the sidewalk.

"Get in here," the woman said. "She goes outside to smoke. I don't want her to see me talking to you."

The last thing Shaye wanted to do was enter the narrow, dim space but what if the woman had information for her? She glanced up and down the street but didn't see anyone lurking around who could help corner her in the space, so she stepped into the alley.

"I heard what you told Mama—that a lady was attacked."

Shaye nodded. "A nurse. A good woman. I'm trying to help her by finding the man who did it."

"You showed Mama two pictures. Can I see them?"

Shaye pulled out her phone and showed the woman the pentagram. She leaned forward, concentrating on the image, her brow screwed up in concentration. "What about the other?" she asked.

Shaye slid the image over to the goat mask and turned the phone back around. The woman gasped and her hand flew over her mouth. Her eyes were wide as she stared at the image.

"Do you know this?" Shaye asked.

The woman nodded. "My grandfather made it. When he passed, my grandmother locked it away."

"Then how did this man get it?"

"Mama took everything out of the attic when my grandmother died. She sold it all, including the mask. I tried to talk her out of it, but grandmother's hospital bills were high and the house wasn't worth enough to cover them."

The woman looked behind her, then back at Shaye. "Mama don't believe in things, even though she claims to for the customers."

"But you do?"

The woman nodded. "I seen things—things that you can't explain—and I've felt the presence of evil." She pointed at the phone. "That mask is strong evil. Ain't nothing good ever come from wearing it and nothing ever will."

Despite the heat and humidity, Shaye felt a chill run through her. The woman's fear was so apparent that it seemed to fill the air surrounding them.

"Do you know who bought the mask?"

The woman nodded. "One of them Derameau bastards."

Shaye's excitement grew. "His last name was Derameau?"

"No. He was one of Derameau's bastard kids. There's a whole lot of them that claim it. Never heard of him to have a wife, but if you believed the stories, he had women with babies all over the French Quarter. The man who bought the mask claimed he was one of those babies. Said his father had given up the old ways, but he was going to do things right."

"Do you know Derameau's first name?"

"No one did." The woman shook her head. "You don't understand. I never believed he was a real person. I thought it was a story unwed women gave their children when they got old enough to ask about their fathers. I ain't ever heard of anyone who's seen Derameau. He's a folk tale."

Shaye's excitement waned. "You don't know anything else about the man who bought the mask? Anything that might help me find him?"

"Only saw him the one time."

"I have a friend, an artist. Could you describe him well enough for my friend to draw him?"

The woman took a step back. "I don't want to be involved. That was sixteen years ago and my memory ain't what it used to be. I did my best to forget the man, and the mask. I suggest you and your friend do the same."

Shaye struggled to control her disappointment, reminding herself that she couldn't be certain that the man who bought the mask was her captor. He might have sold the mask later on or died or given it away. Still, if she could locate him, it would be a starting point.

"Wait, at least tell me what he looked like," Shaye said.

"He was black, accent was Creole. Around twenty years old. Over six feet tall and fit. He was an average-looking guy, except for the eyes." She crossed her arms across her chest. "Had dead eyes. Like a doll. I don't ever want to see something like that again. You and your friend take care." The woman whirled around and hurried off.

The breath Shaye hadn't even realized she was holding came out in a whoosh. It was him. Her abuser. The man with the dead eyes.

She left the alley and hurried back to her car, taking a second to text Jackson that she was leaving. As she pulled away from the curb, the name Derameau kept running through her mind. What if he wasn't a folk tale? If this Derameau existed then she might be able to find the man through someone who knew him, maybe one of his other kids.

If the stories were true.

If Derameau wasn't a folk tale.

If the man who bought the goat mask wasn't lying about his parentage.

She clutched the steering wheel and headed for her apartment. That was a whole bunch of ifs, but she had a feeling about it—dread coupled with excitement. Something told her she was on the right trail. And she planned on hiking it until the bitter end.

Jackson's computer signaled that it had finished running the search he'd requested on the pentagram and he accessed the results. No matches found. He wasn't really surprised. If there was another case involving the brand, the traitor inside the police force would have removed it from evidence as well.

His cell phone buzzed and he grabbed it and checked the display, then let out a breath of relief when he saw Shaye's message. If there had been any way he could have prevented her from going out on her own, he would have, but he knew better than to even suggest it. She was being careful and following all the protocols they'd agreed on. Short of being with her, there wasn't anything else he could do to protect her. And he had no ability to pursue an alternate investigative angle without telling Grayson what he was doing. Until he figured out who the mole was, then Grayson had to be kept in the dark just like everyone else.

Jackson looked down at the list he'd compiled. Sixteen

people currently working in the department who were also employed when Shaye was found, or hired the year following. Only sixteen people who would have had access to the files in the time frame the information would have been removed. Of the sixteen, only Grayson, Elliot, and Bernard were employed in the right time frame and also had access to all information on the Clancy files. One of them or Frank had fed information to Bob, the desk sergeant, who'd fed it to Harold. Was that it? Those four men?

And Vincent.

Jackson rubbed his chin, trying to figure out where and how Vincent figured into things. He was there when Shaye was found and would have had access to the files. He was working the Clancy files now, but his access was supposed to be limited. Still, if he got wind that something on the case involved Shaye, Jackson wouldn't put it past him to do some digging. Even if he wasn't the mole, he hated Shaye so much he'd probably seize any opportunity to get back at her for taking him down with Bernard.

But if Vincent had found something out and wasn't the mole, Jackson had no doubt Shaye would be headline news again. So either he was as lazy and uninterested as everyone thought or he was the mole and he was keeping quiet. Jackson added Vincent's name to the list. He couldn't afford to dismiss the man simply because he was unmotivated. It didn't take much energy to pick up a phone and make a call.

Five names.

Assuming no one else working the Clancy files had shared information with someone other than Bob. And assuming Bob hadn't shared the information with anyone but Harold.

Don't overcomplicate things.

He picked up the paper and folded it in half. These five were a good start. A start of what, he had no idea. How in the world was he supposed to figure out if one of them was the mole? These weren't ordinary men. They were men with decades of experience in how to cover their tracks. Any one of them was capable of hiding something for a decade.

The question was, which one was capable of this level of evil?

"You make all your calls?" Grayson's voice sounded behind him and Jackson shoved the folded paper under his keyboard before turning around.

"Yeah," Jackson said. "The two other nurses assigned to Shaye in the ER both moved away years ago. One married and the other divorced, so both names changed. I don't think it would be easy to find either one, but I made them aware of the situation and suggested they be extra cautious. I told them I'd call when I had more information."

"What about the paramedics?"

"One died two years ago of a heart attack. The other guy dropped off the map. The best I could run down was from an old coworker who said he had a sex change and left town for LA several years ago."

Grayson stared. "Seriously?"

"That's what he said. Anyway, I ran the guy through every database we've got. He's a ghost. No driver's license, no tax returns, no income on his Social. If I can't find him, I don't know how anyone else would. What about you?"

"The X-ray tech is still local, but she was at the airport, leaving for a two-week vacation in Italy. I filled her in but I figure she's pretty safe, at least for two weeks. The admitting nurse retired right after Shaye's stay and is in an assisted living center in Idaho, where her daughter lives. According to the daughter, her memory is completely gone and she's not much longer for this world."

"So no threat."

"Doesn't seem like it."

"What about the cops?"

Grayson's expression shifted from normal to slightly disgusted. "I ran down Peters in Mexico. He was three sheets to the wind even though it's not even noon. I told him what we had going on, but he blew me off. Said he was done with police work and don't call him again with bullshit. If goat man finds Peters, he might be doing Mexico a favor."

Jackson nodded. Harold's opinion of Peters had ranked right up there with Grayson's assessment. "What about Beaumont?"

Jackson knew Harold was safely ensconced in the Ritz-Carlton, but he had to pretend Harold was no different from any other person on the list.

"Couldn't get a hold of him," Grayson said. "HR has

him at an address in Florida. No phone number listed and directory assistance doesn't have one for that address. I called the local PD and asked someone to do a drive-by for me and give Beaumont a message to call, but he wasn't home. They said newspapers were in his yard, the oldest Sunday's."

Jackson straightened in his chair, feigning concern. "Did they check the house?"

Grayson nodded. "I gave them a scaled-down explanation of the problem and they forced a window open, but the house is clear. No sign of a struggle. Kitchen light and a radio on, but that was it."

"Maybe he's out of town. Left the light and radio on to fool potential thieves but forgot to stop the newspaper."

"Maybe. Anyway, the locals promised to check back periodically and get Beaumont in touch with us as soon as they located him."

"So that's it," Jackson said. "Everyone is either dead, in the hospital, out of reach, or warned."

"Looks like. I talked to Reynolds a couple minutes ago. He sent a sketch artist to work with Ms. Mandeville." Grayson opened a folder he'd had tucked under his arm, pulled out a sheet of paper, and passed it to Jackson. "Check that shit out."

Jackson had seen the mask in 3-D and full color, but the sketch was just as disturbing. Clara had done an excellent job describing it and the artist had captured the malevolent feel of it perfectly, especially the eyes.

Jackson shook his head. "I can't imagine keeping my

cool long enough to get away if I was staring at that. Ms. Mandeville is one tough broad."

Grayson took the sketch back and grimaced as he looked down at it. "What have we stepped in the middle of, Lamotte?"

"I don't know, but we're going to find out."

CHAPTER NINETEEN

French Quarter, 1985

He sat in his office, waiting for the clock to strike midnight, as he'd done so many times before. Every time the Haitian had come, he'd been forced to pay. And he'd paid dearly. Over two million dollars in almost three decades. He'd been young and foolish when he'd made that first payment. If he'd been older and wiser, he would have refused and told the Haitian to try his theory with the police. But his wife was the one thing that still made him think twice.

He had no doubt that the Haitian would have killed her, if for no other reason than to make him suffer for not living up to his word. But that first payment had been his undoing. That payment gave the Haitian proof that he was hiding something. If something would have happened to his wife after that first payment, then the Haitian could have gone to the police and shown them withdrawals from his bank account and deposits to the Haitian's that matched up.

Then they might have listened.

After all, why pay someone an enormous sum of money for no reason? So he'd paid and he'd kept paying, year after year. It had crossed his mind once before to track the Haitian down where he lived and kill him. End this for good. But the Haitian was a step ahead of him—the Haitian informed him that if he was murdered, he'd left documents with his attorneys that would be turned over to the police.

So instead of an end, he got yet another worry—that the Haitian would do something that prompted his murder and he would be caught in the cross fire. But months passed, then years, then decades, and the Haitian still turned up a couple times a year for payment. If the Haitian had invested wisely, he should be very well off. His clothes, watch, and car suggested that he didn't need the money. But money had never been about need. Not for certain types of people.

Unfortunately, money was getting to be a scarce commodity even for him. Orders had been decreasing steadily, longtime customers favoring cheaper Chinese-made goods over a proven product. He'd already sold some of his real estate holdings to help with cash flow until he could figure out what direction to take the operation. Clearly, the old business model was no longer a viable one. If the Haitian demanded too much, he might have to sell off more real estate in order to make the payment.

Footsteps sounded in the hallway outside his office just as the clock was about to strike midnight. Seconds later, the door opened and the Haitian stepped in.

The Haitian stared at him until he looked away. He

couldn't take the cold gaze of those blue eyes—his father's eyes. He'd guessed the truth when he was fifteen, but even if he hadn't, the Haitian made sure he knew. Made sure he understood that the Haitian wasn't extorting money from him. He was only taking what he was due. His inheritance. The Haitian always laughed when he used the word.

"How much?" he asked as the Haitian sat down. He didn't want to spend any more time in the man's presence than necessary. The Haitian took far too much pleasure in his discomfort.

"I've not come for money this time," the Haitian said. "I've come to insure my future."

"What are you talking about? I've paid everything you've asked."

"Yes, but my people live long lives. Much longer than a stressed white man with a guilty conscience. I had to ensure that my lifestyle wouldn't change if you were to meet with unfortunate circumstances."

The Haitian pulled some photos out of his pocket and slid them across the desk. He hesitated before reaching for them, already knowing that whatever they contained was going to be bad. He lifted the photos, looked at the first one, and gasped.

"No!" He flipped through the pictures, each one more devastating than the next.

"I believe," the Haitian said, "that your son has embarked on his own career path. I wonder what his employer would think if they knew he was a devil worshipper. So much talk. So much fear of such things these days."

He threw the photos back at the Haitian. "Photos can be manipulated. This proves nothing."

The Haitian smiled. "Of course, but video…so much harder to alter. Your son was such an easy target, celebrating his birthday in the French Quarter, drinking until he no longer remembered who he was or what he was doing. I thought I would have to drug him, but he did all the work for me."

He felt the blood drain from his face and his stomach rolled. "The girl on the altar?"

"A poor confused soul," the Haitian said, "who believed the ceremony would give her special powers."

"What did you make him do?"

"He was too drunk to do anything but exist there, but the footage of him holding a knife above her would be enough to convince the police that he was responsible for the cuts on her body. And if that isn't enough, there's the brand. Oh, your son didn't administer it, but he was holding the poker. His fingerprints are on both."

The man's stomach rolled. "So the girl is…?"

"Dead? Yes. The same poison used to kill your father. The police will find her body in the next day or so. As long as your son understands his responsibility, the police will never see the footage or the photos."

He clutched the armrests of his chair, desperate for a solution that didn't involve telling his son this horrible story. That didn't involve obligating him to this life of constant fear. "I'll give you anything. Name your price. Just don't involve him."

"My price is your son's acceptance of your promise. There is no other option." The Haitian rose. "I'll be back in a week to ensure you've done what you needed to do. Unless you'd prefer to wait until your death and let me tell your son what you did."

He managed to control his rage only long enough for the Haitian to leave the building, then he launched from his chair, yelling and throwing anything he could get his hands on. When his energy was finally spent, he sank onto his knees in the middle of the floor and began to weep.

"What have I done?"

CHAPTER TWENTY

Shaye pushed herself away from her desk and leaned back in her office chair. She'd been searching for any information on the mysterious Derameau for two hours already and had exactly nothing. The name wasn't common, but it wasn't exactly uncommon, either. She'd called every Derameau she could find a phone number for but no one claimed any knowledge of a relative who'd fathered many children and practiced the black arts.

It didn't help that in addition to not knowing the man's first name, she also had a limited idea of his age. The woman at the shop said the man who bought the goat mask was young, maybe twenty, which meant his father could have been forty or so years old up to who knows how old. Men didn't have the same reproductive limitations as women. So if he'd been forty back then he might be midfifties and up now.

Which meant he might be dead.

She did a quick mental calculation. If the man purchased the mask sixteen years ago and he was approximately twenty years old, then that was thirty-six years. Add a little for margin of error and you had someone who was born sometime within the last forty years. She grabbed her phone and called Jackson who answered on the first ring.

"I need a huge favor," she said.

"Did you find out something?"

"Maybe. I don't know. It's a long shot and really thin, I mean paper thin, but I have a feeling about it." She told him about her conversation with the shop owner's daughter and the potentially fictional Derameau. "The guy who bought the mask is him…the man who bought me. The height and build was right and the dead eyes. I just know it's him."

"The woman was certain it was the mask that belonged to her grandfather?"

"You should have seen the look on her face when I showed her the picture. She was frightened."

"Okay, so what do you want me to do?"

"I've run down every Derameau that I could find and haven't gotten any closer to locating the man who might be the father, but if he wanted to keep a low profile, then there might not be anything to find. Unless he's dead."

"The one time you can't hide from paperwork. So you want me to check the death records for any males with the last name Derameau who died in the last…forty years? More?"

"I think forty years should cover it."

"No problem. Give me some time to arrange it and I'll call when I have something."

"Thanks. And Jackson?"

"Yeah?"

"Be careful. You don't know who you can trust."

"I will."

Shaye tossed her phone on the desk and blew out a breath. Now what? She'd pursued this line of investigation as far as she could without help, and she had nothing else.

You've got the house.

She reached for her mouse and brought up the pictures she'd downloaded to her computer. On the big monitor, the house looked even more dark and depressing than it did when looking at the pictures on her cell phone. She clicked through them one at a time, studying every detail captured, silently willing her mind to zero in on something and unlock another door to her past.

Her frustration grew as she moved through photo after photo without even a flicker. She tapped on her desk and stared out the front window. Maybe the photos wouldn't work. Maybe she needed to be inside the house for her mind to really process what she was seeing. Maybe she had to feel it in order to remember it.

But revisiting the house presented a problem as well. Clearly, her captor was targeting the people from her past. She had to assume he was watching her as well. He could have been the one who came in the house when she and Hustle were there. If that was the case, then he was aware of it already and he might be watching it, waiting for her to return.

He can't be everywhere at once.

That was true, but since she couldn't know for certain

where he was, she had to assume that he might be watching her. That meant not taking unnecessary risks. Even if she got desperate or foolish enough to consider doing something stupid, she'd made promises to her mother, her grandfather, and Jackson, and she wasn't about to go back on her word. Still, that didn't mean she could sit inside her apartment and wait for something to happen.

Jackson wasn't an option. He was working and wasn't her personal bodyguard. Besides, she needed him down at the department doing exactly what he was doing. Harold wanted to keep a low profile, and hanging out with her was the last thing that would accomplish that. And then an idea struck her. She might have been annoyed with Pierce for hiring someone to follow her, but the idea of paid protection wasn't exactly a bad one. Not if she controlled the game.

She grabbed her phone and started scrolling through her contacts. When she'd been on an insurance fraud case for Breaux, the detective agency she'd worked for before going solo, she'd met a guy who owned a private security firm. He was former military, and "imposing" was the most polite way to describe him. Surely no one could complain if she had an armed, qualified bodyguard.

Her cell phone rang and she saw her grandfather's name pop up on the screen. She answered the call and could tell immediately that something was wrong by his clipped tone.

"I'm afraid I have some bad news about the house," Pierce said.

"You couldn't locate the owner?"

"No. That was easy enough, and he was quite willing to sell. The lawyers insisted I send an inspector over there to assess the structure since I specifically told them I wanted it to remain intact until further notice."

"Of course." Lawyers didn't like anything that was a potential liability.

"The inspector just called…I'm really sorry but the house burned to the ground last night."

Shaye clutched the phone, her mind trying to process what her grandfather had just said. "How? There wasn't even a storm. The house didn't have power."

"I don't know. The fire department put the fire out early this morning, but they told me they won't bother with an investigation. The house was unoccupied and probably should have been condemned. The owner collected on it after Katrina, so not like he can process another claim for the same property that he's already been paid for."

"They don't care why it caught fire?"

"No one sustained a loss. In the big scheme of things, it's better for everyone if homes in that shape go away. All they do is invite drug dealers, squatters, and injury."

Shaye knew he was right, but it was still frustrating. No way was she willing to believe this was an accident.

"I knew you wouldn't be satisfied with the department's stance on the matter," Pierce said, "so I have my attorney looking for an arson investigator."

"Thank you…for everything."

"I'm really sorry, honey. If there's anything else I can

do, you'll let me know?"

"Yes."

There was a couple seconds of silence, then he cleared his throat. "How are you doing? I mean, other than this?"

"I'm doing fine."

"Have you made any more progress?"

"Unfortunately, it's very slow going. I don't really have anything to report."

She hated lying so she'd carefully couched her words so that they weren't necessarily a lie. The investigation *was* going slowly. And she didn't have anything to report because she, Jackson, and Harold had agreed to keep everything a secret, at least until they uncovered the mole in the police department.

"Try not to let it get to you," he said. "I know it sounds trite but I'm really worried about you."

"I know you are, but I promise I'm all right. And if I'm ever not all right, then I have you and mom and Eleonore to put me back in line."

"Well, don't make it a full-time job, okay?"

"I'm not making any promises."

"I didn't figure you would. I'll let you know when I hear something about the arson investigator. I have to run."

She disconnected the call and tossed her phone onto the desk. One more avenue of investigation gone. The masked man was either ahead of her or right behind her, sealing off potential angles of detection. She had to get ahead of him, but he had all the advantages.

After all, he knew more about her than she did.

Grayson stepped up to Jackson's desk and shook his head. "Reynolds said the forensics team didn't come up with crap from the hospital garage, and the security cameras are old and blurry. All they could make out was that the guy ran south after Ms. Mandeville got away. They searched the streets and parking lots south of the hospital and questioned everyone they could find, but no one was out at that time of the night and none of the businesses with cameras caught anything. Wasn't a lot of them to begin with."

"It was a long shot given the time of night."

"Yeah. What was Shaye's take on it?"

"She doesn't know what to think. She's freaked out, of course, and glad Clara got away, but beyond that, she's as in the dark as the rest of us."

"She's taking extra precautions, right? Her place is secure? She carries her weapon? Not going anywhere alone?"

"She knows the score, probably better than any of us. Think about it, she's been living in this city for nine years now, not knowing if the guy who did that to her was walking past her on the sidewalk."

Grayson nodded. "Gives a whole other meaning to the words living nightmare. Listen, I've got to go over some paperwork with Frank for some cases we need to close out. It will probably take an hour. Why don't you grab some lunch? Maybe we'll catch a break and have something to look into this afternoon."

"Sounds good," Jackson said.

He waited until Grayson left for the conference room, then quickly processed Shaye's request. He had no idea how long it would take to finish. There were too many variables—amount of data, number of jobs ahead of him in the queue, how well their Internet was running today, and that was always questionable.

His cell phone rang, and he saw Shaye's name come up on the display. Worried about two calls back to back, he grabbed it up and answered on the second ring.

"The house I lived in with Lydia burned down last night," she said.

"What?"

"Pierce just called. His lawyers wanted an inspection and instead of a house, the inspector found a smoldering pile of ash."

"Were any other structures affected?"

"Nope. Just that one. Not a cloud in the sky last night and no power on at the property. No footprints in the dust, either, so no one had been squatting there. This can't be a coincidence."

"It's not very likely."

"Anyway, I just wanted to let you know that we lost another avenue of investigation. I've got to go. I need to figure out another way to prompt my mind into giving up its secrets."

She disconnected and Jackson frowned. He hated the sound of defeat in her voice. Shaye wasn't the kind of woman who gave up easily. If she was getting discouraged, she might lose patience. If she got impatient, she might take bigger risks. One slip was all it took for the wrong person to make the right move.

He rose from his chair and as he grabbed his car keys, Sergeant Boyd stepped up to his desk.

"Hey, I saw Vincent in the Ninth Ward late last night," Boyd said. "Are you guys working something over there? I got an assault at a jazz bar down that way. Thought I'd see if you knew anything."

"You haven't heard?" Jackson asked. "I'm not working with Vincent anymore. I'm partnered with Grayson now."

Boyd smiled. "That's great! Hell, I bet you did a song and dance over that one. Grayson's a good cop. You should do well with him."

"Thanks. It's nice to actually do my job and not take any shit for it."

"Good luck and congratulations."

Boyd continued across the floor, and Jackson headed outside and into the parking lot, mulling over what Boyd had said. Why would Vincent be in the Ninth Ward late at night? His house was in the opposite direction. He was a known cheapskate, so no way was he paying bar prices for drinks, and besides, if he was going to do that, there was a bar around the corner that all the cops went to because they got a discount.

He got into his car and backed out of his space. The more he thought about it, the more it bothered him. Vincent was one of the names on his list. One of the men who was there when Shaye was found and had access to the Clancy files. What if he wasn't as lazy and inept as everyone thought? It would make a great cover. If everyone thought you'd checked out until retirement, then they stopped counting on you for anything and didn't go looking for you when they needed something. All of which left Vincent with plenty of time inside and outside the department to pursue something else.

As Jackson pulled out of the parking lot, he saw Vincent's car at the light ahead of him. Speak of the devil. Probably taking one of those two-hour lunches he was famous for. Vincent went left at the light and Jackson floored his vehicle, barely making the corner before the turn signal expired. He was going to find out where Vincent went when he left the police station.

It was long overdue.

He put a car in between them that went the same direction as Vincent for a good six blocks before turning off. Jackson slowed as soon as he saw the car signal and took his time accelerating. A truck pulled out of a side street in front of him and he breathed a sigh of relief. His car was nondescript, so it blended well in traffic, but Vincent had been in it plenty of times. If he was paying attention, then he'd recognize the car. Jackson hoped he wasn't paying attention.

Vincent made a right turn onto a side street and Jackson continued past, then turned right on the next street and increased his speed so that he made it to the end of the street before Vincent disappeared. There was no sign of

Vincent's car at the end of the street. He cursed and looked again, but Vincent's car was nowhere in sight.

He turned right, and when he got to the street Vincent had turned on, he slowed and looked down it. His pulse quickened when he saw Vincent's car parked midway down. He floored his car and made a hard right onto the next street and screeched to a halt at the curb. He jumped out of his car and ran the block back to where Vincent was parked and crossed to the side opposite of his car.

They were outside the busy area of the French Quarter, but it was lunchtime, and hole-in-the-wall restaurants dotted every street surrounding downtown. Plenty of people milled around, looking at menus in windows or standing outside chatting. Jackson fell in step behind a group of women and skirted the far side of the sidewalk, scanning the opposite side of the street as he went. When he reached the spot opposite Vincent's car, he ducked inside a retail shop and moved to the front display, where he had a clear view of the street.

Directly across from him was a sandwich shop. Next door was a bar, then a café. Retail shops made up most of the rest of that side of the street that he could see. He shook his head. The most logical conclusion was that Vincent was in the sandwich shop. It was probably the cheapest po'boys in the French Quarter or the one that gave him extra shrimp. Either way, Jackson had likely wasted his lunch hour tracking Vincent to his eating spot.

He was about to leave when he saw Vincent come out of a shop two doors down from the sandwich shop, carrying a plastic bag. Jackson looked at the name of the shop and frowned. Spirits and Spells. The first word could also be alcohol, but the second didn't fit that product line at all. He waited until Vincent got into his car and left before exiting the store and crossing the street.

The shop was dark and smelled old, like most of the buildings in the French Quarter. The shelves were filled with some things he'd seen in horror movies and a lot of things he didn't recognize at all. But then, this wasn't exactly his knowledge base.

"Can I help you?"

A voice sounded behind him, and he turned to find a tall Creole man standing there.

"I was just looking around," Jackson said. "You have some interesting things here. What are they for?"

The man stared at Jackson, his blank expression not wavering even a twitch. "If you don't know what they're for, then you're probably in the wrong shop."

"Witchcraft?" Jackson asked.

"Witchcraft, sorcery, black arts…whatever you want to call it. If that's your bent, we can hook you up."

"You don't really believe in that stuff, do you?"

The man raised one eyebrow. "If I didn't, I wouldn't be standing here."

"I guess not," Jackson said. "Well, thanks for the information."

He headed out of the shop and down the street. He needed to find out who owned the shop and see if he could get the names of employees. The man he'd spoken to had fit the physical description of the man with the goat mask, but his eyes had been different from the drawing made from Clara's description. Granted, eyes could change and depending on circumstances, a person might see things differently, but for whatever reason, Jackson didn't think he was the guy. But that didn't mean it wasn't someone else connected with the shop.

The one thing Jackson knew for certain was that in all the time he'd worked with Vincent, the man had never once indicated an interest or participation in the black arts. No one else in the department had ever mentioned anything of the sort, either, and if cops knew something like that, it would have made the rounds.

Vincent had just moved up to the top of his list.

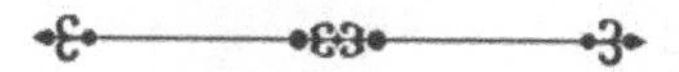

It was almost three o'clock, and Shaye was ready to climb the walls when she finally got a text message from Jackson.

Check your email.

She ran to her computer and accessed her email, then let out a whoop when she saw the file attachment from Jackson. It was the list she'd been waiting on. She opened it and gave it a quick look. A little over a hundred names. More than she'd thought, but it didn't look as if Jackson had filtered it. Given the short text, he probably couldn't risk looking at the file himself.

She printed the list, then started down it, drawing a line

through all the females. Then she made a second pass and reviewed the names more closely, eliminating those with a birth year that made them too young to have been the father. She crossed off several more, then did a quick count. Only twelve names remained. One of them might be the man who'd fathered a monster.

She started to review those twelve names and stopped when she got to number six.

Jonal Derameau.

J.D. The initials on the pentagram. She scanned the other names, but no other first or middle name started with the letter *J*.

This was it. Her hair stood on end. Her heart raced. And she knew with absolute certainty that she'd found the man who didn't exist.

She grabbed her phone and sent a text to Jackson.

Need death certificate for Jonal Derameau.

She pressed Send then stared at the phone, waiting for the message to show as Read. It was probably only seconds, but it felt like forever when she received a text from Jackson.

OK. Give me ten.

She jumped up from her chair, too excited to sit. For the first time in her life, she wished she had a treadmill in her house. What she needed was to expend some energy, and pacing her small apartment wasn't going to get her there. She looked outside. A jog around the block might help, but what if she was half a block away and Jackson sent the certificate sooner than he'd thought? She'd give herself a heart attack sprinting in this heat.

Better she wait inside her apartment for Jackson to send the document.

Ten minutes.

She headed for the kitchen, about to do something she tried to avoid altogether.

Clean.

CHAPTER TWENTY-ONE

August 28, 2006
New Orleans, Louisiana

Jonal Derameau sat in the big comfortable chair in front of the fireplace and stared out across the expansive and elegant living room of his home. It was still hot outside, but at eighty-eight, his bones grew cold easily, especially in the big drafty house. The fire crackled and danced, casting flickering shadows on the walls surrounding him.

He'd lived a long, satisfying life. Not so much in the beginning. His childhood on the plantation had been the kind of hell described in the worst of books and movies on the subject. But without that beginning to harden his heart, he wouldn't be here, in this mansion, surrounded by expensive items.

He reached for the glass of whiskey on the side table and paused when he saw the Bible sitting beside it. His maid was the reason he'd started reading the book. The reason he'd stepped into a church five years ago—the first time in his life. Maybe it was his age that caused his heart to soften. Maybe it was the book.

Or maybe he was just tired and ready to let his anger go.

He'd done a lot of things in his life that he regretted, but there were also a lot of things he'd done that he didn't regret, even though they were immoral. He didn't regret killing the plantation owners. They were all horrible men who abused their wives, children, servants, and workers. Men like them didn't deserve to exist on this earth. For what they did to others, especially what the one did to his mother. That man had started looking at his sister the same way when she was only ten. Jonal believed absolutely that they deserved to die. He would never feel one ounce of sorrow over that.

And he didn't regret taking money from the plantation owner's son. If he hadn't been illegitimate, he would have inherited assets from the man, but no court recognized the black bastard son of a rich white man. He did regret the stress and worry the situation had put on the son. He was a smart businessman but emotionally weak. Jonal often wondered how much the stress of dealing with his demands played into the heart attack that killed the man before he ever made his sixty-third birthday.

The grandson had been stoic and put up a good front when Jonal had gone to see him after his father's death. Jonal knew that his father had told him everything—the poisoning, the payments made over three decades, and finally, the pictures and the film of the grandson with the girl. The grandson knew Jonal's power over him.

When Jonal visited him after the funeral, the grandson tried to hide his fear. But Jonal was too old and too wise. He'd seen too much fear. He'd lived it too many times himself. But he respected the grandson for his composure. Jonal saw him that one time, to make sure that if he ever needed to call in his marker, the grandson understood his place.

Jonal didn't need money. The truth was, he hadn't needed money in many years. The cash he'd taken from the plantation owner's son had financed his nightclubs, which provided cover for the drugs and illegal gambling. The money he'd taken had multiplied until he couldn't imagine ever spending it all. Katrina had destroyed the clubs and he'd thought about rebuilding, but he had grown tired of the business. So he retired to his estate on the outskirts of the city, and the man who was almost never seen had disappeared altogether.

It had been a good life. It was time to relax and enjoy it.

But now, he had a problem. For the first time, something weighed heavily on his conscience, waking him from a dead sleep and disrupting his eating habits. He'd tried to ignore it. After all, he'd never had this sort of problem before, but things had changed. And no matter how hard he wished the problem away or how many times he told himself that it wasn't his to handle, he couldn't stop thinking about it.

It's because of you that he's doing this.

He took a drink of his whiskey.

Emile Samba.

He was the reason Jonal couldn't sleep. He was the reason all the food Jonal used to love now tasted like sawdust. He was the reason Jonal read the book more and more.

Emile claimed he was Jonal's son, but it wasn't true. Jonal had many dalliances with many women and had the children to prove it, but he'd paid off the women long ago and the children after that. None of them contacted him. That was the agreement. And even if they'd thought to try, they didn't know his first name or where to find him. He rarely visited his clubs, leaving their operation to trusted employees who were very well paid and watched by other trusted employees who were paid equally well.

Not a single legal document or deed had his name on it. His attorney had created layer upon layer of corporations and LLCs that it would take a lot of effort to get through, and as Jonal's sole legal representation, he had the authority to sign documents and process money in the clubs' bank accounts. Even this house belonged to a corporation his attorney set up. Jonal paid cash for everything, and he'd kept everything he'd made on the illegal business in cash as well, locked away in cement vaults below this very living room.

He was Mr. Derameau to everyone. Only his attorney knew his full name and where to find him. Even the maid knew him only as "Mr. Derameau" or "the mister" and she handled the hiring and payment of any other household help they might need. But now, the man who had been so careful about not leaving a trace of his existence had a problem that could lead right back to him. And the irony was, it was a situation he hadn't caused. Not directly.

He knew Emile's mother. She'd worked at one of his clubs serving drinks. Jonal recalled his initial assessment of her as pretty but troubled. The kind of woman that would bring problems, therefore, the kind of woman Jonal avoided. He didn't know if Emile's mother had told Emile that Jonal was his father, or if that was a fancy created by Emile, a young man who desperately wanted power and importance. But none of that mattered now.

Emile Samba had managed to do what no one else had done—he'd found Jonal's home.

Found it and taken something from it. The one thing Jonal couldn't afford to lose.

Emile had secured a position through the maid, doing landscaping and general maintenance, which gave him access to the house and the grounds. Jonal had never seen him before, so didn't have any idea of the threat that had walked through the door invited. His heart attack provided Emile with the opportunity he'd been waiting for. Jonal had been hospitalized for over a week, and his maid had spent many hours at the hospital, giving Emile plenty of time to discover the cubby in the floor of Jonal's office.

You should have destroyed them years ago.

It was a mistake he had no doubt he'd pay dearly for. The film and pictures would have been safe if they'd been stored with the money, and he'd considered it at length, but what stopped him *was* the safety of the money vaults, especially in the case of a fire. If a fire broke out, and Jonal didn't survive, the vaults would protect the money, but the film, pictures, and branding iron would melt. And that's the way Jonal wanted it.

The son had lived up to his word every single time he'd asked. The least he owed the man was his continued silence, even in death.

Jonal still remembered the look on Emile's face when he'd confronted Jonal after Jonal returned home from the hospital.

"I thought you were a man of great power," Emile said, his disgust clear. "But you're just a common thief, using pictures to steal money. That man paid you for your silence. Even your altar is wrong. You never knew the power of the One. You're nobody."

"I never claimed that kind of power."

"That's not what everyone says. Everyone says you're a dark priest. That you can call out for the spirits to surround you and they will. Some even say you caused Katrina. I thought I could learn from you—my father. But you have nothing for me except what I've already taken."

"I'm not your father."

"My mother told me you were. I haunted the French Quarter waiting to see you, following you a bit more each time, careful that you wouldn't see me."

"You've wasted your time," Jonal said. "I'm not your father and I don't practice what you do. How much money do you want to return the items you stole?"

Emile laughed. "Money? You think this is about money?"

"Then what do you want?"

"What I've always wanted—greatness."

But Emile had taken money as well—two hundred thousand dollars. Enough to keep someone of simple means living well for a long time. Jonal was still too weak to do anything himself, but he'd hired a private detective to locate Emile. It hadn't been easy. His house was north of New Orleans, on a dirt road in the middle of the woods. The nearest town was ten miles away. The nearest home was five. Jonal wasn't healthy enough now, but as soon as he was stronger, he would go there.

To fix his mistake.

CHAPTER TWENTY-TWO

It took Jackson twenty minutes to send a text that he'd forwarded the death certificate. By that time, Shaye had scrubbed her kitchen counters and picked the polish off two fingernails. As soon as she saw the text, she raced to her computer and pulled up the document.

Damn it!

No home address. No parents.

The informant was a doctor at the hospital. Cause of death was heart failure.

Stonewalled again.

Then a thought occurred to her and she looked at the certificate again. That name sounded familiar. She Googled the doctor and saw he was on staff with New Orleans General. His date of Jonal's death was a couple weeks after she was brought into the same hospital.

The hospital must have gotten information on Derameau. At minimum, someone paid the bill when he died. That person could have been one of his children. She tapped her fingers on the desk. Her chances of getting medical records were absolutely none. The police could request them since Jonal was dead, but they still needed a reason. Hospitals didn't just trot out confidential records for no reason, and getting a reason meant involving Jackson, who would likely have to involve others in order to get the request processed. Involving others in the police department was the last thing they wanted to do.

She jumped up from her chair and grabbed her car keys and purse, practically sprinting out of the apartment. There was someone who had access to the records. It would be breaking the rules, but Shaye was betting that the rules were the last thing on the list of Clara Mandeville's worries.

The drive to the hospital provided her with some time to think about everything she knew so that she could explain it to Clara. She was about to ask the woman to risk her job, and that wasn't something she took lightly. If Clara herself hadn't been attacked, Shaye wouldn't have asked at all. But given the situation, she felt Clara had the right to know the facts, however limited, and make her own decision.

Clara was sitting up in bed, sipping water and watching television, when Shaye entered the room. She smiled as Shaye approached the bed, then her expression sobered. "You didn't come just for a visit."

"No, ma'am."

"Did you find something out?"

Shaye nodded.

"Then you best tell me."

Shaye told Clara about the shop and what the woman had said about the goat mask and Derameau, then explained about the initials on the pentagram and the death certificate. She paused when she finished. Clara stared at her, frowning. Shaye felt her spirits fall a little. Even as she'd told Clara what she knew, Shaye herself had seen how flimsy her facts were. She was making an enormous leap to assume that the man was a Derameau. That Jonal Derameau, in particular, was the father in question. That finding any of the Derameau children might lead to the discovery of the man.

"I know it's a long shot," Shaye said. "And I don't have anything else to offer you but a feeling."

"You think you're on the right track?"

"I do."

Clara nodded. "Then I guess we need to get this Derameau's medical records. There has to be something in them that can get you closer."

"That was my thought, too, but I'm also worried about your job."

"I'm not likely to have a job or a life if he gets another crack at me. I got away once. He won't let that happen again. And quite frankly, I'm not interested in spending the rest of my life looking over my shoulder. That stalker darn near sent poor Emma Frederick into a nervous breakdown. I'm too old for that crap."

Emma Frederick had been a coworker of Clara's, and Shaye's first investigation after opening her own agency. Emma was being stalked, but the police didn't believe her and she didn't know who the stalker was. Shaye had ultimately figured out who was stalking Emma, and Jackson had killed the stalker, but Emma's nerves had been pushed to the breaking point. When it was over, Emma moved to another state, looking forward to a new start.

"It was hard on Emma," Shaye agreed. She'd seen firsthand when the strong nurse had reached the end of her rope.

Clara narrowed her eyes at Shaye. "Hard on you, too. Someone may not be playing around with you, but you've got nine years of walking around not knowing if you're looking that man in the face. Not knowing if he installed your cable or served you coffee. I've thought about it time and time again and each time I do, I wonder how you deal with it."

"I had a choice to live with uncertainty or to hide away inside a fortress and not live at all. I didn't see the second as an option."

Clara reached out and squeezed her hand. "Neither do I. Now, hand me my robe. We've got work to do."

Jackson and Grayson were running down leads on a homicide at a local nightclub when his cell phone vibrated. He pulled it out and saw Corrine Archer's name in the display. Jackson hadn't heard a peep out of Shaye except the thank-you text she'd sent after he'd forwarded the death certificate, and that had been at least an hour ago. He quickly answered, praying that Shaye hadn't done something risky.

"I think I found her," Corrine said, her normally even-keeled voice now high-pitched.

It took Jackson a moment to realize what she was talking about. "The girl that Clancy sold?"

"Yes. I can't be sure, of course, but I found one who fits the criteria, is still missing, and she looks like Shaye. A lot. I sent her information to your and Detective Grayson's emails."

"That's great. Thank you. I'll check it out now."

"Please let me know if there's anything else I can do," Corrine said. "It feels better doing something."

"I understand that completely, and I'll let you know."

He disconnected the call and accessed his email, relaying the call to Grayson. When the image appeared on his phone, his jaw dropped just a little.

"Wow," Grayson said. "That girl looks a lot like Shaye."

Jackson nodded. "Enough to be sisters." He scanned the attached report filed by CPS. "Looks like her aunt and uncle are a nasty piece of goods, but smart enough to avoid leaving any real evidence. The girl wouldn't talk, so CPS couldn't move forward with a case."

"Typical," Grayson said. "So now what? We have a potential ID for the girl, but leaning on the aunt and uncle isn't going to give us anything. She probably ran away. Knowing where she might have run to doesn't give us anything, either, because we already know that Clancy is the one who grabbed her."

"No, it doesn't move the case forward," Jackson

agreed, "but it does support my theory that this guy was trying to pick up where he left off."

"What's your theory on the chances this girl is still alive?"

Jackson shook his head. "With Clancy all over the news, her chances are really low, but we can't stop looking until we're sure."

"I'm not stopping by choice. I just don't know where to look."

"Yeah," Jackson said, frustration coursing through him. "Me either."

Reagan walked around her stone prison, then stumbled and caught herself against the wall to keep from falling. She leaned against the smooth stone, waiting for the dizziness to pass, but it continued until she finally sank onto the ground.

The hamburger had been drugged.

She'd taken a small drink of the water, then waited for thirty minutes to see if anything happened, but when nothing changed, she took a bite of the burger. It had only taken twenty minutes to feel the effect of the drug. She knew the routine. He'd give her the drugged food, then return that night. She wouldn't be completely passed out, but she'd be so looped she couldn't stand without help. Then he'd inject her with something and almost everything went dark. Weird images and sounds would pop up in her mind as she started to regain consciousness, but they were fleeting and she couldn't get her conscious mind to grab hold of them long enough to create a lasting picture.

But this time, things would be different. This time, she wouldn't finish the burger, and when the monster came to inject her with more poison, she'd pretend to be out of it, until exactly the right moment. Then she'd stab him with the dagger and run until she found help, even if it meant running the skin off her bare feet.

She picked up the stone and ran the sharpened edge across the hamburger bun. The razor-thin edge cut the bread into two perfect halves. She smiled.

This asshole was about to get what he had coming.

CHAPTER TWENTY-THREE

September 15, 2006
New Orleans, Louisiana

Jonal waited until the maid left to visit her sister before leaving his house. He was stronger now—almost as strong as he'd been before the heart attack—and it was time to handle Emile. He had his pistol in his pocket. It was an old six-shooter, but he'd had it for a long time and it felt comfortable in his hand, even though he'd never fired it at a human.

Tonight, that would change.

Recovering the film and the pictures from Emile wouldn't be enough. Jonal had done some discreet investigating of his own through old trusted employees and had learned everything he needed to know about Emile. His mother had been committed after killing a neighbor and then trying to kill herself. She'd finally succeeded by throwing herself off the roof of the mental hospital. Everyone said Emile was just as disturbed as his mother. Some went so far as to call him evil. One said Emile frightened him. Given that the man who'd uttered those words was six foot four and three hundred pounds of muscles, Jonal didn't take his words lightly.

Evil didn't need physical strength to blossom. It needed only cunning.

In the garage, he bypassed his Mercedes sedan and took the old pickup truck used by the landscapers instead. The Mercedes would stick out where he was going. A well-worn pickup would pass unnoticed.

The drive took him over an hour. The sun was already setting when he located the dirt road that led to Emile's house. He'd hoped for more daylight, but perhaps this was better. It was easier to hide in the cloak of darkness. He turned onto the dirt road, slowing slightly every time the road narrowed until he was idling. When he reached a bend in the road that the detective said signaled the last stretch of road before the turn into Emile's front yard, he turned off the lights and carefully rounded the corner.

Every couple seconds, Jonal caught sight of a flicker of lights through the trees. That must be the house. He continued inching down the road until he was afraid the motor would be heard inside the house, then he guided the truck into a tiny clearing off to the right and let it roll into the brush until it stopped. He got out of the truck and walked to the edge of the tree line to assess the situation.

The house sat in the middle of a clearing about twenty yards from where he stood. Approaching it directly would leave him out in the open, but he could skirt the edge of the woods and come within fifteen feet of the side of the house. So he set out walking a couple feet inside the wooded area, keeping a close eye on the house as he went.

The forest was eerily quiet, and Jonal found it unsettling. It was as if no other living thing wanted to be here. When he reached the edge of the forest near the house, he looked around, then started to step out when a noise from the woods behind the house made him pause. It was whistling. He took a step back into the foliage and peered through the leaves in the direction of the sound, trying to see something in the dim glow cast by the back porch light.

Several seconds later, Emile emerged from the woods pushing a wheelbarrow. Jonal watched as he approached the house, trying to make out what was inside. It looked like a pile of blankets, but why would Emile carry blankets into the woods? He moved farther down the tree line until he could see the back of the house. Emile had stopped in front of the back steps and was picking the blankets up from the wheelbarrow. He lifted the stack and that's when Jonal saw a thin white leg and foot drop out of the edge of the blankets and twitch as Emile carried the bundle into the house.

Jonal drew in a breath. He had a person in that bundle. Based on the size of the feet, either a young boy or a girl. Jonal was betting on a girl. Emile had made clear his disdain for Jonal's altar in the photos and video and the positioning of the girl, saying Jonal was weak and didn't know how to properly worship the master like Emile did. Jonal would have been the first to agree with that. He didn't know anything about the sort of worship Emile talked about.

Even the girl had been a lie. He'd found her dead behind one of his clubs, a needle in her arm, and decided to use her for the film. He'd put her back where he found her after he'd gotten what he needed.

It wasn't the sort of thing an honorable man did, but it was a far cry from using a live human being in a ritual of evil. Jonal felt his pocket for his pistol. Whatever Emile had been doing, it ended now. He took one step out of the woods, then heard a vehicle approaching. He watched as the headlights swung into the front yard. Four people wearing all black climbed out and went into the house.

Had they seen his truck? It had rolled a good ways into the brush and no moonlight could breach the thick pine trees, but if someone had been looking closely, they might have caught a glimpse of something large in the trees, or noticed the depression in the weeds that the truck had made. He looked back at the house and pulled out his pistol. He'd know in a minute.

He waited for a while, but no one came outside. Whatever was happening inside—and he didn't even want to think about it—the people must have come for it. He had no choice but to wait. One old man and a six-shooter against five people at least half his age were losing odds. He thought briefly about going into the forest behind the house from which Emile had emerged with the girl, but decided against it.

If he wasn't there when the people left, he might lose his chance to get to Emile. Too much time had been spent on his recovery. So he'd wait here until the people left.

Then he'd end the nightmare he'd created.

Two hours passed before the people exited Emile's house. Jonal had long since given up standing and had found an old tree log to sit on. His strength was flagging a bit and standing for hours would have sapped too much out of him. The bugs had been horrible, but they were the least of his problems. He watched as the four got into their car and drove away, then crept from his hiding spot and hurried to the side of the house.

A light was on in the back room and he eased under the window, then rose up high enough to peer into it. The room was a small, outdated kitchen. Peeling wallpaper, broken cabinet doors, and chipped countertops. There was no sign of Emile, but Jonal could see the back door that led from the kitchen onto the porch. Just as he was about to head for the back of the house, a door on the wall opposite the window swung open and Emile entered.

Jonal drew in a breath, his chest burning a bit at the quick intake.

He knew it was Emile based on his size and the way he moved, but that's where all recognition ended. The black robe he wore was hooded and covered his body completely, leaving only his hands and feet exposed. But the mask was the worst. A goat head with giant scrolling horns. He'd seen a similar mask years ago in a trunk hidden beneath one of the plantation workers' beds. But that mask had not been well crafted, rendering it more of an oddity than a fright-invoking piece, as it was intended to be.

This mask was anything but an oddity. It was fear

itself.

Jonal watched as Emile washed his hands in the sink on the far wall, the blood running off his hands in stark contrast to the white porcelain. He waited as Emile wiped his hands and poured a glass of water, then exited the kitchen through a door on the right side wall that probably led to the living room.

This was it. If he was going to enter the house, now was the time to do it, while the back entrance was clear and Emile was in another room. He dropped down and moved around the side of the house to the back. He crept up the cement steps and turned the knob on the back door, hoping it was unlocked. The knob turned easily and he pushed the door open, one inch at a time, then slipped through the small opening and into the room.

The house was pier and beam, like most of the old structures, and Jonal hesitated before each step, worried that the old floor would creak and give him away. Old houses made plenty of odd noises, but the sound of a floor creaking when someone walked upon it was different from the odd rubbing of wood during a storm.

Halfway across the kitchen he paused, wondering if he should go into the other room first and check on the girl, but decided against it. Even if she was alive, he had no medical training and he could hardly drive her to the nearest hospital and check her in. Besides, if the girl could be helped, it made more sense to eliminate Emile first.

He continued across the kitchen, his pistol aimed at the door, when suddenly, the door swung open and Emile stared at him in surprise. He'd removed the goat mask but was still wearing the robe, although the hood was pushed back off his head. He took one look at the six-shooter and laughed.

"You think you can kill me, old man?" Emile asked. "I have power you never even dreamed of. I am everything people thought you were."

"You are nobody," Jonal said. "And you'll die nobody."

He squeezed the trigger and the bullet caught Emile in the right side. Emile's eyes widened in shock and he clutched his side. Jonal leveled the gun at him again and fired another shot, but this one went wide, grazing the sleeve of the robe. Emile cried out again, so Jonal figured he'd gotten a bit of skin at least.

Clutching his side, Emile bolted out of the room and Jonal could hear the sound of pounding footsteps as he ran through the house. Jonal hurried after him and saw the front door standing wide open. Jonal ran through the door and onto the porch, but the dim porch light provided illumination for only a couple of feet. Jonal squinted into the darkness, trying to make out movement, when he heard a car engine fire up. A couple seconds later, Emile's truck went roaring past the house. Jonal fired again, but he missed. The truck left the clearing and turned onto the road, its engine racing as it tore down the dirt road.

Jonal hurried back inside and ran for the door that Emile had come out of wearing the robe and mask. He paused in front of the door, dreading what he expected to find on the other side. Finally, he pushed the door open and gasped.

It was exactly as he'd feared.

The room was an addition onto the house and was made completely of stone. A set of steps led down into it. There was no overhead lighting that Jonal could see. Only the mass of black candles, their collective glow illuminating the girl on the altar in the center of the room.

She was young, probably a teenager, and wearing a tattered red dress. Jonal could see blood dripping down her exposed chest and onto the altar. He moved closer and could then see the extent of the abuse the child had suffered. He turned to the side, gagging, and barely managed to keep his supper down. His chest began to tighten and he drew in a deep breath, praying that his heart didn't give out on him now.

He had to get out of this room. Had to get away from the evil that had created it.

He started to turn, then something moved at the edge of his vision. He whirled around, panicked that someone was in the room or that Emile had a secret entrance and had returned, then realized it was the girl.

She was alive!

Jonal sucked in a breath and stepped closer to the altar. He watched her chest and finally saw the almost imperceptible rise and fall from her breathing. It was so shallow he hadn't even noticed it before.

Now what?

He couldn't leave her here, but he couldn't take her to

a hospital, either. And that was assuming he could get her to his truck, which was questionable. Then he remembered the wheelbarrow. It was outside the back door. If he could get the girl to the wheelbarrow, then he could probably manage pushing her to his truck. If it was too much of a strain, then he'd get the truck and drive back to the house.

He stepped right next to the altar and stuck his arms underneath her, trying not to focus directly on her abused body. Given her emaciated limbs, he'd expected her to be light, but was still surprised when he easily lifted her. He started to turn, then noticed a stone in the center of the altar that didn't have mortar surrounding it. He hurried out of the house with the girl and placed her in the wheelbarrow, then ran back into the room and stuck the tips of his fingers into the gap around the stone and shoved. The stone moved enough to allow him to dig his fingers underneath it and into a gap below. He pulled up as hard as he could and the stone flew backward off the altar and crashed onto the floor.

He leaned over and peered into the opening and saw the photos, film, and branding iron lying inside. He removed the branding iron and grabbed a candle off the floor, then lit the photos on fire, waiting long enough to make sure they burned. The film began to crackle and curl. He pulled one of the photos out and crumbled it, then lit it with the candle and placed it on the second set of film. It didn't take long for the flames to burn the old photos and melt the film.

Clutching the branding iron, he ran out of the house,

then placed the iron in the wheelbarrow with the girl. He lifted the handles on the wheelbarrow and set out at a trot for his truck. Emile might return at any moment. Jonal hoped the shot in his side was fatal, but he couldn't be certain he'd hit an organ. If he hadn't, Emile might be patching up his side now and planning on coming back for revenge.

Even if it wasn't tonight, Jonal knew that unless Emile was dead, he would return.

His house!

Emile knew where he lived. It would be nothing for him to drive to Jonal's house and wait for him to return home. Jonal wouldn't be back tonight for a while. But his maid would. Jonal glanced at the child in the wheelbarrow and thought about what Emile would do to his maid. He pulled his cell phone out of his pocket, but it showed No Service. His stomach rolled and he upped the trot to a jog. He had to get back to New Orleans.

It took him about five minutes to reach his truck. He was breathing heavy and his chest ached some but otherwise, he seemed to be okay. He laid the girl and the branding iron on the seat of the truck and fired up the engine, anxious to get back to the main road. If Emile returned before he made it off the dirt road, there would be nowhere for him to go. There wasn't even enough room on the road to pass, and Emile would know that it was Jonal in the truck. He'd driven the vehicle enough times while working at Jonal's house.

He punched the accelerator and the truck leaped

forward, sliding sideways as he left the clearing and the tires connected again with the slick dirt road. It was impossible to maintain a high speed with all the holes and bumps, but Jonal pushed the limit of the truck.

Wondering if the girl would make the drive.

Wondering if Emile was on his way to Jonal's house.

Wondering how late his maid would visit with her sister.

When he reached the main road, a small bit of relief coursed through him. One hurdle was past, but he had several more to manage. He pressed the accelerator down to the floor, pushing the truck to its limit, praying that a policeman didn't pull him over. There was no explanation in the world that would get him off the hook for this. Cops would never believe he wasn't involved. Hell, he wouldn't believe it, either.

He stopped at the first pay phone he found and dug the phone number for his maid's sister from his wallet. He was relieved to find she was still there. He told her he'd seen someone trying to break into the house and suggested she stay at her sister's that night. She readily agreed and his relief ticked up another notch. Then he hurried back to the truck, grabbed the branding iron, and threw it into a Dumpster before taking off again.

The girl's breathing was noticeable now, and she was starting to move her limbs, jerking like she was having a bad dream. This time, though, he kept his speed right at the limit. No use tempting fate. The problem was what to do with the girl now. Hospitals had security cameras, so even a dump-and-run was out of the question. But he needed to leave her somewhere that she could be found. Out here in the middle of nowhere wouldn't do her any good. She needed to be in New Orleans, where the best doctors were. Maybe they could save her.

He made the drive back into the city as quickly as he dared and headed toward the French Quarter. The hospital he'd been in for his heart was there, and it was a good one. If he could find a place to leave the girl nearby, someone would find her and take her there.

He passed the hospital emergency room entrance and circled around the block, looking for a place that might be trafficked this late by decent people. It wasn't an easy task. But when he rounded the next corner, he hit the jackpot. Two cops were inside an all-night café, picking up coffee. The street was otherwise empty. He pulled around the corner into an alley and checked for security cameras. It was clear.

He jumped out of the truck and lifted the girl, then carried her to the corner. He peered around but the cop car was still parked in front of the café. He stepped around the corner and placed the girl on the sidewalk under a streetlight. She was starting to move more, and he hoped she wouldn't awaken and wander off before the police saw her, but he couldn't risk sticking around any longer. He ran back to his truck and sped off, not slowing until he was three blocks away.

And that's when his left arm went numb.

No! Not now.

But he knew the score.

He raced down the street until he reached the corner, then swung the truck around and parked in front of a bar. His chest felt as if it had been pumped with air and was about to burst. He staggered as he made his way up to the entrance of the bar. The bouncer eyed him as he approached, and Jonal knew the man would think he was drunk.

He walked up clutching his chest. "Heart," he whispered. "Call 911."

Then everything went dark.

Jonal jerked awake and bolted upright. He looked wildly around the room, trying to understand where he was and how he'd gotten here. He felt a hand on his arm and looked over to see his maid.

"Mr. Derameau," she said. "Can you hear me?"

"Yes. What happened?" His eyes, which had been out of focus when he'd first awakened, had cleared now and he realized he was in a hospital room. In a hospital bed.

"You had another heart attack," she said. "You don't remember?"

Jonal tried to recall, but his mind couldn't focus. "The bar. I stopped in front of a bar."

The maid nodded. "The bouncer called the paramedics. You collapsed in front of the club. I don't know what you were doing in the French Quarter that late, though. I was at my sister's. You called to tell me you'd chased off a burglar at your house and asked me to stay put for the night. The hospital found my sister's number in your wallet and called it. That's how I knew to come."

Jonal nodded as it all started to come back to him—the house, the altar, the girl, Emile Samba. "How long have I been here?"

"Three days."

"I need something to drink," he said.

She nodded. "I'll go get the nurse and find out what you can have."

As soon as she left the room, he reached for the television remote and turned the channel to the news. If the girl had been found, maybe the news would have the story. Unless they'd covered it and moved on while he'd been unconscious.

He didn't have to wonder for long.

A photo of the girl popped up on the television screen and he felt his chest tighten. She was awake. Her face was bruised and puffy and her eyes were filled with fear but she was alive. The reporter said the girl had no memory of who she was, and an intensive police search and news campaign had not turned up any information as to her identity.

Maybe it was better, he thought, if she never remembered.

Then another picture flashed on the screen and the reporter announced that Corrine Archer had taken temporary custody of the girl, and planned on filing for permanent custody.

He felt his chest tighten again and reached for the telephone. He needed his lawyer. He had to make sure everything was in order. His time on this earth was almost up.

CHAPTER TWENTY-FOUR

Shaye clutched the steering wheel of her SUV and pressed the accelerator, moving through the traffic as quickly as possible. Things had gone better than expected at the hospital. Clara had been able to secure the information on Jonal Derameau without anyone so much as raising an eyebrow. It was a huge relief for Shaye that no one had questioned Clara. The last thing she wanted on her conscience was Clara's job in jeopardy. The woman had already done so much for her.

Jonal's personal information had been somewhat disappointing in that it still didn't provide a home address or a next of kin. Clearly, the man had taken privacy to an entirely different level than most, leaving Shaye to wonder what he'd been hiding from. Or whom. But the one thing Jonal couldn't control was the fact that his death generated a bill that had to be paid and a body that had to be claimed. In both cases, it was an attorney who'd handled the job.

Shaye had wasted no time locating the attorney, who had an office in the French Quarter and maintained office hours until 6:00 p.m. Professional etiquette called for her to make an appointment, but Shaye wasn't about to be put down on a schedule for a week or two away. It was much harder to tell someone no when they were standing in front of you. She could make a better case for urgency in person.

The office was several blocks from the hospital. She located a parking spot across the street, then hurried into the building and up to the second-floor law office, walking in the door five minutes before closing time. The receptionist at the front desk frowned when Shaye entered. The practice specialized in estate planning and Shaye, in her old jeans and plain T-shirt, obviously didn't fit the standard of dress for their usual clientele.

"Hello," Shaye said, smiling and using her pleasant voice. "I'd like to speak to Mr. Lacoste."

The girl frowned. "Do you have an appointment?" she asked, even though Shaye was certain she already knew Shaye didn't.

"No, but it's a time-sensitive situation." She pulled her business card from her wallet and handed it to the girl. "If you could give him this and ask if he has a few minutes to speak with me. It is really important."

The receptionist didn't even flinch at the private investigator title on the business card, but then where money was concerned, investigation was often part and parcel of the business.

"He's really busy," the receptionist said. "It would be best if you made an appointment."

"It wouldn't be best for me. Look, I'm trying to be polite, but I don't really have any time to waste. Either you take him the card and ask him to speak to me, or the next person standing here asking to speak to him will be a detective with the New Orleans Police Department."

Her eyes widened slightly and she rose from her chair. "Just a minute," she said and headed down a hallway behind her. A minute later, she returned wearing a sheepish look. "I apologize for not realizing who you were, Ms. Archer. Mr. Lacoste is happy to see you now. The second door on the left."

Shaye forced herself to maintain a walk, albeit a quick one, to Lacoste's office. She rapped on the door and heard a voice inside calling for her to enter. She walked into the room and took note of the distinguished, silver-haired man who rose from the desk and came over to greet her, hand extended.

"I'm sorry you were delayed in getting in to see me," he said. "It's a pleasure to meet you."

"Don't apologize. Your receptionist was doing her job, and I barged in here without so much as a phone call, much less an appointment."

"Please." He waved a hand at two chairs in front of his desk. "Can I offer you something to drink?"

"No. Thank you," she said as she sat. "I don't want to take up too much of your time."

He nodded and took his seat. "The receptionist said you had a matter of some urgency that you needed to speak to me about, and that it might involve the police?"

"The police are looking for a missing girl who I think was abducted by the same man I'm looking for."

Lacoste frowned. "And you think I might have

knowledge of this person?"

"Not directly. The identity of the man is what I've been working to determine. My investigation has led me to believe the man I'm looking for might be an illegitimate child of one of your clients, Jonal Derameau."

Lacoste's eyes widened. "Mr. Derameau was an interesting and difficult man. So private that he made it hard for me to do my job. I didn't even know his home address until days before his death."

"Didn't you find that odd?"

"Of course, but Mr. Derameau owned several nightclubs in New Orleans and there were rumors of business that transpired there—the kind of business that the police and the IRS might be interested in. I had no direct knowledge or proof of anything of that nature, but I assumed it might be true and that was the reason for Mr. Derameau's secrecy."

"I see."

"You said you believe one of Mr. Derameau's children abducted a child?"

"I'm not certain, but some facts in the case have led me to this line of investigation. I hoped that as his attorney, you'd have an idea as to where I might find Mr. Derameau's children, or at least start looking."

Lacoste shook his head. "I knew, of course, that he had children. All illegitimate. Mr. Derameau was never married that I am aware of. When I drafted his will, he told me that he had settled with the mothers and children years ago and that there would be no claims to his estate upon his death. I was skeptical, of course, but his words turned out to be truthful. Not a single person has contacted me claiming to be a relative of Mr. Derameau. In fact, no one has ever contacted me about Mr. Derameau until today."

Disappointment coursed through her and her shoulders slumped. Every time she thought she was close, another wall was erected.

"I can't help you locate Mr. Derameau's children," he continued, "but I can give you the information I have on someone who might be able to help you. If she's still alive."

"Who?"

"Mr. Derameau always referred to her as his maid, but I suspect he regarded her as more than just hired help. She handled everything in his household and cared for Mr. Derameau as he aged. She lived in the home with him for many years. I never got the impression that the relationship was romantic, mind you, but I am certain Mr. Derameau had a lot of respect and affection for the woman. In fact, he left his considerable fortune to her."

Shaye's disappointment melted away. If the maid had lived with and cared for Derameau, then she might be the only person who knew the man's secrets. "I would love her information, if you don't mind providing it."

"Of course not. I know your grandfather through a couple of business dealings and your mother from charity events. I've followed your story, of course, as I'm sure most of the city has. You're clearly not someone looking for the next sensational feather to put in your cap. In fact, I suspect you do as much as possible to avoid being the news, which I imagine is a challenge."

"It definitely can be."

He tapped on his computer and jotted down a name and address on a piece of paper, then handed it to Shaye.

"I really appreciate your help."

He nodded. "You were instrumental in taking down that Clancy monster, and that was a service to this city and all of humanity. If I can play even the smallest role in helping you get another one off the streets, then I'm more than happy to do it."

Shaye rose from her chair and he followed. She extended her hand. "It was a pleasure meeting you, sir."

"The pleasure was all mine."

Shaye could barely contain her excitement as she exited the law firm and got into her car. A quick search of the address Lacoste had provided showed that Jonal Derameau's maid, Anna Washington, still resided there. Fingers crossed that she was still alive and kicking in her home, Shaye directed her car toward the Audubon District.

With all the traffic lights and a steady flow of vehicles, the drive took a good thirty minutes, which was about twenty-nine minutes more than Shaye had been prepared to handle. By the time she parked at the curb in front of the attractive white home, she was so jittery she had to take a few minutes to calm down.

Finally, she climbed out of her SUV and headed to the

front door. She rang the doorbell and waited. She was just about to ring it again when she heard footsteps inside and then the door opened a crack. The black woman who looked out at her was probably in her sixties. She was slim and attractive, and wore gray slacks and a cream silk blouse.

"Can I help you?" she asked.

"Are you Anna Washington?" Shaye asked.

"Who's inquiring?"

"I'm sorry." Shaye reached into her purse and pulled out a business card. "My name is Shaye Archer. I'd like to ask you some questions about Jonal Derameau's children."

The woman took the card and her eyes widened. "I think you need to come inside." She stepped back and opened the door wide so that Shaye could enter. Shaye stepped inside, and the woman motioned to her as she set out across the formal living room toward the back of the house.

Shaye followed her through a doorway and into the kitchen. A wide expanse of white marble complemented beautifully crafted cabinets painted a slate color. The woman motioned for her to sit and Shaye took a seat on one of the stools at the counter. The woman pulled a pitcher of iced tea from her refrigerator and poured them both a glass. Shaye noticed that her hands shook as she placed the glass in front of Shaye.

"I'm Anna Washington," the woman said finally. "I apologize for my nerves, but I never really expected for you to come."

"I don't understand."

"Neither do I, but I'll explain what I know. The rest is up to you to figure out." Anna took a drink of tea, then slid onto a stool across from Shaye. "I took care of Mr. Derameau and his estate for almost thirty years. He was a hard man, cold even, but he always treated me fairly and far more than fair in death."

"He left everything to you."

She nodded. "Right before he died, something happened. I was visiting my sister and he called, claiming there had been an intruder at the estate and asking me to stay over with my sister until he could ensure the house was secure. The next morning, a nurse at New Orleans General called my sister's house saying a man with her phone number in his wallet had collapsed in front of a nightclub in the French Quarter and had been brought into the emergency room the night before. He had no identification on him and they were trying to locate the next of kin."

"What had happened to him?"

"He had a bad heart. He had already suffered one heart attack but he was strong as an ox, even for his age, and refused to let it get him. Same thing happened this time, but what I don't know, and what he'd never tell me, was why he was in the French Quarter and why he'd asked me to stay at my sister's house. There was no sign of an intruder at the estate."

"What did he say when you asked him?"

"Only that it was something I never needed to know. Mr. Derameau was a very private man. He wasn't one to talk about his personal business, but I knew something terrible had happened. Something that made his heart give out for good. He died two weeks later."

"You said you never expected for me to come? Why? Why me?"

"Not you specifically, but before he died, Mr. Derameau gave me instructions. He said if anyone showed up here asking about his children, I was to give them something. I'll be the first to admit, I thought the heart attack had affected his mind."

"Mr. Derameau was well off. It isn't really a stretch to think his children might come seeking a share of his estate."

"Mr. Derameau set up trusts for the mothers and the children when they were born. He was very generous. The money is paid out over their lifetime in monthly increments. It was enough money so that invested well, none would ever have to worry about the basics being paid. But there was one condition. No one could contact Mr. Derameau. Not for any reason. If a mother contacted him, she and her child would have their trust revoked. The same for the children. If they attempted to locate and contact Mr. Derameau, their trust and their mother's would be revoked."

"Mr. Derameau really didn't want to be a father, did he?"

"Mr. Derameau had demons and I believe he insulated himself to protect others from them as much as to protect himself. Every afternoon, I spent an hour reading the Bible on the back patio. He'd started coming out there when I read and asked me to read some passages to him and explain them. I think right there at the end, he was on the threshold of a conversion. I pray every day that he was close enough."

"He didn't have any other family?"

"None living. He told me once he had a sister but she died young."

"What did he tell you to give the person who came asking?"

"Wait just a minute and I'll get it." She rose from the stool and headed through a door off the back of the kitchen. She returned a couple minutes later with an ornate wooden box, about a foot long and eight inches wide, and placed it on the counter. Then she pulled an iron key out of her pocket and placed it on top of the box.

Shaye ran a finger across the top of the box. "What's in it?"

Anna shook her head. "I don't know, and I don't think I want to."

Shaye looked up at her and frowned.

"I know who you are, Ms. Archer, and I know your story. Many people think I'm slow because I usually don't say much, but nothing could be further from the truth. The fact that Mr. Derameau had another heart attack and was found in the French Quarter the same night you were brought into the hospital isn't lost on me."

"You think he was involved somehow?"

"I don't think he did those things to you, if that's what you're asking, but you're here, asking about his children, and I wonder. But the answers might not be what I want to hear. I prefer to remember Mr. Derameau the way I knew him. I hope you can respect that."

"I can respect it, but I can only control my own actions as I move forward with this."

Anna nodded and Shaye could tell by the fear and sadness in her expression that she knew the score. Shaye could promise not to tell Anna the truth, but if Jonal Derameau had anything to do with the man who'd abused her, then every news station in the city would be broadcasting it day and night.

"I hope you find what you seek," Anna said. "I know we're supposed to find comfort in the Lord, but I also know there's times in a person's life when we need more. When we need answers on this earth and can't wait for heaven to take away the pain. I'll pray for you."

"Thank you, Ms. Washington. I hope you never need my services, but if you do, please don't hesitate to call."

Anna nodded and followed her to the door. Shaye glanced up at the house as she pulled away and saw her standing there in the front window, the worry on her face plain as day. Shaye made it around the block and parked, then reached for the box, unable to wait another second to see what was inside.

She unlocked the box with the old-fashioned key and lifted the lid. Inside was a leather-bound book. She lifted it out and opened it up. Scrawling handwriting filled the pages. The front page contained only three lines.

A confession of things I have done.

May God forgive me.
Jonal Derameau

Shaye's hands tightened on the edges of the journal and she flipped to the first page and started to read. Jonal's confession began in 1936 on Belles Fleurs sugar cane plantation. The name of the plantation sounded vaguely familiar, but most had changed hands and names once sugar cane farming became a losing proposition. She didn't think it was still operating under that name now, if it was operating at all.

She read about how Jonal convinced the plantation owner's son that he could summon a demon to deal with his abusive father. About how the plantation owner had raped his mother and she'd given birth to him from it. And how Jonal had caught the owner looking at his ten-year-old sister and knew he had to stop the man from raping her as well.

Anger coursed through her at what the young Jonal had been forced to endure. No matter how long she lived or how long she discussed this topic with Eleonore, Shaye would never understand how one human being could treat another as an object—something that didn't merit even basic respect and treatment. Sociopaths were an exception in that they had no conscience, but the world also had a large number of people who were simply cruel and some who were evil for no other reason than they enjoyed it.

She flipped the pages, scanning them, trying not to get slowed by reading too extensively. She paused long enough to read the section on how he extorted money from the plantation owner's son, who'd been very successful. How Jonal had used the money to make himself rich and how he'd ensured that the man's son would be forced to comply with Jonal's demands as his father had.

She took in a breath and slowly blew it out. Jonal Derameau had a lot of sins to confess. If he'd truly had a conversion in spirit, like Anna hoped, then he must have spent a lot of hours bending God's ear. She forced herself to move past the pages that detailed the extortion and explained the video and the pictures. There would be time to process the entire document later, but right now, what she wanted was information on Jonal's children. She turned page after page, her gaze flickering from top to bottom, but there was no mention of children until close to the end.

He says I'm his father, but I know I'm not.

She clutched the book and began to read about how the young man had secured a position in Jonal's house without Jonal or Anna knowing his agenda. How he claimed to be a real worshipper of something he called the One and how he'd mocked Jonal for being a simple thief and a fraud. How he'd stolen the video, pictures, and brand from Jonal's hiding place. How he would gain power through the One and the world would bow to him.

Then she read about how Jonal waited until he was strong enough and went to the man's home. When she got to the part where he saw a human leg hanging out of the bundle that the man carried into the house, she choked back a cry, already knowing what was coming. She read so quickly, the words began to blur, the other people, the goat mask, the room with the altar and the candles, Jonal shooting the man and burning the film and pictures, then carrying her from the house. Lastly, the drive to New Orleans and him placing her on the sidewalk where the cops could find her.

The journal contained only one more entry.

Emile Samba.

Below that, directions to his home.

CHAPTER TWENTY-FIVE

Jackson stood on the sidewalk and watched as Shaye's SUV raced up the street toward his apartment and came to an abrupt stop in front of him. Before he could make a move, she pushed the driver's door open and jumped out.

"I need you to drive," she said, then ran around to the passenger's side.

Completely confused but feeling the urgency of the situation, Jackson hopped into the driver's seat and looked over at her. "Where are we going?"

She looked at Jackson, her excitement clear. "I found him."

Jackson stared. "Him? Goat mask?"

She nodded and gave him a quick rundown on Clara and the medical records, her visit to the attorney, her conversation with the maid, and the journal the maid had given her.

"I have his home address!" Shaye exclaimed. "The place where he held me captive. It's north of here set back in the woods. That's the place where Jonal rescued me."

"Whoa. This Jonal rescued you? From goat mask's house?"

"I'll explain everything on the way, but we have to get there. The other girl might still be alive. We have to save her."

Jackson understood the urgency as well as Shaye did, but what she hadn't seemed to process thoroughly was the risk. "You want just the two of us to go there? Without backup?"

"Who would you get for backup? If you ask for police backup then whoever is working with this man will alert him. He'll kill the girl and escape, and since we know who he is now, he'll never return. We'll lose him forever."

Jackson knew she was right but he didn't like the idea of just the two of them approaching a house in the middle of nowhere. They'd done it before, but Jackson also knew they'd gotten lucky. This killer might have all kinds of booby traps waiting for them, and if he had followers, they could be sitting in the woods just waiting for someone to show up.

"What about Harold?" Jackson asked. "We trust him and I like our odds better with three."

Shaye yanked her phone out and dialed. When Harold answered, she blurted out, "I found his house. Jackson and I are going there now and need backup."

There was a pause, then she disconnected. "Pick him up at the Ritz."

Jackson put the SUV in Drive and pulled away from the curb, directing the car toward the Ritz. It wasn't far from his apartment, and he made the drive quickly. Shaye was silent the entire time, flipping through the pages of the journal.

Harold was standing on the curb in front of the hotel, holding a duffel bag. He tossed it in the backseat and jumped in beside it. "Thought I'd better bring all my weapons and ammo," he said. "Fill me in."

Jackson nodded. "And tell me where I'm going."

Shaye gave Jackson directions, then started at the beginning, this time going into greater length about what she'd found and what she'd read in the journal, sometimes stopping her own narrative to read passages from the journal.

"That's incredible," Harold said. "So this Jonal used the witchcraft, or whatever, to extort money out of the plantation owner's son but Emile is the real deal. Not meaning he can summon a demon, but he thinks he can?"

"That's what Jonal thought. He says here that Emile's mother killed herself in an asylum. I don't think Emile came from mentally healthy stock, then add his daddy issues on top of it, along with his thirst for power, and you have the perfect storm."

Jackson's mind reeled, trying to process everything Shaye had said and read. It was incredible how much damage had been done by one person's desire for revenge, even though Jackson could understand Jonal's reasons for it.

"The brand with the initials," Harold said. "That's why someone in the police department hid evidence. Someone in the department is the plantation owner's grandson. Emile blackmailed him with the film and photos."

Jackson glanced back at Harold, a sense of dread coming over him. He looked over at Shaye. "You said the son made his money in manufacturing, right?"

She nodded. "Why?"

"Grayson," Jackson said, feeling completely ill. "He has this metal thing on his key ring and said it was something his father's company made. He said he was an unexpected late arrival for his parents and an only child. His father died when he was young. The company went under before that."

"All of that fits," Shaye said.

"He requested me as his partner," Jackson said, barely able to force the words out.

"Knowing you were close to Shaye," Harold said. "Jesus."

Everything flooded back to Jackson in a matter of seconds. Grayson's compliments on Jackson's "radar." His insistence that he wanted to hear any theory Jackson developed, regardless of how far-fetched. His interest in Shaye and Corrine. His request to work on the Clancy files.

"I'm sorry," Shaye said.

Jackson shook his head. "And I was beginning to think it was Vincent."

"Why?" Shaye asked.

Jackson told them about Vincent's voodoo shop visit.

Harold frowned. "There are rumors that shop sells the kind of herb that isn't legal."

"Pot?" Jackson asked. "You think Vincent is smoking pot?"

"There were rumors," Harold said, "but I don't think anyone cared enough to look into it."

"Well, at least we know now that it's Grayson," Jackson said. "But I have no idea how to prove it or what to do about it."

"Don't worry about that now," Harold said. "We have a much bigger issue to handle."

"The girl," Shaye said.

"Reagan Dugas," Jackson said. "Corrine called me earlier. She thinks that's who the girl is."

"We have to be careful not to catch her in the cross fire," Shaye said.

"Okay, so let's talk about how we're going to handle this," Jackson said. "According to the satellite image Shaye pulled up, the house is in the middle of the forest, with only one road in or out. With only one way in, he'll see us coming."

Harold nodded. "Depending on how dense the forest is, we'll have to abandon the car at some point and continue on foot. It will be dark soon, and that should help us stay out of sight."

"Yeah, but it helps him as well," Jackson said, "and it's his turf."

"It's not ideal," Harold agreed, "but we have surprise on our side. He doesn't know he's been exposed. He's afraid it will happen, but with us keeping it among ourselves, he's not aware that it has."

Jackson glanced over at Shaye. "Let's hope that's enough."

He was more worried about her than anything else. All three of them were willingly putting themselves in a dangerous situation, but only one of them would literally be confronting the demon from her past. What if she got face-to-face with him and froze? What if he got the jump on them and he couldn't save her? She would die at the hand of the one person in the world she feared the most. It was the most horrible thing he could imagine, and it was also a very real possibility.

"When we get there," Jackson said to Shaye, "maybe you should hang back. At least until we secure the house."

Shaye shook her head. "No way. You said it was a dangerous move with just two of us. Without me, you're back to two."

Jackson struggled to hide his frustration, knowing he was fighting a losing battle. Short of handcuffing Shaye to the vehicle, he wasn't going to keep her from going to that house. The worst part was, he couldn't blame her. If the situation were reversed, he'd be running in, guns blazing. How could he expect her to react differently?

"The turnoff should be right up here," Shaye said.

Jackson scanned the side of the road, looking for the entry point, and finally spotted a dirt road, almost hidden by the weeds and disappearing sunlight. He turned right, and the SUV disappeared into a canopy of brush and trees, what was left of the sunlight extinguishing as he drove. The poorly maintained road forced him to cut his speed in half, and he clutched the steering wheel as the ruts attempted to yank it one direction, then another.

"How much farther?" he asked.

"I don't know," Shaye said. "My service dropped."

Jackson checked his phone. "Mine too."

"And mine," Harold said.

"Good thing we had no intention of calling for backup," Jackson said.

"The journal said the house was several miles into the forest," Shaye said. "Depending on Jonal's definition of 'several' that could mean three or eight or something else entirely."

"Did you form an opinion based on the satellite image?" Jackson asked.

"If I had to guess, I'd say about five miles," Shaye said, "assuming the structure I could see is the one we're looking for. In nine years' time, things could have changed." She blew out a breath. "For all we know, the whole house might be gone and Emile has set up shop somewhere else."

"Let's assume the best," Harold said, "until we know otherwise. If it makes you feel any better, I have a feeling about this. I'm getting edgy, you know?"

Jackson nodded. He knew exactly what Harold was talking about and he felt it himself. It was anticipation bundled with excitement tied up in adrenaline, and when he felt this way, it usually meant something big was about to happen. Jackson just prayed that the three of them were left standing to tell everyone about it when it was over. He didn't have the same desire for Emile. The truth was, he really hoped Emile engaged. The last thing he wanted to think about was Shaye having to deal with that psycho's trial.

"We've gone four miles since we left the road," Jackson said. "I don't see any lights ahead, but it's so dense, I don't know that we would see anything unless we were directly on top of it."

"Go a little farther," Harold suggested, "and then stop. One of us can run ahead and do some reconnaissance."

Jackson went another three-quarters of a mile, then slowed to a stop. Shaye pulled a flashlight out of her glove box and started to get out of the SUV. "Where do you think you're going?" he asked.

"To check ahead," Shaye said. "I run ten miles three times a week."

He already knew it was useless to argue, even though his own workout matched Shaye's. "Stop as soon as you see something and come back. Do not approach the house alone."

"I'm determined," Shaye said. "Not crazy."

She jumped out of the SUV and set off ahead of them at a good clip. Within a couple seconds, all Jackson could see was the light from the flashlight moving farther and farther away until finally, he didn't see it at all.

"Must be a bend in the road," Harold said.

Jackson nodded, mentally counting the seconds since the light had disappeared. He'd reached thirty when the light reappeared, growing larger as it moved closer. Seconds later, she opened the door, her face flushed.

"The house is about fifty yards and to the left. There's a light on inside and an old pickup truck parked out front."

"No other vehicles?" Jackson asked.

Shaye shook her head. "No garage or barn, either."

"We still can't assume he's alone," Harold said, "but I like the odds." He opened his duffel bag and pulled out two pistols and several magazines. He placed the pistols into holsters at his waist and ankle, then stuffed the magazines in his pockets.

Jackson checked his magazine and spare, took a flashlight from Harold, and looked over at Shaye. "Are you ready?"

"I've been waiting nine years for this."

Reagan clutched the homemade dagger and slumped in the corner. She hoped it looked like she'd leaned against the wall, then slid down it as the drugs kicked in, because having her legs beneath her in a crouching position offered her more leverage for a strike. The key was patience, and that was going to be the hardest part. She had to wait until that monster was close enough to her that she was certain she could stab him where it counted. If she moved too soon, he might be able to block her, and then her advantage would be lost.

And there would be no second chances.

She'd heard scuffling above her, as she always did when he was coming, but this time, instead of dreading his arrival, it seemed as if she'd been waiting forever. At one point, she wondered if he wasn't coming at all, but then she decided it was because she wasn't drugged that it seemed to take so long. And because of her plan. The anticipation had her nerves on end. She was practically shaking from it.

Most people probably never experienced anything like this—having to get one thing perfect and knowing they'd die if they didn't. Combat military did, and some firefighters and cops, but that was a small amount of people compared with everyone in the country. The average person died in a car wreck or of some disease and didn't have an opportunity to change it. She had an opportunity, but it was a very narrow one, and required skills she didn't necessarily possess.

You can do this.

She'd been telling herself that all day, and she'd keep saying it over and over and over again, until she was far away from this pit of hell and the devil that controlled it.

The sound of the door sliding open made her stiffen and suck in a breath. She forced herself to loosen her shoulders back to the slump, in order to appear semiconscious. Her plan wouldn't work unless she caught him unaware. She heard the footsteps coming down the stone steps and forced herself to remain relaxed but as he grew closer, it became harder and harder to stay loose.

When he was right in front of her, she opened her eyes a tiny bit—just enough to ascertain his body positioning—then as he reached for his pocket to pull out the needle he would use to knock her completely out, she gathered all of her strength, anger, and will to live and sprang.

She swung the dagger directly at his crotch but he

managed to partially block her and she hit him in the thigh instead. He screamed in pain and she kicked him as hard as possible. The kick threw him off balance and he fell backward, dropping the needle and the key. She jumped over him, but he managed to grab her foot as she went.

She hit the ground, hands first, then her knees crashed into the stone and pain shot through her entire body. She kicked at his head, but he held fast to her foot with one hand while he reached for the needle with the other. She flipped her entire body over and got a good shot directly into his face, but as she connected, he shoved the needle into her calf.

She yanked back before he could finish plunging the needle into her, but any amount of the poison in her bloodstream was a problem. She grabbed the key from the floor and bolted for the steps, pulling the needle out as she ran. When she reached the top of the stairs, she heard what sounded like a small explosion behind her. Bits of the door splintered and the pieces hit her face, cutting her skin.

He was shooting at her!

She jammed the key in the lock and turned it, then shoved the door open and ran out, stopping when she realized she was in the middle of a forest and not the city. She glanced back and her stomach rolled when she realized she'd been held in a crypt. She had no way to know which direction would get her to safety, or even how far it was from here, but she couldn't afford to stick around.

With the dense brush and trees and only a little bit of moonlight, it didn't leave her much to work with. She looked down at the ground surrounding her and saw a section of the brush that was flatter than the rest. That must be the path out of here.

She set off at a slow jog, unable to move any faster without risking going off the path. The stones and briars tore at her bare feet, but she clenched her jaw and kept moving, trying to ignore the pain. As soon as the masked man got that dagger out of his leg, she had no doubt he'd be right behind her. Staying on this trail wasn't an option, but maybe she could make it far enough to find a road with passing cars. If not, she'd find a place to hide until morning.

When she reached a fork in the trail she ripped off a piece of her ragged T-shirt and pulled the worn fabric onto a branch on the right trail, hoping to misdirect him, then she spun around and set out again on the left trail. She made it two steps, then stumbled. She grabbed a tree trunk to keep herself from falling and realized that she was starting to get dizzy.

The needle!

Enough of the drug must have made it into her system for it to affect her. She pushed herself off from the tree and started a slow jog down the trail, but as her vision blurred, she had to slow to a walk. She had to hide before she passed out. It was her only chance. She dropped onto her hands and knees and crawled into a set of thick brush and behind a huge cypress tree.

She leaned against the cypress tree and fought to stay conscious, but all of the energy was quickly draining from her body. This couldn't be how it ended. Not here.

Not with him.

CHAPTER TWENTY-SIX

Shaye turned off her flashlight and motioned to Jackson and Harold to do the same. Without the lights, they had only the tiny slivers of moonlight to see by, but it was enough to get them to the edge of the tree line where they peered around. The house was set back in a clearing, about twenty yards from where they stood, a single light shining inside. An old truck was parked on the side of the house. There were no exterior lights at all.

Jackson scanned the area and looked over at Harold. "I think the best approach is to skirt the tree line to the side of the house."

Harold nodded. "I agree. Too much open area between the front and back of the house and the woods. The side offers cover for longer."

They set out along the tree line. Without the flashlights, it was slow going. Every step was deliberate, and even then, it was difficult to move forward without encountering obstacles. Thorns grabbed at Shaye's pants leg, tearing at the denim. She clutched her pistol in her right hand and used her left to shield her face from the leaves and branches that slapped her body as she moved through them. There was no protection from the spiderwebs, and their silky strands on her bare arms combined with the muggy weather made her itch all over.

Moonlight flickered in and out of the dark clouds, occasionally giving them a patch of light to work with. They moved faster then, anxious to get to the house and confront the evil inside. When they finally reached the side of the home, they stopped and scanned the area. Light streaming from a side window at the back of the house provided a bit of illumination but it also provided a clear way for anyone looking out that window to see them approach.

Harold motioned for them to huddle up. "Here's the thing," he said, "regardless of what we all think or feel, we can't just go busting down the door, because we don't know for certain that the person inside is Emile. I don't want to go giving some eighty-year-old grandpa a heart attack because he had the misfortune to move into this house. Or give him an opportunity to fill us full of buckshot."

"Agreed," Jackson said. "But we don't know what Emile looks like, so even if we got a look at him, it wouldn't help."

"We need to get inside," Shaye said. "If Emile is living there, we'll know. He'll have things—the candles, the mask—that's enough to verify."

"Okay," Jackson said. "I'll move to the side of the house and try to get a look through that window. If the house looks clear, I'll move to the back and see if I can get inside. I'll signal to you if it's okay."

"And if it's not clear?" Shaye asked.

"I think this is where the 'busting down the door' part comes in," Harold said.

"I should be the one going in," Shaye said.

"Why?" Jackson asked. "Harold and I were trained for this and have done it hundreds of times between the two of us. And while Harold probably could have taken me twenty years ago, he's not in the shape I am now. I'm the best option."

Harold nodded. "He's right. We have to give ourselves the best opportunity of success and that's Jackson."

"Be careful," Shaye said.

Jackson clutched her shoulders with both hands. "If this guy is here, we're going to get him. We're not leaving until we do."

"Damn straight," Harold said.

Jackson stepped to the edge of the brush and looked both directions before dashing across the open patch to the side of the house. Shaye watched as he moved to the window and rose up to peer inside. He gave them a thumbs-up and headed for the rear of the house. Shaye and Harold moved down the tree line so that they had a clear shot to the back steps and stood in ready position as Jackson crept up the steps.

Jackson opened the back door and disappeared inside. Shaye mentally counted the seconds, each one seeming longer than the one before, until he finally leaned out the back door and motioned to them. Shaye hurried from the brush for the back of the house, Harold right behind her.

"There's no one inside?" Harold asked.

"No, but he's been here. There was a vial of something on the kitchen counter next to a package of needles. And there's a room with an altar and black candles."

Shaye's breath caught in her throat. "We found him."

"Then where is he?" Harold asked. "I don't like this. We're sitting ducks."

"He must have the girl somewhere else," Shaye said. "Somewhere nearby."

A pop sounded from the forest behind the house and they all froze.

"Did you hear that?" she asked.

Jackson nodded. "Gunfire."

Harold pointed to the woods behind the house. "It came from that direction."

"You're sure?" Jackson said. "Things tend to echo in the woods."

"Been hunting all my life," Harold said. "I'm sure."

Jackson took off across the lawn and Shaye sprinted after him, Harold following close behind. When they reached the tree line, they could make out a path that led into the forest, but as soon as they took a single step into the brush, the thick trees blocked the moonlight and pitched them into darkness.

They stopped and listened, but only the sounds of the night creatures filled the air. Jackson pulled out a penlight and located the path. "We have to risk it," he said. "Stay low and keep moving."

He set off down the trail, hunched over a bit and moving quickly. Shaye fell in step behind him, staying close enough to use his body to guide her down the trail. She could hear Harold right behind her. When they reached a fork in the trail, Jackson stopped and they checked both directions.

"Both have been traveled," Harold whispered. "The ground cover is too thick to tell if one is more recent than the other. The depressions in the taller grass are the same."

Jackson nodded. "You take the right. Shaye and I will take left."

Harold pulled out a penlight and headed to the right. Jackson set off down the left path and Shaye hurried behind him. The forest seemed to close in around her, and she held one hand in front of her face to try to keep the thick brush from scratching her. They were moving at a pretty good clip when suddenly Jackson stopped so quickly that Shaye almost ran into him.

He turned around and tapped her, then pointed in front of him. Shaye peered around him and saw a clearing with odd, square shadows that she couldn't make out in the dim light. She stepped closer and squinted and at that exact moment, the moon came out from behind a cloud and illuminated the area.

She sucked in a breath. It was a cemetery. She scanned the crumbling headstones and broken crosses, then tapped Jackson's arm. "There."

The crypt stood in the back of the cemetery, its stone sides covered with vines and moss, but the vines had been removed around the doorway and she could see it clearly, even from the distance and in dim light.

Jackson nodded. "Let's circle around."

They skirted the edge of the cemetery until they reached the crypt. Jackson dropped down and looked at the dirt. "Footprints."

"She's inside," Shaye said.

"There's only one way in. If he's in there, he'll pick us off when we walk inside."

"We can't leave her there."

"Of course not. Follow me."

Shaye followed him around the side of the crypt. He stopped in front of the door and put his ear to it, then shook his head. He motioned for her to stand on the side of the door and she stood right at the edge of the opening, her back pressed against the stone wall. Jackson pulled the latch back and grabbed the handle. He pulled the door open, moving to the side as he went. Shaye waited for the sound of gunfire, but nothing was forthcoming.

Shaye pulled out her flashlight and Jackson nodded. She clicked it on and was just about to peer into the opening when a shot rang out behind her. The bullet hit the stone wall right beside her head and she automatically ducked and darted into the opening. Jackson jumped back and around the side of the crypt.

"Are you hit?" Jackson called out.

"No. Go after him. I'm going to get the girl."

She heard Jackson's footsteps as he ran away from the crypt. She turned to face the inside of the crypt and shone her light ahead. One glance and she was glad she hadn't stepped two inches farther inside without looking. Otherwise, she would have fallen down the stone steps located right inside the opening.

Clutching the flashlight in her left hand and nine-millimeter in her right, she crept down the stairs, drawing in and expelling a breath with each step. Sweat formed on her brow and ran in rivulets, the salt stinging her eyes. Her heart pounded in her chest, and she counted each beat as she went.

What if the girl was already dead? What if the shot they heard earlier had killed her?

She shook her head and pushed forward. Until she knew for certain, she was moving forward with the assumption that the girl was alive. The walls on the side of the stairs ended and she ducked under a ceiling and looked into the room.

Her vision blurred and she clutched the overhang as a wave of nausea and dizziness raced through her. This was it. The room where he'd held her. Her prison for seven years.

And like a tidal wave, her entire life rushed back in.

CHAPTER TWENTY-SEVEN

Harold shone his penlight on the path and stayed low, hoping the brush hid any sign of the tiny light he was using. This path wasn't as heavily traveled as the one they'd been on before, but he could see signs of passage in the taller grass, which had been bent down and was just starting to lift back up. He clutched his pistol in his right hand as he went, praying that he got a clear shot at Emile Samba.

In his years on the force, he'd shot criminals on several occasions, and he didn't feel one ounce of guilt for the action he'd taken because they'd left him no other option, but this was the first time he'd actually hoped he'd get to shoot someone. The first time he'd wanted someone dead rather than standing in front of a jury. A jury would have no trouble convicting Emile Samba, but that meant Shaye and this other girl, if she were still alive, would have to go through the rigors and emotional heartbreak of a trial. The law might call that justice, but as a human being, Harold just considered it wrong.

If anyone deserved to die, it was Emile Samba.

He stepped in between two cypress trees and shone the light ahead, but a tall bank of weeds covered the trail.

He bent over and studied the ground, but it was clear that no one had passed this way in some time. He scanned the sides of the trail and noticed several depressions leading away from where he stood. He stepped into the brush and slowly moved forward, using the light to scan the ground as he went, then following the barely perceptible signs of passage.

When he reached a huge cypress tree, the ground cover cleared into solid packed dirt and he lost the trail. Cursing silently, he stepped up next to the tree and scanned the area, trying to figure out which direction to go next.

That's when he heard someone exhale.

He froze. The sound had come from the other side of the tree.

He moved his finger to the trigger, then whirled around the side of the tree, gun leveled and ready to fire. When he saw no one standing there, he was momentarily confused. Then he realized his foot had connected with something less solid than the tree. He looked down and saw the girl.

She was slumped down, her back against the tree, her head hanging forward and to the side. He squatted and put his fingers to her neck, letting out a breath of relief when he felt a pulse. It was faint, but it was there. He shone his light on her, looking for a gunshot wound, and saw the scars on her arms, but no sign of a bullet entering her body.

He lifted her head so that he could see her face and gasped. It was like looking at Shaye all over again. The gauntness of her face, the cuts, and bruises and scars. Anger coursed through him as every detail of the night flooded back through his mind as if it were yesterday.

He had to assume she'd been drugged. Maybe she'd gotten away, but when she could no longer continue, she'd left the path and hidden, hoping Emile wouldn't find her before the drug wore off. She needed medical attention.

Harold gathered her up and placed her over his shoulder. It wasn't the most comfortable position for her but she was unconscious, and this position allowed him to move quickly and still hold his gun. He headed back to the path, moving as fast as her weight and stealth allowed, pausing periodically to listen. He had to get the girl to safety. No way did he get this close and fail.

He'd helped save the one before and by God, he wasn't going to let this one die.

Jackson ran through the cemetery in the direction of the shot, leaping over the remnants of a picket fence when he reached the edge and skidding to a stop in the forest. He listened and heard movement off to his left, then another shot rang out. He dropped to the ground as the bullet ripped by his head, splintering wood off the tree behind him. He crawled deeper into the forest until no moonlight crept through the trees, then began to move toward the location of the second shot.

He knew he was at a severe disadvantage. Emile had lived here for a long time and probably knew the forest as well as Jackson knew the layout of the French Quarter. It wouldn't be difficult for him to hide and wait for Jackson to approach or to lead him into a trap. But those were risks he had to take. No way was he letting this monster get away. No way in hell.

He stopped behind a tree and listened, trying to pick up a sound, but all he heard was the rustling of the trees. He crouched and slipped around the tree, and when no shot was forthcoming, he hurried through the brush, farther away from the cemetery and the bit of moonlight that provided him illumination. Now he was operating in pure darkness. With every step forward, his mind filled with one question after another.

Had Emile returned to his house?

Was Reagan still alive?

Was Shaye all right?

What had happened to Harold?

He couldn't fool himself about the severity of the situation, even if he'd wanted to. They'd needed backup. The three of them weren't properly equipped to take a man on his own territory, especially this man. He'd avoided detection for a long time, something stupid people couldn't manage. But if Jackson had asked for backup, he would have asked Grayson, and that would have been a fatal error because then Emile would have been tipped off that they were coming. He could have waited for them in the forest and picked them off, one by one, as they approached his house.

A stick snapped somewhere off to his right and he

turned that direction. When he reached a small clearing, he studied the loose dirt and saw footprints leading right. He set off in that direction and then realized he had made a big loop and was headed back to the cemetery.

Emile had circled around.

He was going after Shaye.

Shaye's legs collapsed beneath her and she slumped down onto the stairs, unable to draw in a breath. Her chest ached, and her head felt as if it were being split in two. Every second of her life rolled through her mind like a horror movie on high speed. Every atrocity, every minute of abuse, every tear, every cry for help, every plea for her freedom, her attempt to take her own life, and finally ending on that street in the French Quarter, when she awakened on the sidewalk and stumbled into the street before collapsing in Harold Beaumont's arms.

She hung her head down between her legs, desperately trying to draw in a breath. It felt as if a giant iron band had been placed around her chest and was preventing any air from entering her body. Every inch of her skin itched and burned, and with even the slightest of movement, her head throbbed harder until she wanted to scream with the pain.

Reagan!

The girl's name ripped through her mind, breaking up the running film of terror. She had to save her. Had to get her out of this pit of hell and back to New Orleans where there were people who could help her have a normal life again.

The breath she'd been trying to draw finally filled her lungs, and her chest ached and burned from the effort. Her eyes watered and she slowly blew the breath out, trying to calm her racing heart, then drew in another breath. This time it was easier.

After a third intake of air, she pushed herself up from the stairs, wobbling as she rose. She leaned against the stone wall that was on one side of the stairs to help stabilize herself, then shone her flashlight into the crypt. Slowly, she scanned every inch of the space as she crept down the stairs, praying that she'd find Reagan alive.

Panic coursed through her when she realized the room was empty. Had Emile shot her and removed her from the room? She stepped off the stairs and shone her light on the floor, looking for any clue as to what had happened here. In the far corner, she caught sight of a dark spot on the ground. She hurried over and crouched down, panicking all over again when she realized the spot was blood.

A couple feet away was an odd-shaped piece of stone that also had bloodstains on it. She picked up the stone and studied it, then realized it had been sharpened into a knife. This didn't belong to Emile. He had a ceremonial knife. The crude structure of this one suggested it had been homemade, and the stone matched those that made up the floors and walls of the crypt. Reagan must have made this. She'd stabbed Emile to escape and he'd shot at her. The question was had he hit her? And more importantly, if she wasn't dead, where was she now?

She had to find Reagan. There was still a chance the girl was alive and if she was, then she desperately needed their help, especially if she'd been drugged. She rose from the squatting position but as she turned around, a gunshot roared through the tiny room.

The bullet hit her right biceps, ripping into the flesh and causing her to drop her gun. Clutching the biceps with her left hand, she scrambled to grab the pistol when a second shot zipped right by her head.

"Don't move again."

The blood rushed from her face at the sound of his voice. She'd didn't have to look up. She knew it was him. Wave after wave of panic coursed through her and she concentrated on keeping her legs from buckling. Her vision blurred and she looked at the stairs where she could barely make out the figure standing halfway down.

She blinked and her vision began to clear. Then she saw him, standing there wearing the robe and the goat mask. She cried out involuntarily, trying to control the feelings of dread, revulsion, and despair that threatened to take over her mind and deliver the final crushing blow that would break her forever.

"I told him to bring you to me," Emile said. "I knew he wouldn't, but you're here anyway."

"Were you and your sick buddies planning to kill me this time?"

"My followers weren't as committed as I was. They had to be sacrificed to protect his work. But now I can write the final chapter—just like I saw in the vision the One sent me. Killing you will allow me to ascend to my rightful place. I'll have power over mankind forever. I'll never die and for all of eternity, everyone will worship me or suffer the consequences."

"No one will ever worship you," Shaye said. "They'll strap you onto a bed and put a needle of death into your arm. You'll be forever known as the delusional monster that you are."

"I won't be caught. I can't be. Don't you understand? I am the messenger of death. I am the harbinger of all that is dark. I am the end."

Shaye scrambled to find something to keep him talking. Surely Jackson was tracking Emile and would come back here. "Then why are you using a gun? I thought you used a knife to serve the One."

"The One will understand, especially if I give him you. You're going to be his bride, you know? That was always your place…next to him in hell."

He leveled the gun at her, and what little strength she had left disappeared. She leaned back against the wall, trying to remain standing, but her body began a slow slide down the wall. Emile pulled the mask off with his left hand, the gun still clenched in his right, and smiled at her. His smile was even worse than the mask.

The words Shaye wanted to share with Corrine, Jackson, Eleonore, and all the other people who loved her and whom she loved rolled through her mind. All the things she would never have a chance to say to them, but most importantly, to thank them all for making her life the incredible experience it had been for the past nine years.

She closed her eyes and waited for the darkness that was coming.

When the sound of gunfire engulfed the tiny room, she cried out, knowing that pain was certain to follow long before she faded into black and no pain at all. But as the moments ticked by and only the pain in her arm remained, she opened her eyes and looked up.

Emile was collapsed facedown at the bottom of the stairs, blood seeping from under his head. Footsteps sounded on the stairs and she looked up as a set of black slacks began to come into view.

A wave of nausea passed through her. "No!"

She knew those pants and suddenly, she knew why the plantation name sounded familiar. She watched in horror as Pierce Archer descended into the crypt.

"You were the plantation owner's grandson," she said. "Jonal Derameau framed your father for murder and extorted millions from him. Then he drugged you and staged you performing an occult ritual with a girl on an altar so that he could take pictures and video, guaranteeing that if he needed more money, you would have to comply like your father did."

Pierce looked down at her, his shoulders slumped, his expression one of a man who'd reached bottom. "I'm so sorry, Shaye. I swear to you, I didn't know how to find him. Until this moment, I didn't even know his name. I don't know the name of the man I killed, either."

"Emile Samba. You might not have known his name, but you knew he was my captor. You saw the brand."

"I recognized the brand when you were found, but I had no way of finding the man who did it. I saw the man who framed my father and I only once, after my father's funeral. He wasn't a young man then, so when decades passed and I never heard anything, I thought he had died. I thought I was finally free. Then this…thing contacted me today. He told me he had the brand, pictures, and video and he wanted to exchange them for you."

"You could have told the police where to find him," Shaye said.

"Then everyone would have known. It would have ruined my life and yours and Corrine's. I came here tonight to kill him. To end this forever. I didn't know that you'd be here. I didn't know that you knew about my father and me."

"Jonal left a journal that confessed everything he did, including rescuing me. Emile's name and address was in the journal."

"And now you know it all. I failed. The scandal will ruin everything my father and I worked for. Everything that you and Corrine accomplished for yourselves."

"You didn't do anything wrong."

"I knew my father plotted to murder my grandfather. I knew the man who held you captive was somehow related to all of that. And I never told the police. Maybe if I had, they would have been able to find him sooner. Before he could torture another child."

Shaye looked down at the ground for several seconds before looking back up at him. She couldn't argue with him on those points. Even though she understood his reasons, she also believed he should have told the truth all those years ago. And then something else occurred to her.

"You made sure Corrine got custody of me, didn't you?" she asked.

He nodded. "If you ever remembered, I wanted to know. I wanted to find the man who did that to you and kill him, and being close to you was the easiest way to know if your memory returned. But my feelings for you were never a lie. You *are* my granddaughter. I swear that helping Corrine get custody wasn't about me. I wanted to help you. But not telling the cops what I knew was selfish. I won't make that mistake again."

Fear coursed through her. "What are you saying?"

He looked down at her, completely defeated, ultimately miserable, and so very sad. "I love you, Shaye. Tell Corrine I love her more than anything in the world. You won't have to stand by me through an investigation. I won't do that to you. This all ends now."

"No!" Shaye launched up from the ground but it was too late.

Pierce Archer placed the gun in his mouth and pulled the trigger.

CHAPTER TWENTY-EIGHT

Wednesday, July 29, 2015
Algiers Point, New Orleans, Louisiana

Harold Beaumont knocked on the front door but no one answered. He twisted the knob and the door opened. He stepped inside the living room that he'd been in a hundred times before and glanced around. Everything was in its place. Every lamp, vase, and potted plant. Just like it had been before the man's wife died three years before.

He walked toward the back of the house, where the kitchen was located, figuring he'd find the man he sought there. He was right. The man sat at the kitchen table, a half-empty bottle of whiskey in front of him. He looked up as Harold entered the room, then sighed.

"When I heard you were in the middle of this, I knew you'd figure it out," he said.

Harold pulled out a chair and sat across from the man who'd served as his police chief for fifteen years of his career. "Jonal Derameau only told the story of a single plantation owner in his journal—Pierce Archer's grandfather. But when I did some poking around, I found that not one but three plantation owners died within a two week period, each with a single son as an heir."

Bernard looked out the kitchen window but didn't respond.

"I figure," Harold continued, "that Jonal saw the news about Corrine Archer getting custody of the girl he'd rescued, and he wrote that journal because he knew if anyone ever came looking for him, it would be about the girl. The journal was his way of protecting both Shaye and Pierce. He probably thought you were safe."

Bernard shook his head. "Jonal was an old man who didn't think everything through. Otherwise he would have known that people wouldn't be able to leave this alone. Not until the entire story was told."

"I don't know the entire story, but I think I know enough. I remember you telling me that your father inherited a plantation when he was still a teen. That he lost everything when he had to go to war. That he came home and joined the New Orleans police force. He didn't have money to offer Jonal Derameau, but he could do his best to keep the police from investigating the gambling and drug trafficking that went on in Jonal's clubs."

"My father told me he tried to find Jonal, but he was a ghost. No one knew where he lived or how to contact him."

"Do you believe that's the truth?"

Bernard shrugged. "I don't know. Jonal told my father that he'd left documents with an attorney and that if he died by anything other than natural causes, those documents would become public."

"And then later, Jonal framed you so that he ensured your cooperation once your father retired."

"He never asked me for anything," Bernard said. "I saw him one time only—after my father's funeral. He reminded me of the power he had over me, but I never heard from him again. I wasn't really surprised. I think the clubs had gone legit years before. Hell, maybe he didn't even own them any longer. He was probably just making sure I never talked."

"That's a good possibility."

"I didn't do those awful things—in the film, those pictures. You have to believe me."

"I believe you. Jonal drugged Pierce. He said so in his journal. Everything was staged for Pierce as I'm certain it was staged for you."

Bernard looked at Harold, clearly miserable. "I destroyed evidence from Shaye Archer's case file and lied to you about it. I recognized the brand and I knew what it would tie me to."

"But you didn't know who her captor was or how to find him." Harold leaned on the table. "You're not to blame for what Jonal or Emile did, but there is one thing you are responsible for. You gave Emile my home address. There is no other way he could have found me."

Bernard's eyes widened. "No! I never gave him your address, even when he demanded it. I lied to him and told him our records had never been updated after you moved." Bernard frowned. "But I think someone was in my house a couple weeks ago. The back door was unlocked, but since nothing was missing, I assumed I'd forgotten to lock it myself."

"You have my address here?"

"In a book in my desk. I didn't remember until now."

Harold sighed. He believed Bernard was telling the truth but that didn't change the fact that he'd destroyed evidence and failed to report his contact with Emile. Harold understood the impossible position Bernard and Pierce had been placed in, but he still liked to think he would have handled things differently.

"What are you going to do?" Harold asked.

Harold had no doubt there would be an investigation. Jonal's journal and Pierce's suicide had unleashed a media storm like he'd never seen before. When the police and the media dug up the same information Harold had—that three plantation owners had died in a short time frame, not just one—their next step would be identifying those sons. It was a short jump to Bernard as one of the grandsons. His entire career would come under scrutiny. Every decision he'd ever made would be gone over with a fine-toothed comb.

"I'll turn in my resignation tomorrow," Bernard said. "I'll lose my pension, my reputation, and the respect of everyone who ever served with me or under me. Ultimately, I could lose my freedom."

"I think the mitigating circumstances and your record hold enough weight to keep your freedom."

"Maybe." He stared at Harold. "But do I deserve it?"

Harold rose from the table, feeling old and tired for the first time since his retirement. "Only you can answer that." He left the house and got into his car, certain that he'd just seen Bernard for the last time.

The empty bottle of sleeping pills on his counter hadn't gone unnoticed.

CHAPTER TWENTY-NINE

One week later

Jackson entered the building, his usual swagger completely gone. It had been the hardest week of his life. Pierce's suicide, Shaye's collapse, Chief Bernard's suicide, and the thousands of hours of media attention had turned the police department and his personal life into a circus. Walking up to the building, he fended off two crews of reporters camped out on the sidewalk. Unfortunately, his professional life wasn't much better, with the entire department under scrutiny and Grayson miffed at him once he'd figured out Jackson thought he had been the mole.

There were a few silver linings. Emile Samba was dead and would never harm another child. Reagan Dugas had been placed with a foster family who were helping her heal. Dr. Thompson had finally awakened and it looked like he was going to be fine. And Clara Mandeville was on the mend in the comfort of her own home, without having to worry about another attack.

Jackson knocked on the door and because he didn't expect her to answer, he called out. "It's Jackson Lamotte."

He heard rustling inside, and a minute later the door swung open and Eleonore Blanchet looked out at him. She motioned him inside and he walked into her office, noting the empty bottle of wine on her desk.

"Backsliding," she said, noticing his gaze. "The best I can say for it is at least it wasn't a bottle of the expensive stuff."

Jackson sat across from her and took in her appearance. The woman who always looked so put together now appeared to be falling apart. The dark circles under her eyes told of the many nights of lost sleep. The puffy eyelids and bloodshot eyes belied the tears she'd shed. The slump of her shoulders and sagging jaw were those of a woman who'd been emotionally beaten down.

"Are you okay?" he asked, even though the answer was right in front of him.

"If you have to ask, you already know the answer."

He nodded. "I know you can't tell me anything relayed to you as her therapist, but can you tell me as her friend if Shaye is all right?"

Eleonore shook her head.

Jackson sighed. "I guess I already knew the answer to that question, too."

"They're devastated," Eleonore said. "So am I. Shaye's past rushing back in…Pierce's connection with Jonal and Emile…it's so much to process that they don't even know where to start. Honestly, neither do I."

Eleonore grabbed a tissue from the box on her desk and wiped her eyes. "For the first time in my career, I don't know how to help someone."

Jackson nodded. "And now it feels like everything you did right up until this point no longer counts."

Eleonore stared at him for a moment. "Yes. That's exactly it."

"Can you at least tell me if they're safe?"

The last time Jackson had seen Shaye was when she'd been put into an ambulance and taken to the hospital. She'd told him about Pierce before collapsing in the crypt. Corrine had been admitted as well, but no one would tell Jackson what had happened to her and no one but Eleonore was allowed in their rooms.

This morning, Jackson had gone to the hospital, as he had every day, hoping that this would be the time he could see them. But when he arrived, the desk nurse told him both Corrine and Shaye had been discharged the night before. He'd driven to Shaye's apartment and Corrine's house, but both appeared empty. By the time he'd driven to Eleonore's office, he was at wit's end.

"I'm sure they're safe," Eleonore said, "but I don't know where they are. Corrine asked me to bring their passports to the hospital. They left last night on Pierce's jet."

Jackson's mind eased a tiny bit. It wasn't the answer he wanted but it wasn't a horrible one, either. Getting away from New Orleans was probably the best thing they could do. Until the media found something new to focus on, they wouldn't have a moment's peace outside of their homes. And that was no way to live. After only a week of it,

Jackson was at the brink of asking for unpaid leave and going away himself.

"Will they be back?" he asked, even though he already knew the answer.

"I don't know."

"What do you think?"

"I think I miss them, and I love them, and more than anything I want them back but I don't want them to live the way they'd have to right now."

"Me either."

Eleonore gave him a sad smile. "You're a good man, Jackson, and you've been through hell yourself. If you ever want to talk, you know where to find me."

"Are you saying I need professional help?"

"We all need professional help, but I meant as my friend."

Anna Washington turned off the television and reached for the stack of mail she'd retrieved earlier from the box. The news had been filled with speculation about Mr. Derameau, that evil Emile Samba, Pierce Archer's suicide, and police involvement. She'd always thought Mr. Derameau went overboard with secrecy, even insisting that she not give anyone associated with him her full name.

But now she appreciated his reasons.

Every day she worried that someone would knock on her door. That someone would connect her with Mr.

Derameau and ask her to answer for the things he'd done. Ask her to answer for Emile Samba, who'd worked in Mr. Derameau's home. So far, her home remained quiet, but Anna knew that day of reckoning was coming. The attorney had provided her information to Shaye Archer and he would do the same for the police. Anna only hoped they believed her when she said she never knew about any of it.

She flipped through the envelopes, setting the junk mail in a stack for recycling. When she got to the last envelope, she frowned. It was hand-addressed to her but had no return address. She opened the envelope and slid out a single sheet of paper that contained three sentences.

In the end, Jonal did the right thing.
Your prayers weren't in vain.
Shaye Archer

Anna clutched the paper to her chest and began to cry.

Chapter Thirty

One month later

Shaye sat in a chair on the patio, looking over the cliff at the ocean below. Ultimately, Pierce had gotten his wish—she and Corrine had left the country. Under different circumstances, she would have thought the view beautiful, but at the moment, she couldn't appreciate it. Right now, the surf breaking against the rocks didn't look majestic. It looked bleak.

Just as everything felt.

"Do you need anything?" Corrine's voice sounded from inside the house behind her.

"I need you to sit down," Shaye said.

Corrine was trying to put on a brave front, but Shaye knew better. Pierce's suicide had shaken her mother to the core. The woman who had the emotional strength and heart to face any challenge life threw at her had finally met her match.

Corrine stepped out onto the patio and dropped into the chair next to Shaye. She handed Shaye a glass of iced tea and gazed out at the ocean, her expression completely vacant. Shaye took a drink of the tea and frowned.

"We can't stay here forever," Shaye said.

"Sure we can. We can buy the place if we want to."

"You know what I meant. Sooner or later, we have to go back to New Orleans and deal with this. The press is not going to go away. Not until they get their pound of flesh. No matter how long we stay, they will still be waiting for us when we return."

Corinne slapped her hands down on the arms of the chair. "Damn them! Why can't they leave us alone? Haven't we been through enough?"

Shaye didn't bother to reply because they both knew the answer.

Corrine turned to look at her. "Are you telling me you're ready? You're ready to face all the questions about your past? About your time with that monster?"

"I don't have to answer anything I don't want to. My injuries told the story nine years ago. I don't need to recount the gory details in order for people to know what happened to me. And I have no intention of doing so."

"But they'll ask."

"And I'll tell them to go to hell. Eventually, they'll go away." She turned to face her mother. "Look, as much as I hate it, you have responsibilities that you can't ignore much longer. You're the CEO of Archer Manufacturing. You need to take control."

"I have no desire to control Archer Manufacturing or any other business."

"You have to do something."

"I will. I'm going to sell it. All of it. The manufacturing company, the real estate, everything."

Shaye stared at Corrine for a bit, surprised at the conviction in her voice. It was the first time since leaving New Orleans that her mother had sounded so certain. It was both comforting and concerning. Granted, Corrine had never had an interest in her father's business, but Shaye wondered if selling was Corrine's way of separating herself from everything that had happened. Her way of dealing with Pierce's choice to leave her.

"What about you?" Corrine asked. "What are you going to do if we go back?"

"I'm going back to work."

Corrine's dismay was clear. "Not investigating. Please tell me you're not going to go right back into that dangerous line of work."

"There's nothing else I want to do. I can help people with what I do. People the police can't or won't help. And I have the luxury of not having to work for money if I want to. If I hadn't been there for Hustle, what would have happened to him or Jinx? To any of those street kids?"

"Someone else could do it," Corrine argued.

"But no one else wants to, and I don't want to do anything else."

"Are you really ready to take on that kind of work again? Seeing all the horrible things people do to each other?"

"What can I see that's worse than what I lived through? That's worse than what I've already seen?" She took her mother's hand. "I've been broken into a lot of pieces, but the glue that I put them back together with—you and Eleonore—you're the strongest adhesive out there. I'm going to be fine."

Corrine squeezed her hand, her eyes filling with tears. "I never wanted this for you. I wanted to make your life perfect."

"You gave me a chance at life. That *is* perfect."

What happens when Shaye returns to New Orleans? Find out in 2017.

To receive notice when a new book is available, please sign up for my newsletter.

CPSIA information can be obtained
at www.ICGtesting.com
Printed in the USA
LVHW091721080820
662695LV00001B/135

9 781940 270388